YOUNG AGAIN .... AND AGAIN ... AND AGAIN

YOUNG AGAIN ...
AND AGAIN ...
AND AGAIN

A contemporary fantasy

CHUCK VAN SOYE

ABSOLUTELY AMAZING eBOOKS

ABSOLUTELY AMAZING eBOOKS

Published by Whiz Bang LLC, 926 Truman Avenue, Key West, Florida 33040, USA

For information contact:
Publisher@AbsolutelyAmazingEbooks.com

ISBN-13: 978-1945772375 (Absolutely Amazing Ebooks)
ISBN-10: 1945772379

Dedicated to my sweet patient wife, Judy, who listened quietly as I read each chapter to her on completion, then smiled and told me "how good it was." That encouragement kept the story moving along to its completion.

YOUNG AGAIN ....
AND AGAIN ...
AND AGAIN

PROLOGUE

JAKE by now had stepped way back near the hallway to the front door. It shortly opened, and in walked Cody.

"You're Mr. Harding, aren't you," he said to Jake. "I remember going to your Attorney office in Dothan once with my dad."

Without waiting for a response, he looked around the living room; saw his mother and father seated on the couch, and two teenagers standing nearby, all with drinks in their hand, and all participating in a heated conversation. Not wanting to interrupt, he continued standing next to Jake, and whispered, "Where's grandma and grandpa?" And after a slight pause, "Wow, that's a cute little chick standing there, just about my age. Could you introduce me to her?"

Jake almost broke into laughter, but suppressed it, and seeing the opportunity to inject a little merriment into the all-too-serious conversation in the room, gently pushed Cody along as he walked toward Jennie, saying, "Jennie, this young man thinks you're cute, and wants to be introduced to you."

Cody said, "Hi Jennie, wanna' go watch a new DVD movie with me out in my folks' SUV?"

Clay couldn't suppress his laughter, and let it flow all the way out from his belly up through his mouth into the otherwise silent room.

Jake quickly interrupted, "Cody, Jennie is your grandma."

"She is not my grandma; my grandma's an old lady!"

CHAPTER 1

"**54** YEARS!" I can't believe we've been married that long," exclaimed Clay Evans as he stared into the bathroom mirror, trimming his mustache.

"I can," impishly responded Jennie, his still-shapely bride of 54 years, as she peered intently into the same mirror. Simultaneously, she allowed a tiny giggle to escape her lips while adeptly applying greenish shadow over one eye.

"Then again, maybe I can," Clay continued, viewing all the light brown and darkish spots growing in number all over the wrinkled skin on his bare chest. "I asked the doctor once about these spots, showing my consternation, and he had the gall to laugh and call them barnacles."

"I think that's really funny, honey; he was just making fun of your concern. Besides, look at my grey hair, this spot on my nose, and the loose skin under my chin. We're just getting real old."

"Well, at 81, I don't feel old and don't want to be old and don't want to look old. Look at this silver hair; if it gets any thinner, the girls will stop trying to pick me up!"

"Ha!" shot back Jennie, "that stopped three decades ago. And besides, they'd have to get past me anyway."

With that, Clay took a short sidestep, leaned over and gave her a quick kiss on her cheek.

"You know, even though it's not one of the big milestones, our 54th Anniversary is something we really ought to celebrate."

"I do too, Clay. Got any ideas?"

"Nope, but let's kick a few around during breakfast, okay?"

≈ ≈ ≈

Clay Evans had a decisive nature. Even when he was a young man, fresh out of college, his ability to make wise decisions quickly, combined with his physical stature and good looks, moved him up rapidly through the lower echelons of management into a marketing leadership position at Johnson & Johnson. At age 27, while attending a health products convention in New York City, he met Jennie Jackson for the second time in his life.

As a presenter in one of the booths at the convention's related exhibition center, she was speaking about her employer's medical devices to a group of doctors that had stopped at that company's booth. From a distance, Clay noticed that while she spoke, pointing to various components being displayed, most of the doctors were looking at her, not the products she was promoting.

No wonder. She was gorgeous. Her knockout body was clothed in a sleek well-fit red dress, cut well above her knees, leaving very little to the imagination. Her facial features were highlighted by perfect makeup and framed by long black hair.

"Somehow she looks familiar," he mumbled to himself. "But I can't place her; too bad, I wish I could." Clay turned

2

and walked away, anxious to get to the afternoon J & J seminar.

Later that evening, he saw her again, chatting with a group of girls in his hotel's cocktail lounge. This time he approached her and said, "Hi, I saw you perform at the convention booth. You were great, and I couldn't help but notice how beautiful you are, and that you look familiar. Could it be that we've crossed paths somewhere?"

Being used to guys trying different pick-up lines, Jennie would normally have brushed Clay off with a smile and a thank you. But as she studied his curly blonde hair and handsome features, she thought, *I know this hunk somehow.*

Her eyes quickly scanned him as she tried to remember more. His height, well-fitting suit, shined shoes, white shirt and power tie certainly didn't escape her notice. She responded, "Do I know you?"

"My name is Clay Evans. What's yours?"

As soon as he said "Clay," she caught her breath, suddenly remembering him and that they had briefly met years earlier at a Memorial Day barbeque.

"Hi Clay, my name is Jennie Jackson, and we have indeed crossed paths. Back in 1950, we met at my uncle's Memorial Day backyard barbeque. I was only 15 then, and you were three or four years older, and on your way back to college."

She didn't reveal to Clay that she had instantly developed a teenage crush on him when their hands had touched briefly during a casual handshake as they were being introduced to each other.

"Wow, yeah, now I remember," said Clay. "What a memory you have. Would you care to reminisce with me over a cocktail?"

"I'd like to do that, Mr. Evans."

The cocktail was followed by a dinner date, hours of small talk, dozens more dates, an eventual engagement months later, meetings with parents, and ultimately a wedding. It took place in her small-town home church, celebrated by both families and dozens of friends. The date was August 2, 1958. Joshua was born in 1961, and Deborah in 1963.

≈ ≈ ≈

Reminiscing again about those long-ago memories as he shaved the rest of his face clean and brushed his teeth, Clay told himself that he was one lucky guy to have Jennie as his wife. He also began to think about the kinds of things that Jennie and he might do to celebrate their anniversary.

Within the hour, make-up applied and dressed for a day of grocery shopping and housework, Jennie busied herself in the kitchen preparing bacon, eggs and toast. Clay was in front of his computer, checking the news, emails and the August 2012 Evans stock portfolio.

At the breakfast table, Clay spoke first. "How about a few days on a Caribbean island? I've noticed a few TV commercials for a resort called 'Sandals.' It must be their off-season now, because they're offering two-thirds off normal pricing, and sweetening that offer with $350 towards airfare."

"Oh honey, that sounds wonderful, but a trip like that takes a lot of preparation, advance planning, getting resort and plane reservations, packing and all that stuff, and we need to celebrate tomorrow, or at least during the next couple of days."

Jennie then suggested, "How about just picking one of your favorite overpriced restaurants in town, and we can build a party around it tomorrow night. We could start here with a couple of your special homemade margaritas, and maybe find a place to go dancing later."

"Hmm. I agree. A trip involving flight is unrealistic. But Jen, we could still go someplace by car, just so that we could get away from our local routine for a couple of days. Let's think of someplace we haven't ever been to, but could drive there in one or two days."

By the time breakfast was over, they'd decided to leave the following morning for St. Augustine, FL, a place famous as the oldest city in the United States. It was about 600 miles from their Florence, AL home, a long tiring drive, but they grew excited about the prospects of the trip as they read some promotional material downloaded from Google. It was too far to drive in one day, they decided, but with an overnight stay in a motel along the way, it would turn out to be a comfortable plan that would get them there right on their Anniversary.

After a day and a half of driving, lunch on the road, and check-in at a St. Augustine motel, Jennie said, "Clay, after we unpack, why don't we head over to see Old Town. All the stuff we downloaded makes it sound so interesting, and a place we should see."

"Babe, I agree that we should see it while we're here, but we've got several more days to do so, and I'm pooped from all the driving. Why don't we take a nap instead, and go there tomorrow?"

"Well, remember that one article we read, Clay, the one about the Old Town Trolley, how it loops around and winds in and out of all the streets in the old part of the city. It said the driver points out over a hundred points of interest, particularly 23 special attractions we might like.

"So, I thought that this afternoon we should go down there, get on that trolley for the ride, kick back and sightsee, learning all about the city and its history. Then tonight, we'd be better equipped to choose which attractions to visit tomorrow, doing much less walking, which would help save your bum knee."

"Yeah, the knee's been on my mind, thinking about walking around on this trip. You've made some good points, Jen. Forget the nap. Let's go; we can unpack tonight."

As they headed out the door, Clay stopped short, turned around and went toward the living room, leaned over the coffee table in front of the couch, picked up something and came back out waving it, saying, "Almost forgot my iPhone, Jennie. Couldn't get there without that Google Map thing.

"These new electronic toys are really something. Can you remember when only Dick Tracy in the comics had a portable telephone . . . in his watch! Now this gizmo in my hand is like having an entire portable Atlas book of maps, and one that sweetly speaks to tell you 'Turn around, you're going the wrong way; I told you to turn right at the next light, not left, stupid!'"

Jennie giggled out loud.

A little less than an hour later, the Evanses were seated comfortably on the open-air Old Town Trolley, along with perhaps two-dozen other tourists. As they drove along, the conductor spoke over the intercom.

"Coming up on your left side, folks, is 'America's Oldest Drug Store.' If you get off the trolley here and go inside, you won't see any computers. Instead, there's an antique cash register, wood floors and bottles of remedies, elixirs and tonics. You'll feel like you're in an era gone by. Whenever you want to get back on one of our trolleys, you won't have to wait long. One comes by every 15 minutes."

The trolley bell clanged; the trolley stopped a minute, letting passengers off and others on; the bell clanged again, and the tour continued.

Originally, the Evanses had agreed to just ride, and not to get off to visit any of the attractions that day. But after the hour-long tour was almost over, however, Jenny said, "We ought to get off this trolley at least once before heading back to the motel. This brochure says the last attraction coming up is 'The Fountain of Youth'. Why don't we take a half hour or so, and check it out? We can do all the rest we want to see tomorrow."

"Good idea, Jennie. Let's do it."

CHAPTER 2

"**O**KAY, folks, we're almost to the 'Fountain of Youth National Archaeological Park' attraction," advised the trolley's conductor. "Get off here if you want to take a drink from the famous spring, relive the days of the conquistadors and discover many colorful facts about Ponce de Leon's arrival in Florida in 1513. You'll be walking the grounds of the actual site where Spanish explorers first came ashore in America. You can learn about the first Christian Indian burials, and listen to a Timucuan Indian actor tell about their settlement here, see relics, and much more."

The trolley made a hard right, leaving the main road behind, and traveled about a quarter mile to a main square bounded on the left by a concession building offering food and drink, and adjoining benches filled with waiting tourists. On the right, a banner proclaiming 'The Fountain of Youth' fluttered above the attraction's walk-in entry path.

As the Evanses stepped off the trolley and headed down that path, they promptly came to a ticket booth where they paid the senior's rate for two tickets. A map they were given showed the layout to the grounds, which were expansive, encompassing many acres.

Clay spoke as he studied the map, "Jen, this place is huge. I'm not sure my bum knee will be willing to cooperate if we have to walk around the whole thing."

Jennie responded, "I hear you, hon, so for now let's skip the building that houses the Fountain of Youth, and while your knee is still good, head right down to the far end, next to the water. The program says that in 10 minutes, they're going to fire an antique cannon for the last time today to celebrate the landing of Ponce de Leon, and I'd love to watch that."

She grabbed his hand and led the way across acres of green grass toward the water. Clay forgot about his knee, and enjoyed watching how spry she was, considering she was 77 years old. *Not bad for an old gal*, he mused.

Thankfully, the cannoneer warned all the tourists standing next to the rope marking off the safe zone, "Folks, unless you're already deaf, you'd better cover your ears before I light this black powder fuse."

Instantly, dozens of hands flew up to heads, accompanied by female squeals, as half the crowd took several quick steps back away from the rope. A few macho men laughed the warning off, and probably wouldn't have covered their ears if he was detonating a bucket of TNT.

KABOOOM! Subsonic shock waves rattled everyone present, as billows of pungent smoke covered the crowd, driven by the wind coming off the water. Then quick multiple conversations, jokes and laughter followed, as everyone recovered their cool, and started walking toward the nearby Indian Village attraction. There a half-naked male in ancient native garb awaited the crowd to apprise them of early Timucuan village lifestyle. He adeptly kept the crowd's interest high as he displayed numerous native artifacts while repeating his well-rehearsed lines.

There was so much yet to see, an archeological dig, a statue of Ponce de Leon and more, but Clay reluctantly quashed Jennie's expectations to see it all, saying, "My knee is starting to complain. Let's head back slowly instead of trying to keep up with this rushing crowd."

Jennie knowingly agreed, saying, "Yeah, hon, we better go. But couldn't we at least stop at the building actually housing 'The Fountain of Youth.' It's on the way back."

Clay, grimacing, nodded agreement.

Once inside the air-conditioned structure, they were alone except for an attendant who approached them with a tray of tiny paper cups half-filled with water from the 'Fountain of Youth' spring, which was located a few feet away, visible as a small circular rock-rimmed pool.

The smiling attendant recited her lines: "Welcome to the famous 'Fountain of Youth.' If you like, you can have a taste of our famous spring water. It's safe to drink, but we make no promises that you'll get any younger."

Both Clay and Jennie plucked one of the tiny cups off the tray, saying "Why not" and "Thank you," respectively. Clay followed up with "Down the hatch," as he emptied his cup. Jennie followed suit.

The attendant then added, "Folks, you'll have to excuse me for a few minutes while I put up 'Closed' signs outside the attraction's entrance, as it's 5:00 pm. You can stay as long as you wish, and leave when ready, as the locked entrance door is open from the inside. Please help yourself if you'd like another cup." With that, she set the tray of cups down next to the pool, and left hurriedly.

Standing alone as the only tourists in the empty building, Clay and Jennie shrugged and smiled at each other. "It's time for us to leave," said Clay, "but I've got to take one of my pain pills for this knee, and need some water right now. I think I'll just pick up a couple of those little cups, and do so." With that, he stepped towards the tray, intending to straddle it while picking up a few cups. But as he did so, his right foot clipped one of the rocks rimming the pool, he lost his balance, and his left foot kicked the tray, sending it and its contents flying.

And with a yelp, he fell in.

Jennie screamed, and ran towards the pool to help him get out, shouting, "Are you hurt, Clay?"

"No, Jen. But I can't find anything to grab hold of to help pull myself out. Gimme a hand." She promptly sat on the floor, feet braced against the rocks, and clasped his hand and pulled, exhibiting strength she didn't know she still had. Out he came, rolling on his side to get one leg up on the floor first, then the other. Once clear of the pool, he stood up, water dripping off him from head to toe. Clothes wet, watch wet, wallet wet, shoes wet. For most, it would be a disaster. But instead, Clay was laughing so hard, he could barely stand. Soon Jennie was too.

"Come on; let's get out of here before the attendant comes back. We'll go get something to eat or drink at the concession stand, and allow time for me to dry off enough so that they'll let me get back on the trolley."

Jennie giggled at the thought of Clay, dripping wet, being shooed away by the conductor. Clay didn't hold back; he again roared with laughter as they joined hands and ran together out the door, barely missing the returning attendant.

As it was after 5:40 by the time they reached their car and departed for the motel, the Evanses decided to stop at the first nice restaurant they might pass by, and have an early dinner. A couple miles down the road, they spotted a Red Lobster, and went in. As they were studying the menu, Clay complained, "I don't feel too well. Maybe we shouldn't have drunk that water in Old Town. How are you feeling, Jen?"

"I feel fine. You'll probably feel better, Clay, as soon as you get some food in your belly. Let's have a glass of wine to start." After a sumptuous dinner, they continued their drive to the motel, and settled in for the evening.

After a little stretching out in the suite's chairs, Jennie suggested, "Let's watch a movie. They were offering microwave popcorn at the front desk."

"You go ahead, Jen. Not for me, though. I'm starting to ache all over. Check my forehead and see if I have a temperature."

She placed a palm above his eyes. "Nope, you're as cool as a cucumber. I do hope you're not coming down with the flu or something."

"I think I'm going to go to bed early tonight, like right now. Enjoy your movie. I'll be all right. Good night, baby. I won't kiss you just in case I have something contagious."

CHAPTER 3

EVEN though they were on a mini-vacation, Clay had set an alarm to awaken him at the usual 6:30 am. He was a creature of habit and had been an early riser most of his life. When the alarm sounded the following morning, he reached over, turned it off quickly in hopes that Jennie wouldn't wake up if she wanted more rest. He stood up, stretched, yawned and headed for the bathroom. Since there was a nightlight on, he didn't flip on the lights. In a few minutes though, as the haze of sleepiness left him, he realized that he couldn't shave or brush his teeth in the near-dark of a strange bathroom. So he quietly closed the door to shield Jennie from the light, flipping it on.

He glanced casually towards the mirror, and did an immediate double take. The image staring back at him startled him, and he immediately became wide-awake. He even let out a loud "What the...?" It was his reflection indeed, but it had a full head of curly blonde hair.

Jenny, awakened by his exclamation, rushed toward the bathroom, rubbing the cobwebs out of her eyes, looked in, screamed and slammed the door shut. Leaning her weight against the closed door, she frantically tried to size up the situation, finally managing to yell, "Who are you and what are you doing in our bathroom?"

A voice from within yelled back, "Jennie, it's me, Clay."

She paused, then turned and opened the door a few inches, looked through at Clay standing there naked, and came to the realization that it might indeed be Clay. She opened the door all the way and exclaimed, "Oh my god! Is that you Clay? Is that really you?"

She walked to him, touched his face, his hair, his body. "Yup, it's really me," Clay said.

For the next few minutes, neither spoke, but just stood there totally shocked as they studied the male body standing there. The old man had disappeared. In his place stood a different man, his slightly taller, lean, muscled body topped by a handsome young chiseled face, crowned with a crop of glorious blonde hair.

Clay spoke first. "Look, he doesn't . . . I mean, I . . . don't have any brown spots on my chest, and there's no wrinkles . . . anywhere!"

Jennie, her eyes now wide open, exclaimed, "Oh Clay, you look just like you did when we met the first time as teenagers. You were gorgeous then, and you're gorgeous now! I remember having a crush on you back then. Wow! As I look at you now, I'm getting that same feeling. Whoopee! I think I'm just falling in love with you all over again.

"Can you remember that day? I was 15, almost 16, and you were 19. You dropped by to say hello to some friends at my uncle's Memorial Day barbeque. Remember? You politely shook my hand when we were introduced, and I was instantly crazy about you. I was crushed when you left the party to return to college without even saying goodbye to me."

"Jen, I didn't know you had feelings toward me way back then. You were just a kid. A beautiful sweet-sixteen female kid. Why would you have been interested in me?

Besides, I had a girlfriend waiting for me back at school when the new term began."

"Yes, I was a kid, but I had the feelings of a woman even then, and all I wanted to do was wrap my arms around you and kiss you. It was like love at first sight. But I had to wait eight years to get that kiss, not long after we met again at that New York convention. You may be 81 years old now, but oh boy, you've now got the same wonderful body of that 19-year-old hunk I met back then."

After several delicious moments of contemplation, she said, "Clay, how is all this possible?"

"Beats me, Jen. Could it be that my falling into that 'Fountain of Youth' pool is responsible? I mean, an actual fountain of youth is just a legend, isn't it?"

"I've always thought it was. That's what they taught us in grammar school," answered Jennie.

Clay continued expressing his thoughts, "I certainly do believe that a Spanish explorer named Ponce de Leon landed on the shores of Florida centuries ago. That's real history. But was he really searching for a so-called fountain of youth? I don't think so. For sure, I don't believe that any such 'fountain' ever existed, never mind that today it's supposedly located there in Old Town, St. Augustine in a money-making tourist attraction."

"Yeah, Clay. But look at you. What else could have caused that change?"

Clay just shook his head slowly and said, "It's a logical conclusion, I guess. But growing young again overnight! That's a fantasy. It doesn't happen in real life."

As he glanced at his image in the mirror again, he added, "But it did."

He continued, "Jen, I don't think we're going to come up with real answers standing here talking about it. Let's go get something to eat, and talk more about this over food. I'm looking forward to those do-it-yourself waffles. After all, I'm a growing boy now, he said with a grin."

"Skip the waffles, Clay. I need a drink." But, acknowledging he really was hungry, she agreed they should head for the motel's breakfast room.

≈ ≈ ≈

As usual, they held hands as they walked along. Jennie continued to express her delight with her handsome 'new' 19-year-old husband, prompting Clay to plant a nice full kiss on her lips as they entered the breakfast room. A small boy seated at a nearby table facing the entry door leaned over toward his parents and said, in a muted voice, but still loud enough for everyone in the room to hear, "Did you see that, Mom, that boy just kissed his grandma's lips and patted her on the fanny!"

Jennie visibly clenched her teeth, frowning on hearing the boy's remark. "Grandma!" she said aloud, "How rude!"

In the boy's eyes, she had been clearly defined as an old lady, and not young and pretty. Although she knew that she really was old, by her own admission in the bathroom two mornings earlier, she simply did not want to hear it expressed in public. The fact that Clay was trying to suppress a grin when he heard the comment didn't help matters any.

"Let's get out of here," Jennie said, as she even briefly found herself resenting his youthful appearance.

In fact, after a few seconds of no response from Clay, she turned around smartly and stormed out of the room.

Clay, by this time standing in front of the waffle maker pouring the batter, stopped mid-pour and hurried out of the room in chase.

"Jen, wait!" he yelled, trying to catch up with her down the hall.

"I won't eat in that place!" she yelled back. "Did you hear all those snickers from everyone? I want to go find a restaurant somewhere else . . . and keep your hands off me!"

"Honey, he was just a little kid. You raised enough of them to know they can say the darndest things when you least expect it. He didn't mean to offend you. What he said was actually sort of funny." *Oops*, he thought, I shouldn't have added that last comment.

"It was not funny! I don't look like a 'grandma,'" she said with emphasis as she started to cry. I want to look young and pretty like I used to. I want to be young like you."

"Oh, baby, you look wonderful to me, always have, and always will. I love you just like you are."

But the die was cast, and the thought of possibly being young like Clay was embedded in her mind.

≈ ≈ ≈

The rest of that day, the Evanses toured many of the other attractions in Old Town, as had been their original plan. But neither of them fully appreciated what they were seeing and hearing during the tour, as both were deep in thought, mentally reviewing the amazing impact on their lives that had taken place just a few hours earlier in their motel bathroom. Jennie also felt strange, holding hands with Clay as they walked together, something they'd done for most of their marriage.

She couldn't help but notice the suddenly turned heads and second looks directed at them by passers-by, and from people glancing and even pointing toward them from the moving trolleys going by. She also felt threatened by the stares and smiles that pretty young women projected towards Clay. He didn't seem to mind that attention at all, and that aroused feelings of resentment within Jennie. She began to feel a sense of urgency to get away from the tourist crowd, and suggested several times to Clay that they should leave.

They eventually retreated to their car, heading for the motel. Along the way, Clay observed a nautically embellished sign, "The Retired Pirate's Bar." "You know, I'm real thirsty, Jen. What do you think about stopping there for a quick brew?"

"Good idea, hon; let's do it."

Since all tables were occupied, they headed for the bar. Jen, as usual, ordered a margarita, and Clay asked for a beer. The bartender gal, costumed as a pirate wench, looked carefully at Clay and said, "Sorry sir, I have to card you. May I see your ID?"

This took Clay by surprise, but he didn't show it in his face or action, and calmly pulled out his wallet, took out his driver's license, and handed it to her. She took it to the register where there was more light, and studied it. Walking back to Clay, she handed it to him and said, "Sorry sir, but that won't do the trick. The picture's that of an old guy, and it says you're 81 years old. That ain't you, and I can't serve you here. Please leave."

Clay, taken aback as he realized the disconnect caused by his new youth, turned red, muttered, "Oops, sorry," got up and joined

Jennie, who had already by now left her stool. Together, hand in hand, they hurried out the door, heading for the motel.

"Good grief, Clay, we can't even buy a drink when we're out together."

"Yeah, kind of awkward wasn't it?" he said.

≈ ≈ ≈

That evening they watched the 9:00 pm television series, *Bering Sea Gold*. Jen said, "I'm wrung out from this day, and am heading to bed."

Clay responded, "I'm going to watch the news first, then take a shower, so you go ahead. I'll try not to awaken you."

As Jen lay in bed, unable to sleep, her thoughts were on what might happen later when Clay turned in. *This is really another awkward situation*, she thought. *In a little while, a 19-year-old kid is going to climb into bed with me. I have to think this thing through. He's a real hunk, and he's my husband, but holy cow, it might be weird. What will he want, and what will I want?*

About this time, Clay finished drying off after the shower, and slowly and quietly approached the bed. Jenny pretended to be asleep. Clay assumed she was, climbed in quietly, rolled over and fell asleep. At last, Jenny could sleep too, with her final thought of the day, *We really have to do something about this situation!*

CHAPTER 4

JENNIE woke up several times during the night, ruminating through the previous day's positive and negative events, recollections that were invading her sleep, and churning over and over in her mind. First there was the incredible delight at seeing her wonderful new husband's body, then the dismay she felt when the little boy called her Clay's 'grandma.' Then there was the embarrassment of Clay being refused service in the bar; and these were topped off by the memory that she resorted to pretending sleep because she didn't know how to handle Clay's arrival in bed.

She finally forced sleep to come, pushing these thoughts out of her mind. She replaced them with a promise to herself that in the morning she'd draw Clay into a serious conversation about their mixed-up ages. Jennie was determined that they needed to take action to prevent recurrence of further awkward situations. But what, how and when?

Clay woke up that next morning, rolled over and saw that Jennie was awake and said, "Good morning, beautiful."

She happily responded to his compliment with, "Hi handsome. I love you. Got a kiss for me?" He did, several times, starting to feel frisky. Jennie, suddenly gripped by the same sensation of awkwardness as the night before, turned away, arose quickly and started dressing, saying, "Clay we need to talk."

Uh oh, here comes trouble, he thought. "About what, Jen?"

"About me being 77 years old and you looking like you're 19."

"Strange, huh?"

"Yes, strange . . . and awkward . . . and a situation that's been making me want to cry because I love the way you look, but I can't stand the unpleasant things that are happening." She stepped over and briefly hugged Clay. "Let's get ready for the new day, go out and get breakfast somewhere. Then we can talk more about all this, and develop an action plan real soon . . . like before lunch. Okay?"

That kind of action-oriented speech was not typical of Jennie, so Clay knew the situation was serious, and would require his total cooperation. "Jen, you've got my attention, and I'm fully onboard. It's your show. Let's go."

They found a franchise eatery just a couple miles away that fit the bill. The aromas of fresh coffee and pancakes cooking greeted their entry. Rows of brightly colored booths, all paralleling the plate glass wall fronting the building, were virtually empty. A waitress arrived with menus, water and silverware almost as soon as they sat down. When the coffee was served, Clay again said, "Okay, Jen, it's your show."

Jennie picked at her meal quietly, so Clay, deferring to her anticipated lead of the discussion, ate his breakfast silently. As the last cup of coffee was being drained, Jennie finally spoke up: "Clay, what are we going to do about this. Our apparent age difference caused all kinds of problems the very first day. Can you imagine what pitfalls and catastrophes are ahead of us? We have to do something!"

"I dunno, Jen. I don't think things are as serious as you do. I mean, nobody got hurt or anything. We just have to keep our feelings in check. I think I'll be able to handle whatever happens. Don't you?"

Filled with emotion, Jen responded, tears causing her eyes to glisten, "No, I don't think I can handle it. I was awake most of the night worrying about this."

"You got any ideas, honey? I want to cooperate. I want you to be happy."

"Yes, I did get one idea that I believe is the only way to prevent future distress. I think I should try to become young too."

"Holy mackerel, Jen, how can we make that happen?" Then suddenly realizing the obvious answer, he chuckled, "I got it; I bet you want to get into the Fountain of Youth pool and see if it makes you young too. Right?"

Dead serious, she said "Yes."

After a minute or two, with both of them in deep thought, Clay said, "Well, even if we could pull that off, what if it didn't work? It was probably just a fluke with me, and might not happen again to anyone for another thousand years, if ever."

"I'll worry about that if the situation arises. Come on, Clay; let's agree it's worth a try."

"Okay, but we've got to develop some kind of plan. We were lucky when we visited there the first time because we were all alone. There're probably dozens of tourists in that building most of the time. And even if there wasn't a single one, the attendant would still be there, and she'd probably call Security the moment you stepped near that water."

More silence. "Maybe we could bribe her," Jen suggested, "or get in after the place closed for the night."

"I don't think the bribe offer is a good idea, because if she rejected it, the whole concept would be blown. Jen, if you're really, really serious about the need to do this, I think we should be thinking about breaking in at night. If we're caught, we'll be arrested, I'm sure. Are you ready to risk that?"

"Yes, I'd take all the blame, so they'd let you go free."

"It doesn't work that way. We'd both end up in the hoosegow. And you're too pretty, and I'm too young for that," he joked. Clay continued, after several more minutes of thought, "Why don't we go there now, and while everyone else is listening to the attendant, and looking at the pool, we could wander around and discover if there's any way we could get in after it's locked up. Let's say we find a fire door that we could prop open, or an open window or something. Then we could go back at midnight and do the deed."

"I'm game, Clay. Whoopee, let's go!"

As they reached the Fountain of Youth ticket booth, Clay placed his credit card on the counter and said, without thinking, "Two senior tickets, please."

"I don't think so, buddy," said the guy inside, amazed at the brazen request by a kid with his grandma.

"Oh, sorry; I'm so used to saying that. One senior and one adult, please." After signing the receipt, feeling the glow of his reddened face, he ignored Jennie's grin, grabbed her hand and hurried away down the path towards the main Fountain of Youth building.

On entering, they observed that there were at least two or three-dozen tourists there, listening to an attendant's detailed history of Ponce de Leon's arrival in Florida after leaving Puerto Rico.

Clay walked alone straight to the first of two fire doors. Then he went to the opposite side of the building and checked out the other. In the meantime, Jennie went to the Ladies Room. Clay went to the Men's Room next. When they finished their surveillance, they met in the center of the room.

"The fire doors aren't an option," Clay whispered. "They both have alarms on them that go off when they're opened. There's a window in the Men's Room, but it has bars on it."

"The Ladies Room also has a window, Clay, but there aren't any bars. There's a locking mechanism on top of the lower pane that prevents it from being lifted. I unlocked it, and I was able to crack it open as a test. Then I closed it, but left the lock open."

"You've got to be kidding! What a break. I never thought it'd be possible. Let's get out of here before we attract attention. Maybe we'll be able to see whether that Ladies Room window is easily accessible from the outside."

After exiting the building, Clay stationed Jennie in a path heading towards the distant Indian Village exhibit. When he could see no one coming in either direction, he left the path, passed through an opening in some bushes, and took a half-dozen steps in the dirt to a point behind the building where he could observe the Ladies Room window. There was absolutely nothing hindering access, but the window was up too high for easy entrance. He quickly returned to Jennie.

"Jen, we can easily get to that window if we can find how to get here after dark."

So they walked along the path, looking for ways that they could enter the exhibit grounds without passing through the main front gate, which might be blocked or have a security guard present. There did appear to be a few unprotected openings in the high thick foliage that encompassed the acreage.

"Jen, I'm pretty sure we'll be able to sneak through that high hedge via one of those openings, which probably can be accessed from an adjacent street. Are you sure you still want to do it?"

"Yes . . . I think."

"I think? Are you chickening out, babe?"

"I have to admit I'm a wee bit scared, Clay, now that we've started to put this plan in action."

"Me too, Jen. But we can pull it off, I'm certain." However, his mind was silently screaming: *Don't be so sure, Clay; all kinds of things could go wrong, and you know it.*

Clay added, "Let's get out of here now and head back to the parking lot."

As they walked along, Clay cautioned, "We have to remember to bring a stool or stepladder tonight."

CHAPTER 5

SINCE their trolley ticket was still valid for a third day, and they were in no rush to go anywhere else, the Evanses decided to spend the rest of daylight seeing more of the attractions that Old Town had to offer.

Later, after a fancy seafood dinner in the Bistro de Leon, Clay said, "Jen, we have to find a store that sells the stool we'll need tonight. So I Googled for it while you were in the ladies room. There's a K-Mart a couple miles from here. Let's jump into the car and head over there now."

"Okay. That reminds me. I need to buy some cheap clothes to replace my wet ones after I climb out of that pool. There's no sun to help me dry off, like you had, and it's going to be cool there at midnight. I don't want to sit in the car shivering all the way back to the motel."

At the store, Clay located a collapsible kitchen stool he could buy for less than twenty bucks, while Jennie found what she wanted. After paying for them, they locked the clothes and stool safely in the car's trunk for use later that night, and took in a movie playing in a theatre just across the street from the K-Mart parking lot.

As the movie ended, Clay looked at his watch and said, "It's 22:35, so I think we should head for the perimeter of the 'Fountain of Youth,' find a side street nearby, park the car, and walk to our target area."

"There you go again, Clay, using that army lingo: '22:35,' 'perimeter' and 'target area!' And what time is that, anyway?"

"It's 10:35 pm. I explained it to you a hundred times. To convert military time, just subtract 12:00 for any time that you don't understand."

"Cripes, you haven't been in the army for 60 years, honey. Please talk like a civilian, okay?"

Well before midnight, they found an obscure parking spot, grabbed the clothes and stool from the trunk, and searched along the east edge of the attraction's acreage, looking for an entry point through the heavy fence-like foliage.

"Whoa, here's a small opening. Duck down and hold my hand as we squeeze through this high green stuff onto the grounds," said Clay.

They carefully picked their way through the row of tangled brush and bushes bordering the attraction's grounds, and found to their relief that there was another parallel thinner row of foliage a few feet away. That greenery partially screened them from view of anyone that might be on the main acreage.

"Phew, we made it. Now we only have to cover about a hundred yards or so to reach the building."

"Oh Clay, I'm so scared now. This isn't legal, is it? I mean, we're trespassing, right? What if we get caught?"

"You're right. If we're caught outside, we'd likely get charged with trespassing, and hopefully just get fined. If we're caught inside the building, however, we'd really be in trouble for breaking and entering, and could be jailed. Do you want to change your mind and not do this, Jen?"

A long silence followed while Jennie chewed these realities over in her mind, realities offset though by her fervent desire to be young again with Clay. Finally she said through quivering lips, "I want to do it, honey. It's worth the risk."

"Okay, follow me as quietly as you can. Stay close. Keep low, just in case. If someone sees us and shouts or comes in our direction, run as fast as you're able, following me."

After they had moved about 40 yards toward the building, stooped over to minimize their silhouette against the night sky, Clay abruptly stopped, dropped to his knees and whispered, "Shhhh. Get down and don't move. It looks like they have a nighttime security guard."

A male figure appeared on the far side of the building, walking the perimeter of the grounds. He had something in his hand. A leash. There was a huge dog, bigger than a police dog, behind him, tugging on the leash to go in the opposite direction. The figure stopped, yanked hard on the leash to get the dog alongside him, and continued coming in their direction.

"Lie on your belly, Jen," whispered Clay. "Don't move."

"Ugh, it smells awful where I'm lying, Clay. Like manure."

"Probably is manure fertilizer. That's good. The dog won't be able to catch our scent."

The dog, obviously not well-trained, had a mind of its own and now wanted to run, tugging the grunting guard behind him hard enough to cause him to jog a little to keep up with the beast. "Slow down, Bruno, damn it. They must be feeding you 'speed' or something."

Even though the brush row screening them was thin, it was enough so that the preoccupied guard and the straining, nearly choking, huffing and puffing dog passed them by less than 15 feet away, without seeing them. The security detail was heading in a hurry towards the far end of the acreage, right towards the water where two days earlier the Evanses had watched and heard the cannon's roar.

"Jen, it's safe to stand up. Let's quickly head to the back of the building now, and do what we planned."

Once there, Clay opened the collapsible kitchen stool, placing it against the building just beneath the Ladies Room window. Jen put the bag of clothes beneath the stool. He stood on the top step, put his fingers along the top edge of the window's lower half, and pushed up. It worked. The window was open enough for them to climb through.

"Jen, you go first," he said, "and I'll follow right behind you."

Jennie, with a gentle lift and push from Clay got halfway through, lying on her belly with her upper torso inside, and her lower torso and legs outside. "What do I do now, Clay?" she asked.

"Bend at your waist, and drop to the floor on your hands. Then I'll push your legs through."

"I can't drop to the floor; there's a toilet in the way."

"You mean the window's right over the toilet?"

"Yes, this morning I had to stand on the toilet stool to open the lock on the window."

"Well, support yourself by putting your hands on the bowl cover as I push your legs through."

"I can't. There is no cover. It was lying on the floor in the corner this morning. It must have been broken, waiting to be fixed."

"So there's nothing directly beneath you but toilet water?"

"Yes."

Clay groaned, and then suggested, "Grab hold of the front part of the porcelain, and pull yourself forward, and lean down to put your hands on the floor in front of the toilet."

"It might not be clean, Clay."

"What might not be clean, the toilet or the floor?"

"Both."

"Just do it anyway."

She did, and allowed her body to slide over the front part of the toilet, and ended up lying on her belly on the floor.

"I'm in," she said in a semi-whisper.

"Good, I'm coming right behind you."

Both were now inside. Clay cautiously opened the door to the main room. It was empty. And it was dark. Pitch black.

Clay said, "I goofed; I should have brought a flashlight."

He thought a moment, and then said, "I've got an idea; I'll turn on my iPhone to the brightest screen, and we'll be able to see with that. Let's go."

"Wait, I have to wash my hands," said Jen.

"What?"

"Well, I had to grab the filthy toilet to pull myself in, and put my hands on the dirty floor, and I'm soon going to get into the Fountain pool, and they give that to people to drink."

Clay grimaced and said, "Okay, hurry up, we've got to get out of here fast, before that guard and dog come back. We might not be so lucky the next time."

Using the barely sufficient light from his phone, Clay led the way to the edge of the rock-rimmed pool. "Go ahead and get in now, Jen."

"I need something to sit on to remove my shoes."

"Sit on your butt on the floor."

"Then I can't reach my feet; you'll have to do it."

"Okay, sit," he said, as he squatted to untie her shoes and pull them off.

"Now, roll over onto your belly and scoot backwards until you can lower your legs into the water."

"Okay, now what."

"Grab hold of the rocks and push yourself backwards the rest of the way over the edge, gently lowering your whole body in."

"Oh, this is so refreshing," she said as she dunked her head.

"Yes, but get out right now, because for all we know, if you stay in too long, you'll end up as a baby tomorrow."

That worked miracles. Without a single word of further guidance from Clay, Jen almost flew out. . Dripping wet, she sat for a minute at the pool's edge while Clay helped her put on her shoes.

After they worked their way back to the Ladies Room, Clay put his iPhone back in his pocket, and climbed onto the toilet.

"Oh darn," he exclaimed in the darkness.

"What happened," she asked.

"The bowl is slippery, and my right foot just splashed in. Be careful it doesn't happen to you when you follow me out."

Clay made the rest of the way out. Jennie followed, with Clay on the stool supporting almost all her weight as she wiggled out, and stepped down the stool to the ground. Then he climbed back up and closed the window, and collapsed the stool. Jennie quickly changed her clothes right there, and packed the wet ones into the bag that had held the store clothes. A quick run to the brush opening to the street, and in just minutes they were walking towards their car.

"Let's go home!" said Clay triumphantly, his right shoe wetly squishing with each step.

"Right on!" she responded.

As they drove towards the motel, Jennie said, "Clay, do you think it'll work for me like it did for you? Do you think I'll be young in the morning?"

"We'll just have to wait and see, babe."

But they didn't have to wait long. About five miles down the road, Jennie said, "Stop the car, Clay."

"What? Uh . . . why?"

"Stop the car and pull over. Now!"

Clay responded promptly, and pulled off the road onto the soft shoulder. Jennie opened the door, stepped out, bent over and threw up.

"I guess that answers your last question, Jen. Remember how I got nauseas after I fell in? Here, take a swallow of this water. You'll feel better."

"I'm also starting to ache all over. It's all happening a lot faster than it did with you. Now I know why you wanted to go to bed so early that night. I feel terrible, Clay."

"We'll be home in just twenty minutes, Jen. Hang on, and you can jump into bed as soon as we get there."

She did. He watched *Red Eye* alone that night.

CHAPTER 6

C LAY awoke at 6:25 am, just before the alarm clock was ready to ring. He reached over and turned it off. After a few minutes of debating with himself whether to sleep in or get up, he rolled over to face Jennie and kiss her good morning. He stopped short. She lay motionless with the sheet pulled up covering most of her head.

I'll let her sleep, he thought. She had suffered a tough night with a lot of discomfort. So he quietly got up, and headed for the bathroom to shave and brush his teeth. By the time he finished, he hoped, she'd be up and around. He could hardly contain his desire to see if she had changed age-wise, and if so, how.

But as he exited the bathroom, she was still asleep, so he headed for the kitchenette to make coffee; later, he retrieved the paper off the sidewalk to read while enjoying that first cup of java.

Meanwhile, Jennie did awaken. While still lying in bed, she started to examine her body. She noticed first that tresses of her hair, now black and not grey, and much fuller and longer, were spread over her face after a night of tossing and turning. Then she looked at her hands, which were smaller and smooth-skinned without a trace of age spots. Her arms were slimmer than the night before. Next, while still lying prone, she lifted the sheet and noted slender, almost skinny legs, and to her delight, her belly fat was gone.

With growing excitement, she got out of bed, aiming to head for the bathroom mirror to see her face. But she almost tripped over her panties. They were so big for her new body that they had fallen off her waist to the top of her feet. Now she was alarmed; her body had changed shape so much that she'd have to buy a whole new wardrobe. But then, giggling softly, she became elated that she'd soon be buying new clothes.

She wondered out loud to herself as she reached the bathroom, "Just how young did I get?" Standing in front of the full-length mirror, she studied her features. The wrinkles in her forehead and under her nose and eyes were gone, as were all age spots. Her neck skin was tight, and the hated flap of loose skin under her chin was missing. Full of joy, she loudly exclaimed, "Oh Clay, come and look at me."

He dropped the newspaper and nearly ran to the bathroom, anticipating the sight of a younger woman, closer to his apparent age. As he rounded the turn into the bathroom, he saw her standing naked in front of the mirror. "Good grief, Jen! You stayed in the water too long. Wow, you look just like you did the day we first met. How old were you then?" he stuttered in shock, not sure as to what to say.

"Almost sixteen," she said, in a teenage girl's voice. "I'm so happy, I can hardly stand it. Are you pleased, Clay?"

"Jen, you look terrific. Wow, I suddenly have this strong urge to hug and kiss you."

"What are you waiting for, handsome?"

Clay hesitated, momentarily reticent due to decades of belief that a grown, mature, aged man has no business touching, never mind hugging and kissing, a naked 16-year old girl. But then, realizing the truth that he had a 19-year old body, and that they were married, he walked over to her and obliged. They hugged and kissed with fervent intensity. His hands explored her soft, warm skin, all over her torso, as her tongue searched for his. They both enjoyed the moment immensely, neither wanting to stop.

But shortly, Jennie pushed him back and said, "We'd better stop now. What do you want your young wife to make you for breakfast this morning, hon?"

"Oh baby, who wants to eat?"

"Later," she said. We've got to go home today, and you told me checkout time was 10:00 am. Besides, I'm famished. Remember, I lost my dinner last night."

Reluctantly, Clay released her.

At breakfast, Jennie suggested, "Let's drive only half-way home today. That way, we'll be stopping before dark, and can find some restaurant where we can have a nice meal before checking in at a nearby motel.

"Otherwise, I know you'll just want to keep driving to get closer and closer to home. And then it'll be too late to have a memorable unrushed evening together, just like newlyweds."

That message registered loud and clear, music to Clay's ears. "Okay, Jen, we'll stop after three hundred miles; maybe sooner," he chuckled.

It was an uneventful six-hour drive that found Jennie napping and Clay in prolonged deep thought. Clay eventually broke the silence as she woke up, saying, "I think we both have to be very careful to avoid revealing how we became youthful again. If the facts of our new reality ever became public, there'd be a stampede of humans clawing over each other to access the Fountain of Youth waters. It could become a tragedy of our making."

"Yeah, you're right, hon. Especially when meeting those family members and friends who've known us for decades, and see us as we are today. They must either be kept in the dark, or after a revelation of necessity, promise to keep what they've learned in total confidence."

Somewhere close to 5:00 pm, as they neared Dothan, AL, Clay started looking for a motel. None appeared for miles. Finally he spotted an older mom-and-pop motel and family-style restaurant, side by side just off the highway. He drove into their entrance, and parked in front of the eatery.

Once seated with menus in hand, Jen said, "We're going to have to change our habits, and skip our cocktail or beer before dinner. It'll be years before any establishment will be willing to serve us anything alcoholic."

"Yeah, if we want to eat out, we'll have to have our drinks at home."

"Well, Clay, we could act our new age, and give up drinking until we're legal."

"I'll give up beer when pigs fly."

A waitress interrupted their conversation, "What would you young folks like to eat?"

Orders were placed, dinners quickly served and hastily consumed, and the bill paid. The Evanses left, moved the car a few dozen yards to the adjoining motel's parking area, and walked into the office to register.

A middle-age woman emerged from a room behind the front desk. She had little if any makeup, her hair in a bun, and a shaggy old sweater draped over her shoulders. Her tattered appearance reminded Clay of his long-forgotten high-school principal. The woman looked over the top of her glasses, without smiling, and said, "What do you folks want?"

Clay said, "We'd like a room for just one night, please."

"How do you intend to pay?" the woman asked.

"American Express," Clay responded, as he laid his credit card on the counter.

She looked over her glasses again, contemplating the youth of the couple, and ran the card through the machine that copied it. "Are you brother and sister," she asked?

"No ma'am, we're married."

"Here's the key to Room 128, down at the end. Check out time is 10:00 am. If you stay beyond that, you'll have to pay for another night."

Jennie walked in first, noticing how small and plain the room was, just a small dresser with an aged TV on top, a single wooden chair, no table, no decorations and one double bed. The bathroom was clean but tiny, and outfitted with an old tub and shower curtain.

Clay moved just enough luggage for one night from the car's trunk, shut the room's entry door, closed the drapes, and turned on the TV. Jen walked over to the TV, and turned it off. "Clay, we're finally alone now. Do you really want to watch television?"

In short order, clothes were thrown on the floor and the bed turned down. They climbed in. Finally, after so many delays following their emergence from the Fountain's waters, the first chance to fully express their love had arrived. Clay caressed Jennie's hair, and gently encircled her in his arms, while tenderly kissing her closed eyes, her cheeks and her lips.

Suddenly, there was loud knocking on the door, and a shocking voice on the other side, "Police, open the door at once or we'll knock it down."

Surprised and astonished, Clay jumped out of bed, pulled up his shorts, and scurried across the room to the door, and opened it. Three Dothan police, one of them a female, barged in.

"The motel manager contacted us and told us she suspected that you, sir, could be a sexual predator and child molester!"

"That's preposterous!" said Clay. "What right do you have to disturb our privacy?"

Then turning to Jennie, huddled beneath the covers, "Miss, you'll have to get out of bed and get dressed. Officer Janice Austin will give you a blanket to cover yourself en route to the bathroom. Bring your clothes with you."

Jennie, whining, said "Clay, what's happening?"

"I'm not sure, Jen, but you'd better do what they say." She did.

"Mister, you get dressed too, right now."

When both Clay and Jennie were fully dressed and standing there together in front of the police, Clay was asked, "Who are you, how old are you and what are you doing here in this motel with a young girl?"

"I'm Clay Evans, and I'm 81 years old. And we're on our way home to Florence."

"Oh yeah, and I'm Forrest Gump, and we're on the way to my shrimp boat!"

One of the officers picked Clay's wallet off the table, opened it and took out his driver's license. "Sarge, this ID says he's 81, and that his name is Clay Evans, but the picture shows an old guy."

"Son, you're in real trouble. Who's the girl?"

"Her name is Jennie, and she's my wife."

Addressing Jennie, the female officer said, "What's your real name and age, honey?"

"My real name is Jennie Evans, and I'm 77 years old."

The female officer opened Jennie's purse, removed her ID, and noted that the name and age were correct, but the photo was that of an old woman.

Sarge said to Jennie, "You're wisecracker too, huh? Where did you two get these wallets? Did you steal them from an old couple? Where is that couple? Did you hurt them?

"I'm arresting you two on suspicion of robbery. And in addition, Mr. so-called Evans, I'm arresting you as a sexual offender and child molester."

Clay was put into handcuffs and led to a police car. Jennie was led to another vehicle, but without handcuffs applied. Their own car was impounded, along with all their belongings in the trunk and room, including Clay's computer.

At the station, both were photographed, fingerprinted and swabbed for DNA. After booking, Clay was taken to a county detention center, and ended up spending the night sitting with a stranger in a jail cell. Jennie was turned over to Child Protective Services, and eventually ended up in a dormitory with a few other teenage girls. Both were in a state of shock, and could only wonder what fate had awaiting them ahead.

CHAPTER 7

A S she was led from the motel room to Officer Janice's car, a frightened and angry Jennie watched through tears as Clay was roughly stuffed into the back of the other police car by the two male policemen. Officer Janice, trying to calm her said, "Sweetheart, I know he's convinced you to think he's a wonderful guy, but he's just been taking advantage of a nice girl like you. Did you run away from your mom and dad? We can call them, and they'll be thrilled to see you again. You'll feel better as soon as Child Protective Services finds them. In the meantime, they'll feed you and let you spend some time with other young girls your age in a nice dormitory facility."

Jennie knew it was futile to explain the truth of the situation, so she remained silent in the back of the squad car.

Once Officer Janice delivered her to the CPS Assessment Center, a 24-hour facility, Jennie was led by hand to a series of offices and rooms where second-shift administrative clerks, social workers, and medical professionals awaited her. The first stop was the admissions clerk, who took her picture and asked and recorded her routine information, excluding her stated birth date of 'May 9, 1935,' which the incredulous clerk replaced with 'Refused.'

Then, in the next room, a social worker interviewed her.

"What's your real name, honey?"

"Jennie Evans."

"Is that Jennifer?"

"No, it's Jennie, J-E-N-N-I-E."

"How old are you, Jennifer?"

"I know I look 16, but I'm really 77 years old, going on 78."

"I'll put down '15 or16', Jennifer, if that's alright with you."

"I believe in telling the truth. I'm 77. Put down what you like."

"Who are your parents, Jennie, and where do they live?"

"Both my parents are deceased. They died in an auto accident when I was 53."

"Okay, so you don't wish to tell me. I'll put down 'Unknown.'"

"Oh, that's a clever move. Avoid the facts if they don't jibe with your personal view."

Eventually, Jennie's address, race, hair color, weight and height were discussed and recorded, and she was shuttled along to the next room by Hattie, the volunteer escort. A physician and nurse awaited her there.

"Hello Miss. Please state your full name," said Dr. Hanes.

"Jennie Evans. What's your full name?"

"Dr. Thomas Hanes. Now, Jennie, please tell me, how are you feeling right now? Do you feel sick? Does anything hurt? Are you bleeding anywhere?"

"Okay, no, no and no," Jennie responded.

"Please remove your clothes."

"What?"

"Strip down to your panties and bra please."

"What are you, some kind of pervert? I'm not going to take my clothes off in front of you," said Jennie. "Why should I, why the heck am I here, and who are you, anyway?"

"It should be pretty obvious from my white coat that I'm a doctor."

"Yeah, it should be pretty obvious from my blue boot jeans that I'm a rodeo queen."

"There's a curtain over there; when you have your clothes off, put on this white gown. The nurse will help you."

"What's her full name?" Jennie shot back. But she reluctantly complied, feeling as a prisoner under threat.

After completing a routine physical exam of Jennie, the doctor inquired, "Did that man in the motel molest you?"

"None of your darn business! He happens to be my husband. Do you molest your wife?"

"Actually, Jennie, it doesn't matter how you answer; at the request of the prosecutor assigned to that man's case, the nurse will have to swab some samples from your intimate areas for forensic analysis. If you're embarrassed to have me here, I'll leave the room."

"Okay, leave!"

When Jennie was finally escorted out of that room, her face was burning red. She muttered to her escort, Hattie, "How dare they subject a 77-year-old lady to that awful procedure?"

The escort was baffled by Jennie's age claim. That evening, Hattie couldn't wait to tell her boyfriend about the crazy teenager just admitted who thought she was 77 years old.

In the next room Jennie was asked to enter, she was greeted by a man seated in an overstuffed chair, dressed in suit and tie. "Hello Jennie, I'm Doctor Johansen. I'm a psychiatrist. I'd like to chat with you."

"How come everyone in this place seems to know my name?"

"Would you like to sit down on that couch?"

"Not really. I'd like to be out of this room, and out of this building." But she did sit down.

"Jennie, you seem agitated. Why?"

"Who wouldn't be agitated? First they barge into my private motel room while I was in bed. Then they put my husband in handcuffs and cart him off in a cop car. Then they take me to this place, ask me a bunch of mindless questions, and put me into a room with some guy that wants me to expose myself. Then I'm forced to submit to some woman who pokes and wipes my private parts, both front and back. Now what kind of indignity are you going to subject me to?"

"Whoa, young miss; I'm just going to sit here and have a little chat with you for awhile. Okay?"

"We'll see."

"You say that you and your husband were in a motel room. Both of you in bed?"

"Yes, we'd just gotten into bed when the cops started banging on the door, threatening to knock it down. My husband, Clay, jumped out of bed and opened the door, and the rest is history, which you probably already know anyway, mister psychiatrist."

"Jennie, how long have you and your husband been married?"

"Three days ago was our 54th wedding anniversary."

"Hmm, that's quite a feat these days. Your husband must be getting up there in age."

"He's a very young-looking 81. And I'm 77."

"Let's see, if you are 77, and have been married 54 years, you must have been married at age 23 in the year 1958. Is that correct?"

"My, you certainly do excel in arithmetic, doctor."

"I love that comment, Jennie. I'm pleased to hear that your belligerence has changed to sarcasm. We're making progress."

"Well, progress this: I'm Jennie Evans, I'm 77 years old, and I haven't done anything wrong. I want to leave this place and go find my husband. That's all you all need to know. I'm done talking."

Dr. Johansen shrugged his shoulders, pressed a button on his desk, and the escort appeared. "Hattie, please take Jennie to the holding area for teenage girls. In case she has to stay overnight, stop on the way and pick up some bedding for her, and help her select a bunk. Oh, and please introduce her to the other girls."

Dr. Johansen picked up a phone and called the social worker assigned to Jennie's case. "Trudy, I think you'd best petition the judge to authorize movement of Jennie to the CPS Shelter tomorrow, pending any interviews requested by police. Because of her delusional state of mind right now, I'd encourage overnight supervision."

Later that evening, Hattie's boyfriend typed on his Facebook page, "Here's a hot one. My girlfriend met a 16-year-old teenager at work today that seriously thinks she's

77 years old. She musta run away from parents that really screwed up her brain. Sad, but also kind of funny."

Somehow that Facebook entry went viral, and was tweeted and retweeted until the humor blogs started writing about it. Eventually, it was quipped as part of a skit on the following 'Saturday Night Live.'

But Jennie didn't see that Saturday Night Live program. Even if she had access to a TV, she wouldn't have been watching. All her thoughts were centered on Clay: *Where is he? When will I see him again? Is he safe? Is he alive?*

CHAPTER 8

THE morning after Clay's arrest, Houston County Detention Center staff allowed him to make one phone call. He phoned Jake Harding, the Evans family attorney for decades. Jake's office was on the other side of Dothan, not many miles away.

"Good Morning, Jake. This is Clay. Are you still alive and kicking?"

"Nice to hear from you, Clay. How's the world treating you and Jennie up there in Florence?"

"Jake, I'm going to cut to the chase. I can't talk long. I'm in jail. Please come to the Houston County Detention Center in Dothan as soon as you can. I need your help. We really need to talk face to face."

"What? You're kidding me, Clay; Mr. Straight-Laced in the pokey?"

"No, I'm not joking. I'm really behind bars."

"I have a court hearing this morning," said Jake, "but I'll be over there to see you this afternoon. What are you charged with?"

"Robbery and child molestation."

"I don't believe this! You've gotta tell me a lot more. I'll see you in a few hours. Bye."

"Bye."

After decades of being in the legal trade, Jake Harding knew a few key staff personnel at HCDC, phoned one, and was able to reserve one of the attorney-client rooms for

2:00 that afternoon. On arrival, he signed in at the control room, got a badge and permission to walk unescorted to the reserved room.

An escort officer brought Clay from his cell to the meeting room, unlocked the door allowing Clay to enter, and walked away as the door shut audibly. Jake, who had been seated at a small plain wooden table reading a charge sheet about Clay, stood up and turned around to shake hands with him.

Jake, hand outstretched as he turned, said, "Hello Cl … uh, sorry son, they brought you to the wrong room."

Clay, dressed in the usual inmate orange jump suit, chuckled and said, "Jake, it's me, Clay Evans."

"There must be some kind of mistake. The Clay Evans I'm waiting for is over 80 years old. Is this a joke, or what?"

"I know you must be terribly confused, Jake, but I really am Clay Evans. I'm really 81 years old, but I have this wonderful new youthful body. Look closely at my face, it's me. I just look like a teenager."

"No, I don't believe you. Nobody turns young again."

"Jake, if I can't convince you by my facial features, perhaps I can help bridge your disbelief by reminding you of some of the things we've done together in the past. You defended me in that lawsuit related to misrepresentation of one of our products in a health-store advertisement. You also prepared our family trust, and are named as the executor in our wills."

"I don't know who you are, buddy, but anybody could've looked that lawsuit case up, and there were witnesses to the signing of the estate papers. One of them might be involved in this hoax."

"Okay, how about this, Jake. Jennie and I picked you and Annie up one Friday afternoon about 30 years ago. We drove you two to our summer home on Sardis Lake in Mississippi for the weekend. We took a ride on our speedboat, and you fell overboard. I threw you a life preserver, and you swam to the ladder. I gave you my hand to help you aboard, and fell in myself. We spent the rest of that afternoon sitting with the girls in front of the fireplace, warming up and drinking whiskey sours. Remember?"

"I'll be darned, Clay, it is you!" After a minute of silence recovering from his shock, Jake continued, "No one else could know about that great trip! Except Jennie. What does she think about all this, you turning young and being in jail?"

"Jake, she's being held somewhere by Child Protective Services. She looks like she's 16 years old."

"This is just too much. You're blowing my mind! How did all this happen, Clay?"

"We checked into a motel en route back home after a trip to St. Augustine, and the nosey manager must have called police because of our apparent ages. Three cops came barging into our room just after we got into bed. They're holding me for child molestation because Jennie looks so young. We couldn't prove who we were since our ID pictures show an old man and old woman. So, the cops thought we beat up some old couple, and stole their licenses or something, and that's why they charged us with robbery."

"What an incredible situation! At some point, Clay, you're going to have to explain to me how or why you look so young. But, I assume right now you want me to spring you. I'll be able to arrange a bail bond, I think, but proving you're not guilty is going to be much more difficult."

"Well, after you get me out of here, Jake, we can work on that together. I've got some ideas. But, more importantly, we absolutely have to investigate Jennie's situation. She must be scared stiff. Maybe you could at least find out where she is, visit her and let her know we're working on our release."

Jake concluded the conversation, saying, "I need to get out of here if I'm going to get anything going in a reasonable time. Clay, it'll possibly be several days, so don't give up on me. And for your own safety, stay away from trouble in your cellblock. There're some bad dudes in this place. Keep a low profile. See you later."

At that week's hearing, Jake appeared with Clay before Judge Pamela Suarez. When she called out Clay's name from among a dozen other inmates in the room, Clay and Jake walked to the rostrum.

"Mr. Evans, if that's your real name, which seems unlikely based on the police report before me, you are accused of robbery and child molestation. How do you plead?"

"Your honor, I'm Attorney Jake Harding, representing Mr. Evans. Mr. Evans pleads 'Not Guilty.' I hereby request that you set bail for him."

"Mr. Harding, do you realize the seriousness of the charges against this young man?"

"Yes, your honor, I do, but I've been his family's attorney for many years, and have always known him to be an honest, upstanding citizen. I firmly believe that if you grant him bail, we can present evidence in a matter of weeks that he is completely innocent of the charges."

"Given the circumstances of this case, bail is set at two hundred and fifty thousand dollars," said Judge Suarez.

"Thank you your honor. I'll arrange for that within a day or two. When would the court entertain the next motion on Mr. Evans' case?"

"Mr. Harding, the court calendar shows that the next opening for a brief motion and hearing would be six weeks from today."

"Thank you, your honor. We'll be here."

As the guard prepared to take Clay back to his cell, Jake said to him, "Clay, I'll front twenty-five grand for your bond. You can reimburse me with a check as soon as you're out of here."

"Thanks, Jake. Not a problem. See you later."

"Remember what I told you; keep a low profile in there. Bye."

Later that afternoon, Jake phoned a woman he knew, Jan Bishop, who used to work in Alabama's Department of Human Resources. It had been years since he'd spoken to her, but hoped she was still there.

"Hello, Jan? Jake Harding here. So you're still working for the State?"

"Hello back to you, Jake. Yes, but I've only got a year and a half until retirement. I can hardly wait. What brings you into my world today?"

"A question and a favor. I want to locate a young person that I understand is in the custody of Child Protective Services. How would I go about that?"

"Normally, Jake, you'd have to contact the Family Services Division of our Department, jump through all kinds of hoops, and fill out a myriad of forms. But give me his name, age and circumstances that led CPS to get involved, assuming you know them, and I'll find out where he is."

"Wow, thanks Jan. It's a female, not a male, and she says her name is Jennie Evans, but the authorities don't believe it. She's only around 16, I've been told, and apparently thinks she's 77 years old. She was picked up by the police in a Dothan motel room along with an older male, who's been arrested for child molestation."

"I'll look into it, Jake, and get back to you. Same cell phone number?"

"Yup, I owe you one, Jan. Bye."

The following morning, Clancy James, a detective with the Dothan Police Department, phoned the Florence, AL Police Department.

"Good morning, this is Detective James from the Dothan PD. I'd like to speak to the ranking officer of your criminal investigations division."

"That'd be our Lieutenant Detective, Peter Aspen. I'll ring his line."

"Lieutenant Aspen here."

"Lieutenant, this is Detective Paul James from the Dothan PD. We'd sure appreciate a little help from your people. We suspect that there may possibly be a crime scene in your town, and would like a detective and forensics specialist to go to a residential address we have, and check it out. If it's occupied when they get there by a Mr. Clay

Evans and his wife, Jennie, we'd like to know whether their wallets were stolen, where, when and how.

"If it's unoccupied, we'd like to know whether it might be a crime scene. In particular, if you gain entrance and find no evidence of any crime, we'd sure like you to gather up the toothbrushes, hairbrushes and combs, and send them to us here in Dothan. We need some DNA specimens to compare with others we have here."

"Okay, Detective James, fax me your reports on this so I can get a search warrant."

"Would all this be possible in the next day or so?"

"Sure, we'll do it today, assuming I can get the warrant quickly. What's the address?"

"It's 188 Honeysuckle Lane. Thanks for your help, Peter."

"No problem, Paul. I'll keep you informed. Good bye."

"Bye."

CHAPTER 9

THAT afternoon, Jake and the bondsman presented the necessary paperwork at the detention center, and Clay was released. His wallet, however, was retained as evidence in the case. Jake and Clay walked to Jake's car, parked about a block away. Once underway, Jake suggested, "Why don't we go to my home to talk. If we go to my office, there'll be too many distractions. We need peace and quiet to be able to think and talk this thing through, and come up with a plan of action to keep you from ending up in prison."

When they arrived at Jake's, Clay quipped, "Got any beer in your fridge? You can't get in trouble for giving alcohol to an 81-year-old, even if he does look like he's 19."

"Yeah, but we'd have to prove that you really are 81, Clay. However, I'll take the chance."

"I've had a lot of time to think, sitting in that cell, Jake. I've watched enough TV dramas to know that the police use dental records to identify bodies. I'm wondering whether the dental records for a guy in his 60's, 70's and 80's could be used to identify that same guy when he's reverted back to a teenager. My dentist for the last 20 years must have all those x-rays. If we got hold of those records, and brought them to a local dentist, maybe he'd be able look at my teeth today and be able to match them to the ones sent from Florence?"

"If so, Clay, that information might be strong enough to prod the authorities in Dothan to duplicate such a comparison. It's worth a try. Give me your dentist's information, and I'll have my office get those x-rays. Hopefully, it'll only take a few days to pull this off."

"Clay, another thought's just crossed my mind. Dental records aren't the only way forensics can confirm the identity of humans, dead or alive. DNA is even better. When you were arrested and booked, I'm almost certain they took a DNA swab from the inside of your mouth. If we could get Dothan PD's forensic people to obtain samples of DNA from your Florence home, they could be compared with the one taken here. That'd be solid proof that you're who you say you are. It'd help me get them to drop the case against you. I'll work on this concept with a couple PD people I know here."

"Super idea, Jake!"

"Here, have another beer, Clay, and tell me now how the heck you've become a kid again."

"Okay Jake, I'll trust you to keep my explanation a secret. I don't want to become an international curiosity. Agreed?"

"Agreed."

"I got careless while we were in St. Augustine, and fell into the Old Town tourist attractions' 'Fountain of Youth' pool. The following morning, I woke up like you see me now."

"But a real Fountain of Youth never existed, Clay. No one, including Ponce de Leon, ever found it, and the story that he was actually looking for it in 1513, when he landed in Florida, is pure bunk. We all learned that in grammar school. It's a legend that's been perpetuated through the ages."

"I too believe it's nothing but a myth, Jake, but nevertheless, look at me. If it wasn't those waters, what the heck did do this to me? Besides, those same waters made Jennie young too. But," Clay continued, "that's another part of the story that we don't have time to get into now. I know we both have other things to do today, and I want to get moving on mine?

"Jake, do you have a spare cell phone you can let me use for a few days; then could you take me to a car rental office so I can get some wheels to drive the 300 miles back home? I need to get my checkbook, as well as a few unused credit cards from my desk drawer. I need to get some cash, and write you a check. I can also write one as a retainer for your services, if you like."

"Yes for the cell phone, Clay. My wife has two for some unfathomable reason. As for the rental car, they won't rent one to you because you don't have a license and credit card. We can both drive there, though, and you can drive my car back here. I'll rent a car in my name, and when I get back here, it's yours to use. Please drive carefully, though; my insurance policy's expensive enough already. If you get arrested for anything, don't call me," he smirked.

"Jake, thanks for all this help, and for your friendship over the years," said Clay about an hour later as he was getting ready to back the rental car out of Jake's driveway. "Please find a way to see Jennie; ease her mind about all this, and tell her I love her."

"It's as good as done, Clay. I'll phone you and tell you all about it. Stay out of trouble."

CHAPTER 10

GLEN and Sonny Sanger were enjoying an evening of television. She had just tuned in one of their favorite programs, "Saturday Night Live."

During the initial commercials, Glen asked his wife, "More popcorn, honey?"

She put the bowl on her lap as the SNL stars ran through their usual banter and humor routines. When a routine about "a teenager that insists she's 77 years old being held in Dothan, Alabama's Child Protective Services" was mentioned in a skit about southern folk who marry their cousins, Glen jumped up and spoke with excitement, "Did you hear that?"

Sonny responded, "Sure did; we really ought to look into it. It's been years since we found one."

"We have to go to Dothan!"

Since Dothan was only a two-hour drive from Montgomery, where the Sanger's residence was located, Glen made a note to phone one of his contacts in CPS there the following Monday morning. He was hopeful she'd arrange a visit enabling him and Sonny to interview that teenage girl. The Sangers were well known in CPS circles as foster parents that took in teenagers, and after a period of a few years each, turned them loose to become model citizens.

"Good morning, this is Glen Sanger up in Montgomery; may I please speak with Cynthia Sherwood?"

Only a few minutes passed as he waited.

"Hello Glen. It's been years since we've heard from you. I hope everything's fine with you and Sonny. How is she?"

"Oh, she's just fine, and just aching to get down there to Dothan. We've heard about an unusual teenager that you've sheltered. Something about her thinking she's in her seventies or something."

"That has to be the Evans girl, Jennie Evans. At least that's what she calls herself. Glen, we never ran across one like her before. She's a beautiful sweet-sixteen-type kid, but real weird. Swears she's 77 years old. I owe it to you to brief you on the circumstances that led her to become a ward here." And Cynthia did so, noting that the male involved was in jail in the Houston County Detention Center.

"Well, Cindy, you know us. We look for the hard ones, and we're getting lonely again, so we're hoping we could come and have an interview with her."

"That could be arranged, Glen, assuming she's cooperative. How soon?"

"Would it be asking too much for us to show up tomorrow afternoon?"

"Go ahead and plan on it. If a complication pops up, I'll call you."

"Wonderful! See you then, Cindy."

After he hung up, Glen turned to Sonny and said, "If our suspicions are right, we'll have to find out which social worker is assigned to the girl's case. Then we'd work together with her to set up a joint meeting with Judge Rodriguez, as necessary. He knows the successes we've had in the past."

"It's hard to argue with success," responded Sonny.

64

≈ ≈ ≈

Later that afternoon, Jan Bishop from the Alabama Department of Human Resource phoned Jake Harding.

"Jake, I found that girl, Jennie Evans, who you asked me to locate for you. She's in a CPS facility on Front Street in Dothan. Do you need the names of staff personnel?"

"Thanks for that, Jan. That's all I needed. I know that building well, as it's only a few blocks from my office. I'll take it from here. As I said before, I owe you one. Bye."

Jake left his office and walked to Front Street. He entered and presented his business card to the receptionist, and said, "I'm Jake Harding, and I'm the attorney for the Evans family. I understand you have a young girl named Jennie Evans in custody, and I'd like to meet with her. I need to determine whether she's part of the Evans family that I represent."

The receptionist got up from her desk, and walked Jake's card to an office down an adjacent hallway, came back and announced, "Mr. Harding, our Director, Mrs. Sherwood, will be right out to speak with you."

Cynthia Sherwood soon walked down the hall to meet Jake, shook his hand, and said, "Mr. Harding, give us fifteen minutes and we'll have Jennie Evans escorted to an Attorney-Client room where you can speak with her in private. I feel obliged to add that your visit may be a waste of time as she likely is not part of the Evans family you represent. I also suggest you do not take seriously any of the wild claims she's likely to make."

"Thanks for your courtesy, Mrs. Sherwood, and for your warning."

Twenty minutes later, Jake entered the Attorney-Client Room. "Good grief, Jennie, is that really you?"

"Oh Jake, it really is me. You've got to get me out of here before I lose my mind!"

"I was astonished when I first saw Clay in jail, but you absolutely bowl me over. You're so . . . uh . . . young-looking."

"Is Clay alright? I miss him so much. I was terrified when I saw the cops take him away in handcuffs."

"He's fine, Jennie, loves you like crazy and is concerned for your well-being. Before you start trying to explain all that's happened, don't. I know all about it already. Clay explained everything, and swore me to secrecy."

"Can you get him out of jail? Can you get me out of here?"

"I've already sprung him out of jail on bond, and we've started working together to clear him of molestation charges. But, Jennie, it's going to be a little more difficult to spring you. Be patient; Clay and I are going to do whatever's necessary to make it happen. But it may take some time."

"I can hardly wait. They treat me like a child here, with no rights. And I have to sleep in a dorm bunk with real teenagers, who drive me nuts. But I'll be patient. After all, I'm 77 years old, and have learned how."

"I can't stay Jennie; I don't want the time I spend here to appear like I know you. We want to keep the secret."

As he left and walked down the hall, he stuck his head inside Cynthia Sherwood's office and said, "I didn't recognize her. And, no kidding, she told me she was 77 years old. Thanks anyway for allowing me to check her out. I have to look at some paperwork in my office about the extended

Evans family, and may have to phone you again and possibly see her one more time. Good bye."

"Have a nice day Mr. Harding."

≈ ≈ ≈

The following afternoon, Glen and Sonny Sanger walked into that same CPS facility and spoke to the receptionist, "Hi, we're the Sangers. Mrs. Sherwood is expecting us. Would you please tell her we've arrived?"

A few minutes later, Cynthia Sherwood appeared. "Welcome Sanger family," she said. "A volunteer is escorting Jenny Evans to the Interview Room as we speak."

"Wow, Cindy, you look great," said Glen. "You always did, but something's changed."

"So nice you noticed, Glen. Yes, I've lost almost 20 pounds."

"Nice going," added Sonny. "Do you think she'll talk with us today?"

"You'll have to find out when you see her. Ready to go? Follow me. I'll join your chat with Jennie for just a few minutes to make sure she understands why you're here. I won't need to monitor your whole visit; you certainly know the ropes and rules, thanks to your experience and success with several of our other girls."

CHAPTER 11

THE Sangers sat down at the table directly across from Jennie, who was already seated. Cynthia stood at the end of the table and said, "Jennie, this facility where you're currently staying is charged by the State to be responsible for the care of children that are runaways, or that may have lost their parents and have no other family, or are in limbo. But sometimes, rather than housing the children in a state-run shelter such as this one, we prefer to place them with good families that volunteer to take them in as if their own. Mr. and Mrs. Sanger have years of experience as such a foster family, and wanted to meet you.

Sonny smiled at Jennie and said, "Hello Jennie, I'm Sonny and this is Glen. We're ordinary folk who have an interest in you and your happiness,"

Jennie, straight-faced, said nothing and just looked bored, staring down at the table.

Glen continued, "We've been foster family to quite a few teenage girls over the years, Jennie. Decades ago, we lost our own teenage daughter in an auto accident, and ever since, we've found happiness by opening our home to young ladies like yourself that don't seem to have a family or home of their own."

Jennie looked up, and seemed to start taking interest in her visitors.

"Sometimes it's just for a month or two, and sometimes for a year or two," Glen added. "So we'd like to chat with you a little to learn about you. You can learn about us, and determine whether you'd want to stay with us in our home in the Cloverdale neighborhood of Montgomery, as opposed to being here in this Shelter."

At this point, Cynthia excused herself and left the room.

"Before we start the chat, do you have any questions you'd like to ask?"

Jennie thought to herself: *They look like they're in their fifties. I could be their mother, and here they are treating me like a lost child.* Then she said, "I feel like a prisoner here. Nothing but painted concrete pink walls to look at, noisy kids keeping me awake at night, no phone and lousy food. What would it be like if I was your foster kid?"

Inwardly, Glen and Sonny beamed, and silently exclaimed: *Hurray; she might be open to the concept.* But before they could respond to Jennie's question, she said, "So Okay, let's chat."

"Jennie, is that your real name, and is your last name Evans," asked Glen.

"Yes, I'm Jennie Evans for real."

"You look like you're about 15 or 16, but the CPS staff told us you claimed to be 77. How old are you, actually?"

"Does it really matter, Mr. Sanger, for the purposes of whether we're going to be compatible?"

"Well, no Jennie, I guess not. But we've only been given information based on a police report. We'd very much like to hear from you first hand why you were brought to CPS."

Jennie thought about this request for a few minutes, and then described in detail the incident at the motel, ending in tears as she described seeing Clay in handcuffs, being put into a police car as she was being taken to CPS. With empathy, Sonny handed her a tissue.

Glen then asked, "Have you ever done drugs, or been in trouble with the law."

"No to both. Now, I have a few questions," said Jennie. "Would I be the only teenager in your home? Would I have telephone privileges; the police took my cell phone? Would I have my own room? Would I be able to go outside the house? Would I get to go shopping with you? Would I get to eat the same food as you?"

"That's a bunch of questions all at once, Jennie, but the answers are 'Yes,' 'Yes,' 'Yes,' 'Yes,' 'Yes' and 'Yes.' We'd treat you as if you were our own daughter. The only difference would be that a social worker would come to the house at various intervals to see how you were doing, and to see if we wanted to continue having you in our home."

"How long would I have to stay?"

"That'd depend on a lot of circumstances, Jennie, but you technically have to be a ward of the State until you're 18 years old. You might be with us, or if not, with a different foster family, or with the Shelter. Now, if some of your family members showed up and claimed you, and the claim was proven valid, you'd obviously be released to them, and no longer be a State ward."

Jennie smiled, thinking: *I could be released to Clay, as he's an adult in the State's eyes. If only he can stay out of prison.* Then she said, "It sounds like a wonderful opportunity to me, if you want me, and they let us do this."

Glen and Sonny looked at each other, nodded, and said in unison, "We want you, Jennie."

Glen added, "Now let's see if we can make this happen. Jennie, we'll leave you for now and start working on it. It shouldn't take more than a day or two if we're lucky. So be good in the meantime."

Sonny added, "Jennie, it's been so nice meeting you. I can't wait to take you home."

As the Sangers walked away from the room and down the hall, Sonny commented, "She is so mature and intelligent for her age. She speaks and acts like an adult, not at all childish."

Glen added, "Indeed, I think she is one." As an afterthought, he added, "I wonder whether that guy that was arrested in the motel, claiming to be her husband, is one too?"

Cynthia Sherwood met them in the lobby. Glen Sanger said, "It's a 'go,' both for us and for Jennie. We seem to be well matched. How soon can we meet with the social worker assigned to Jennie's case? We want to start the ball rolling to make this happen."

Cynthia responded, "Wait here for a minute, and I'll check the roster on my desk to confirm, but as I remember, the Evans girl was going to be assigned to Trudy Buckley."

Cynthia left them seated in the lobby and walked to her office. She confirmed Trudy's assignment, and phoned her to see when she'd be available. When she returned to the lobby, she said, "Trudy is the individual you'll need to work with. She's a Senior Investigator with years of experience. She can see you in the morning. How about 10:00?"

"That's just fine," said Glen. "We'll be here. And thanks so much for your help, Cindy. Bye."

≈ ≈ ≈

The following morning, the Sangers met with Trudy Buckley. After the formalities of polite introductions and small talk, Trudy got down to business. "So, I understand you want to take the Evans girl into your home. When I talked with her shortly after the police dropped her off here, she seemed very upset and was quite belligerent, not to mention that she seemed a bit mentally deficient, defiantly claiming that her age was 77. I've since talked with the examining physician and psychiatrist, and they say she's healthy and stable, but has a sharp tongue. Do these facts modify your stance?"

"Not at all," said Glen. "We've spent over an hour with her, and she seems pleasant, intelligent and quite mature for her age. My wife and I have had a lot of experience with foster teenage girls in our home, and Jennie looks to be an easy adaptation by comparison."

"I have the prerogative to place her in your home on my own, but I'd feel better if we ran it by a judge, either Judge Jones or Judge Rodriguez."

Glen said, "We've worked with Judge Rodriguez several times in the past, and he knows of our success with other teenage girls. We'd prefer him if he's available."

"I'll see if I can set it up with him. Are you available this afternoon?" asked Trudy.

"Yes, and anytime tomorrow, if necessary."

"It's almost noon, why don't you two go find a nice lunch place. I'll reach the judge, set something up over at the courthouse, and phone you after 1:00."

"Okay, Trudy, hope to see you then."

≈ ≈ ≈

Judge Rodriguez, wearing a suit rather than court attire, walked from behind his mahogany desk and welcomed Trudy and the Sangers into his tastefully decorated private chambers that afternoon. A gold-framed picture of the President hung on one mahogany paneled wall, and one of the Governors on another. The room, well lit by a large French window behind the desk, featured a large Turkish carpet on the polished hardwood floor, and a leather-upholstered sofa, where the guests were asked to sit.

"So, Mr. and Mrs. Sanger," said the Judge, "once again you'd like my blessing to welcome some young lady into your home; is that a fact?"

"Yes sir, Your Honor. There's a sweet young girl who calls herself Jennie Evans that we've met, chatted with, and want to take home with us," said Sonny. "She's not very happy with the Shelter atmosphere, and is highly receptive to our invitation. Trudy sees no problem, but thought we should run it by you first."

"What's your opinion, Mrs. Buckley," the judge asked.

"I think the arrangement should work out well for the girl. An escort is currently on the way with Jennie in case you wish to question her directly."

At that point, Jennie entered and was invited by Trudy to approach the group. "Jennie, come on over here and meet Judge Rodriquez."

"Hello Jennie," the judge said. "These folks have been telling me that you'd like to leave the Shelter here, and go to live with Mr. and Mrs. Sanger in Montgomery. Is that true?"

"Yes, Your Honor."

"Remember, Jennie, that the Sangers deserve your respect and cooperation, as they always will have your best interests at heart. I've known other young ladies like you that spent part of their teenage years with them, and are now living happy and successful lives."

"I promise to do my best," she responded.

Speaking to the group, Judge Rodriquez concluded, "As long as you all are satisfied, I am too. I've had enough time to peruse CPS's paperwork on Jennie earlier, and everything seems in order. I'll issue a finding in favor of your and her verbal motions, and email it to Cynthia Sherwood. I hope all goes as well with Jennie as it did with all the other teenagers you folks have fostered. You're doing a great service."

"Thank you, Judge! We'll keep everyone in the loop, and take her home with us tonight if that's okay with the CPS supervision. We appreciate your time, sir."

CHAPTER 12

A T the same time that the Sangers and Jennie started driving to Montgomery, it was ten hours later, near dawn local time, in a small remote rural community of more than 800 people in northeastern Kenya, Africa. A 13-year-old girl there threw the aging half blanket covering her off to the side, rolled off her mat, rose to her feet, brushed the wrinkles from her faded floral dress, and stood barefoot on the cool dirt floor, ready to start the new day. Her name was Farhani, and she was the only girl child of the Iweala family, proud members of a Turkana tribal community. Her two brothers, sleeping on a separate mat to her left, wouldn't have to start their day for another hour. She was the family's early riser because she had one of the most critical responsibilities of family life there: she had to get water every morning to help meet the family's minimal needs for survival.

Farhani stepped outside the hut and picked up the two empty six-liter plastic containers used to carry water from the river, a nine-kilometer walk down the dirt path toward the sun, still below the horizon. There was just enough light to gaze a hundred meters down that path to make sure no wild beasts had arrived during the night, and might be standing in her way. This daily task was so routine, she could almost do it with her eyes shut, but didn't dare to do so while the sky was black, except for the glow on the horizon. It was an easy walk going to the river when the containers were empty, but very tiring on the return trip, three hours later. She was always afraid that her arms would grow too long from carrying the water weight, and then no man would want her as a wife.

Bakkir, the oldest male child at 15, got up an hour after Farhani left for the river. His dad, Waitimu, the village Chief, had also just arisen. Soon they would gather their snares and leave to trap meat for the Iweala family, a weekly effort. They would most likely snare a *diki-diki* miniature antelope if their efforts were successful, an irregular supplement to their normal, infrequent goat meat diet. In the afternoon, Bakkir would tend to the cows and goatherd.

Adani, mother of Farhani, the second to arise, had been up for about half an hour and was making the family's morning meal, consisting of *chapatti* flatbread and *githeri* corn and bean stew. She had to use up the last half-liter of remaining water in the third plastic container. She too would daily walk to the river to get water each afternoon for family and animal use, but only after her other responsibilities were completed.

The youngest boy, Keriuki, was too sick to get up today. The river water sometimes made him weak from diarrhea, especially when the river level was down due to drought, and the animals stood too close to where the water was drawn. Bakkir would have to tend to the herds alone again that afternoon, without Keriuki's help.

During the evening meal, Waitimu told his family that during the day he'd met a village friend who sometimes worked as a driver for a safari guide service near Wamba. He'd heard news that the Soit Elotimi community, hundreds of kilometers to the south of theirs, had a deep well installed last month right inside the common area by an organization known as the Samburu Project. No longer would the girls and women of that community have to walk for hours each day to get water. Now all they had to do was walk a few meters to the well, push a handle up and down, and the water flowed out of a pipe right into their containers. And because that water was clean and pure, the children wouldn't sicken or die from contaminated river water any more. Moreover, he said that the women and older girls had much more time now, enabling them to teach or go to the new school that they were starting to build next to the well.

As much as Waitimu longed for a similar community well, the Samburu Project was too far away, and had to put in wells at too many villages in the east and south that needed help. If only somehow, someone, or some organization that had the know-how and equipment, as well as the money and people to do it, would come to their community and put in a well.

Later that night, after the rest of the family was asleep, Waitimu rested on his mat, still thinking about how important a well could be for their people. His final wishful thought before closing his eyes to sleep was, *Maybe someday it will happen.*

As Waitimu was falling asleep that night in Kenya, Clay Evans was driving that very morning from Florence to Dothan for a meeting with Jake.

CHAPTER 13

CLAY drove the car into the jammed parking lot of a busy well-maintained hamburger joint about 100 miles west of Dothan, and made a cell phone call. "Hi Jake, are you still going to be at your office later today?"

"Yeah, Clay, I'll be here all afternoon. What have you been doing?"

"I've locked up and buttoned down our Florence home, taken care of bills and finances, and acquired key papers from our safe deposit box. I also rooted through some attic boxes to find Jennie's high school yearbook, as well as my own. All this stuff might come in handy. So as soon as I can grab a quick bite to eat, I'll drive to your office and arrive about 2:00 pm, if that's okay with you."

"I'll be glad to see you," agreed Jake.

"What's new with Jennie?" Clay asked.

"As I mentioned last night, I was able to see her and affirm that she's safe and well, although not too happy about being in a CPS shelter. I'm planning to phone the Director there sometime this morning to keep my pathway open to see her, if necessary."

"Okay, my burger just arrived. Bye."

Shortly after 2:15, Clay walked into Jake's office. Jake took him by the shoulder and said, "I got through to the Director just about an hour ago. She told me that Jennie left the shelter as a foster child in the care of a couple from Montgomery. Jennie and the couple appeared before a judge who approved the transfer. I also spoke with the social worker directly involved, and she said Jennie was delighted with the move. As an attorney investigating the case, I was able to obtain the couple's name, address and phone number."

Clay turned white. "Good grief, Jake. What am I going to do? How am I ever going to get this mess straightened out if she's in a foster home in Montgomery and I'm out on bail in Dothan? Who knows where I'll be if I end up in prison. Poor Jennie!"

"Calm down, Clay. Look at the bright side. Jennie's safe there, especially if you're incarcerated. Otherwise, how safe would any pretty 16-year-old girl be, walking around alone in any town. Montgomery's not that far away, and maybe, just maybe, we can get to see her there."

"Let's try, Jake, as soon as we can."

Jake thought a minute or two, as Clay was walking circles on the office carpet. He picked up the phone, dialed the number that the social worker gave him, and asked for Mr. or Mrs. Sanger.

"Hello. This is Sonny Sanger."

"Mrs. Sanger, my name is Jake Harding, and I'm an attorney down here in Dothan. The CPS people I've been working with on the Evans case gave me your number, and advised that Jennie Evans is now in your custody."

"Yes, that's correct. Is something wrong?"

"No, Mrs. Sanger, not at all. But I wonder whether you might be willing to let me stop by and see her for a few minutes someday soon?"

"Well of course, Mr. Harding. Glen and I are usually around the house all day, every day, except when there's shopping to be done. When would you like to come?"

"How about late tomorrow morning?"

Sonny, shouting through the open kitchen window, "Glen, will you be done with that tree trimming today? A lawyer wants to come by tomorrow to see Jennie before noon."

From the back yard, Glen shouted, "Yeah, I think so."

"Mr. Harding, tomorrow morning will be fine. Does Jennie know you?"

"Yes Ma'am. And I look forward to meeting you and Glen as well."

The next morning, the drive to Montgomery along Route 231 took only a little over two hours. During that time, Jake and Clay discussed strategies for the coming meeting. The problem: How could Clay enter the Sanger home without causing an uproar and confusion? The Sangers were expecting only one guest, Jake. How could he explain Clay's presence?

Surely the Sangers knew the background of the molestation charges that led Jennie into CPS custody. And possibly then, they might be suspicious that Clay, if he were present, could be the accused male offender. Then, if Jennie were brought into the presence of Clay, she obviously would be so thrilled and excited to see him that she'd happily and noisily run into his arms.

Indeed, there would be great confusion and an uproar experienced by everyone present except Jake. Clearly, Clay could not enter the house without a lot of prior explanation.

So the strategy was decided. Clay would have to sit in the car while Jake entered to meet the Sangers. Jake would have to bite the bullet, and tell the Sangers the truth about what happened in the motel room. If they believed him, he could reveal that he got Clay out of jail on bail, and that he was sitting in the car. And then the Sangers could allow or refuse to allow the lovers to meet for the first time in over a week.

Jake rang the doorbell.

"Come on in, Mr. Harding, the door's open," Sonny yelled from the kitchen. "Glen, come on down; we'll all be in the living room."

"Please call me Jake," he said, as Sonny approached him drying her hands with a dishtowel.

"Okay, Jake. You can call me Sonny," she said as she shook his extended hand. Glen, right behind her, said, "And I'm Glen," shaking Jake's hand too.

"I have a confession to make; please don't call Jennie to join us for awhile," said Jake. "I didn't come alone. I have a friend in the car. Please bear with me for a few minutes, and don't kick me out just yet. I must tell you a true story first."

"Goodness, Jake, we'd never kick you out. You just got here. Tell us your story."

Jake continued, "I trust that the staff at CPS briefed you on how Jennie came to be a ward of the state. However, the folks there were given false information by the police. Yes, Jennie was with an older man in that motel. The police made the assumption, after being prodded by a nosey motel manager, that the man was molesting Jennie.

"Nothing could be further from the truth. The man, just a few years older than Jennie, was truly her husband. The couple had just finished dinner at the nearby restaurant after driving all the way from St. Augustine. Since they had another 300 miles to drive to their home in Florence, they'd decided to spend the night at the motel before resuming their travel.

"While Jennie was detained and transported to CPS, her husband was handcuffed and arrested for child molestation, and subsequently jailed in the Houston County Detention Center. Since I've been his family's attorney for two decades, I was able to have him released on bail. That man's name is Clay Evans, and he's outside sitting in the car."

"Land sakes, Jake, what a terrible injustice to both Jennie and Clay," said Sonny, with Glen nodding agreement, secretly delighted that another one was there.

Jake continued, "Now Clay is still accused of serious charges, and if we cannot prove his innocence, he's facing years of confinement in prison. That'd be most unjust. In that event, he has solace in knowing that Jennie will be safe in a good home with loving and experienced foster parents. He understands that you folks may not want him to meet Jennie today, and that you may not personally be interested in ever meeting and talking with him. That's why he decided to remain in the car."

"My gosh, Glen, don't you think we should invite Clay in and meet him?" asked Sonny, grinning inwardly.

"Absolutely," said Glen, expecting there had to be a lot more to the story, especially related to Jennie's youth and statements of her age being 77. His hidden excitement was also growing.

"Then with your permission," Jake said, "shall I go out and ask him to come in now?"

"Indeed," the Sangers said in near unison.

Jake excused himself, walked out to the car, opened the door and spoke to Clay, filling him in on the conversation that had just taken place. Clay stepped out, and straightened his clothes.

"My, isn't he a handsome young man?" Sonny said to Glen, as they looked out the window. "I think our hunches are going to prove true. But what about Jake? How can we talk freely with Jennie and Clay when he's right there, listening?"

"I dunno, Sonny, let's wait and see how things break."

CHAPTER 14

CLAY and Jake walked up to the front door. Clay looked ill at ease.

"Hello, Clay," said Glen Sanger, extending his hand to welcome the new visitor. "I'm Glen."

"And I'm Sonny. I suppose Jake has told you that we've just brought Jennie home as a foster daughter."

As he respectfully shook hands with both, he replied, "Yes, and I think Jennie is very lucky to be invited into your home. I appreciate your openness to meet and speak with me."

After everyone was seated, and soft drinks were served, Sonny broke the ice, saying, "Jake told us about what happened in the motel and afterward. He also mentioned that you and Jennie were married, Clay."

"Yes, we are married."

"When did you two get married?" asked Glen.

"I . . . uhh, don't know how to answer that question," stammered Clay, turning red. Sonny, realizing the embarrassing predicament Clay was in, said, "Clay, if you like, we can invite Jennie down to join our group. She's in her room writing emails to her friends."

"Oh yes, please do; we haven't seen each other since the motel room incident, and I miss her very much."

Sonny disappeared up the stairs. Clay stood up in anticipation. In just a few minutes, Sonny and Jennie walked down the stairs. Jennie could barely restrain herself from jumping over the railing to get past Sonny. As soon as both of her feet were on the floor, Jennie squealed and ran into Clay's waiting arms. They hugged and kissed each other. A very tender moment. Even Jake noticed his eyes were peering through a thin watery film.

Sonny broke the silence, "Okay, everybody, let's all sit down."

Jennie and Clay sat together on the couch, hanging on to each other.

Glen picked up on his quest, "You young folks make such a beautiful couple. How long have you been married?"

Clay and Jennie looked at each other, stalling, not knowing how to truthfully answer that question. So neither spoke; both just looked down at their feet.

Jake broke the silence, reaching into his suit coat's inner pocket, "Mr. and Mrs. Sanger, Clay gave me this document yesterday after returning to Dothan from their home in Florence. It's their Wedding Certificate. It states that they were married on August 2nd, 1958."

"Why, that's 54 years ago," said Glen, playing along. "How can that be?"

Jake responded, "I don't know how to rationally explain this to you, but Jennie's real age is 77, and Clay is really 81 years old. As their attorney and confidant for many decades, I too was astonished to meet them again last week, as they now appear to be teenagers rather than the old couple I remember so well. Clay explained to me that they'd both been immersed in the Fountain of Youth pool attraction in Old Town, St. Augustine, and as a result became young again overnight. Neither Clay, nor Jennie, nor I can even begin to explain how or why. Please hold this very private personal information in confidence. If this ever became public, the whole world would soon know, and would all go nuts."

When Jake finished speaking, Glen and Sonny stood up, turned to face each other, did a high five, and embraced. Everyone's jaw dropped as they watched, wondering in silence what next would happen.

Glen then turned to his visitors and said, "You asked us to keep your age status confidential. We're now asking you to do the same for us, as we're about to reveal very unusual and private realities to you."

Sonny continued the revelation and said, "Clay and Jennie, we too are 'Renewables.' We're many decades older than we appear."

Glen continued, as Clay and Jennie jumped to their feet, "Welcome, Clay and Jennie, to the most exclusive cultural group in the world. You are both 'Renewables!'"

Jake, his jaw still hanging low, stared and listened in utter amazement. He finally spoke, "I feel as though I'm sitting here as a monitor during the filming of a sci-fi movie. Except that the main characters aren't actors. They're real live people rejoicing that they're extra-human. Someone please explain."

"I'll try," Glen responded. "First, Jake, I must ask you again to please hold in utter confidence everything you hear and learn about Renewables, today and ever hereafter. Do you solemnly promise?"

"Yes, I promise."

"As it's been explained to me, there's a unique underground stream that flows beneath several of these United States. We call it 'PDL water.' Rarely, its tributaries pop to the surface here and there as small springs, some with sufficient flow to create a small surface pool, or even a small remote swimming hole. These waters have an inexplicable power to react with an extremely rare type of human DNA, accessed via minute seepage. This seepage gains entry through body cavities, damaged skin or even possibly transition right through normal skin. The molecules of this unique water quickly migrate as though they were super viruses, to and through the cell structures of all organs. The net effect is that all body parts that have suffered aging are restored to their optimal youthful state, which occurs between the ages of 15 and 25. The body transformations are apparently completed within 8 to 12 hours after exposure to the water."

Jake, still aghast, said, "Glen, you started your explanation with the preface, 'As it has been explained to me.' Who was it that explained that to you?"

Glen answered, "A member of a highly secret national organization that most Renewables belong to, known as the Renewables Society. He'd lived through many cycles of transformation, and his real age was double or triple mine before he died during an attempt to save some children from a fire. He was the Chairman of the Society at the time."

"Okay," asked Clay, "then how old are you, really?

"I'm really 132 years old, and Sonny is 127. You see, the fluke in the DNA structure that permits the transformation to occur is implausibly passed on to a spouse during many decades of life together. Perhaps it's some kind of natural gene-splicing; no one knows.

"If either one of such an old couple is exposed to PDL water, and is thereby transformed, the other one will also seek transformation by subsequently exposing himself or herself to that water. That's why most Renewables are old married couples. Clay, did one of you become immersed in the Fountain of Youth first, or both simultaneously?"

"I fell in, and then a couple nights later, Jennie intentionally immersed herself."

"That's usually what happens. One spouse by accident, and the other on purpose. But it couldn't have happened to Jennie if she didn't have the unique DNA type; one of you most likely acquired it from the other sometimes during your five decades of marriage."

Jake, his head now swimming in near disbelief, asked, "Glen, how many Renewables are there in existence?"

"To the best of my knowledge, there're fewer than three hundred currently alive today. We try to meet at least annually, as any society should, but it's infrequent that all members are present because many are engaged in their chosen activities, frequently overseas. I don't know the total number that ever existed, but it's probably under a few thousand. I do know who the first one was."

"Who?" Jennie asked.

"It was Ponce de Leon. He really did find the Fountain of Youth, contrary to popular belief. The Society has a diary page that he wrote and initialed. It was acquired from descendants of the Timucuan Indian tribe, who preserved it over the years as a memorial to Ponce, who sacrificed his life attempting to save the tribe from extinction during a smallpox epidemic during the late 1500's."

"Aha," said Jake, "that's not possible. Ponce de Leon died in 1521 in Cuba, a victim of an Indian arrow that wounded him during a skirmish when he and some colonists briefly returned to Florida from Puerto Rico."

Glen replied, "That may be what the historians say, but Jake, the diary page confirms that the colonists left for Cuba after the fight, but he stayed behind, expecting to die there quickly. But some Timucuan women mercifully bathed him and gave him some spring water to drink, and the next day he awoke as a young man. He remained with the tribe as the first Renewable until his death caring for others during the tribal epidemic. Incidentally, in case you didn't pick up on it, the name that's been given to our mystical water, 'PDL water,' comes from Ponce's name."

Jake responded, "This is all so unreal; someone please pinch me."

CHAPTER 15

SONNY suggested, "I've got a nice stew simmering on the stove, Jennie. We can continue this wonderful discussion over supper, if your visitors are agreeable."

Jake said, "Clay and I'd love to stay, Sonny, but he and I have to appear in court on some minor pretrial motions in the morning, and we still have the two-hour drive back to Dothan ahead of us. Besides, I don't think I could stand any more revelations today. My mind is smoking from overwork trying to digest it all. We all could probably use some quiet time to think through the ramifications of this situation. Clay and I'll be back in a day or two, as our mutual schedules permit. Or perhaps, Clay can return alone to visit with Jennie and you folks if I can't make it."

"Either way would be fine with us," said Sonny.

Handshakes, hugs and kisses behind them, Jake and Clay left the side street where the Sangers resided, and drove towards Route 231.

≈ ≈ ≈

Two days later, Clay did return by himself. Jake was tied up in court on a different case.

"Hi everyone," said Clay, as he entered the Sanger residence, Jennie holding the door open. "I have some interesting news. Jake learned from some of his police friends that the Dothan PD had asked the Florence PD to procure some of Jennie's and my personal hygiene articles from our house. Those items are currently being processed by the Dothan forensics people, looking for DNA to compare with the swabs they took from Jennie and me on the day we were detained. Jake feels that if the results are positive, and he can access the test data, he can use it to help vindicate me of the molestation charges."

"Oh Clay, that's wonderful news," squealed Jennie.

"Well, Jake says don't get your hopes up too high that anything's going to happen real soon. There're a lot of bridges to cross. And there may be foot-dragging by City folks worrying that the release of such a report might open the door to false arrest charges."

Glen wanted to change the subject. "Time will tell. That's great news Clay, in any event. But here we are all standing around by the front door. It's such a nice day; why don't we all go sit down on the shaded patio."

Sonny added, "I'll bring us all an ice tea."

Once seated and settled, Glen said, "Sonny and I want to brief you two about a couple major issues you're gonna' face as Renewables. I don't know if you two have thought about this first issue, but eventually you're going to have to decide what to say the next time your adult kids show up at your home. They'll want to know where their Mom and Dad are, and ask 'Who the heck are you?'"

"Good grief, I never foresaw that issue," said Clay. Both of our kids, now in their 50's, are in other parts of the state, but either one of them, with or without their family, could show up at any time."

"I thought about it a little," said Jennie, "but I don't know how we'll handle it. Clay, the holidays are just around the corner, so we'd better work on it soon."

"Yep, I agree, but first and more immediate, Jake and I have to make sure I don't end up behind bars in some prison on the other side of the state. If that happened, the kids would have to wish me 'Happy Thanksgiving' or 'Merry Christmas' through a Visitors window."

Sonny offered, "Well, we know a few Renewable couples that've been through it, and we can give you some input based on their experiences. We didn't go through that crisis ourselves, as our only child died when we were young."

Glen took a sip of his tea, and continued, "Okay, now let's change to the second subject. Have you two kids given any thought at all about what your life is going to be like decades from now? For example, how are you going to support yourselves financially through what could be another full lifetime?"

Clay confidently responded, "We're well set. I have a pretty good pension, and we're getting two social security checks each month."

Jennie added, "In addition, I inherited a very sizeable chunk of money that's well-invested to bring us regular interest and dividend checks. Actually, neither of us will ever have to work for income again, even when Clay's pension and social security checks stop. I guess they will when the systems determine they're going to someone aged beyond a normal lifetime."

"Sonny and I are delighted to hear that, you two. Actually, we sort of expected that kind of answer. It follows the Renewables pattern we've seen over the decades. As I mentioned the last time we met, virtually all Renewables seem to be married couples, and most seem financially independent. Those characteristics are critical to our Society's Grand Project."

"Grand Project?" queried Clay. "What project is that, Glen?"

Glen avoided directly answering that query, but said, "Look, before you became Renewables, you two had lived a long life, were seemingly healthy, and undoubtedly hoped for at least a few more years together. But you were both getting to the age where suddenly an unhappy event could have removed either of you from the scene. If you'll excuse my blunt lingo, in the long-term scheme of things, you were as good as dead.

"But now, instead, you have a whole new life ahead of you, with no responsibilities and no entanglements. But, trust me, without past family and with very few friends left, without work and without responsibility, your lives could become boring and wasted.

"Instead, as Renewables, you've a wonderful opportunity to use your new lives to give back, to render help to the earth's peoples in need. Of course, you absolutely have no such obligation to do so. But, you are in a unique position that enables you to self-sacrifice your time and energy for the benefit of humanity, for the less fortunate, the sick, the impaired, for those struggling with other pitfalls of living, and for unbounded societal improvement. Sonny and I charge you two to make that a significant part of your new lives."

Clay, feeling a sudden burden coupled with bewilderment responded, "We wouldn't have the faintest idea how we could even begin fulfilling such a commission."

"We know what you're feeling," said Glen, "as we've been there. That's where the Renewables Society comes in. It's partly designed to help folks exactly like you. We encourage you to eventually consider applying for membership in this organization when the time is right. Of course, you've got a lot of business to attend to before you're ready for that action, like securing your freedom from prosecution. But when you're ready, let us know, and we'll help you get involved."

Wide-eyed, Jennie said, "Clay, joining really sounds fantastic, and it might open doors that could make our new lives adventurous and exciting. Let's do that."

"We'd better think and talk about it after we solve our real and immediate problems," said Clay.

Sonny then grabbed Glen by the shirt, started towards the door and said to him, "Don't we have some shopping to do today? These kids won't mind if we duck out for a few hours."

"Huh . . . oh yeah, we sure do need to go shopping, don't we. Excuse us for awhile, Jennie. I don't think you'll mind being here alone with Clay. Bye."

CHAPTER 16

J AKE phoned the County Prosecutor, Harry Stansfield. "Good morning Harry, this is Jake Harding, your favorite court opponent."

"What have you been smoking, Jake? Favorite opponent? That's some stretch of the imagination. Okay, so 'good morning' back to you. What's on your mind?"

"Remember our conversation over cocktails a couple of Fridays ago, about the underage couple routed out of that motel by the police?"

"Yeah, real strange case. I can understand the guy, uhh . . . Clay, lying about his identity and age to protect his butt, but the girl child that he was with, insisting that she was 77 years old, and his wife to boot; that has me stumped."

"Well, I've taken their case."

"What? I thought you were smarter than that, Jake. It's an automatic loser. You'll screw up your reputation."

"Harry, I have some very interesting evidence in their favor. I'd like to do a formal deposition of both Clay and Jennie together, with you personally being present, not one of your deputies."

"It seems a bit premature to be doing depositions, Jake, but if you feel it's something that should be done soon, I'll set it up."

"If possible, Harry, let's shoot for seven to ten days from now."

Two days later, Jake and Clay went to a nearby Dothan bank where Clay had temporarily deposited important documents he'd retrieved from his Florence safe deposit box. They emptied the local box, removing its contents of birth certificates, marriage certificate, mortgage papers that Clay and Jennie had executed and paid off decades ago, as well as various sales documents for car leases, a boat purchase and others.

From there they went to a downtown office building. On the fourth floor, they entered a rented room and met two other men, introduced as Dick White and Hans Vanderhoest.

Hans, who was a signature verification expert, asked of Clay, "Please sign your name six times on this blank sheet of paper. Thank you."

Jake handed the documents from the bank to Hans, who then departed saying, "I'll get these papers back to you as soon as I'm finished with my analysis, Jake."

Dick, who was a polygraph expert, hooked Clay up to his machine and asked a long series of questions, which Clay answered without hesitation.

"After I examine the results, Jake, I'll email you an official court-ready report, probably within three days," said Dick as he left. All necessary business being completed, Jake and Clay went their separate ways.

Thanks to prior pressure by Jake, and subsequent approval and release papers from Harry Stansfield, Clay was able to recover his car from the Dothan PD impound lot, and their luggage from the PD's property room. He then checked in at a local motel, where he could spend time catching up on weeks of email, phone calls, etc. Jake headed to Front Street to get permission from CPS allowing him to bring Jennie to Dothan for the upcoming deposition. Several days later, he drove to Montgomery to pick her up.

Clay's deposition, with Jennie present, took place at 9:00 am the following day in a private room adjacent to Harry's office. Jake wasted no words or time getting right to the point, as he addressed Harry, "I believe that after you consider the evidence my client is prepared to present, Mr. Prosecutor, you'll concur that I'm duty-bound to prepare a motion petitioning the Court to dismiss all charges against Clay Evans, and to expunge the records of his arrest."

"Come on Jake, the police walked in on Clay and this underage girl, Jennie, in bed in that motel; both of them lied and showed phony or stolen ID's."

"You're partially correct, Harry, in that they were in bed in the motel room, but they are who they say they are. The ID's were truly theirs, and they are married!" Jake said with emphasis. "We have evidence here today to prove it.

"First, take a look at this Dothan PD forensics report that affirms that Clay's and Jennie's DNA specimens, which were taken immediately after their arrest, perfectly match the DNA taken from personal hygiene articles removed from their home by the Florence PD forensics people."

Harry studied the report, shaking his head, and asked, "What other evidence do you have? There may be ways that the DNA could have been planted in their home."

"Here's a report from Dick White, the same polygraph expert you've hired many times, Harry. It confirms that Clay is who he says he is, and that he and Jennie are married, without doubt."

Jake continued, "Here's another report that shows that Clay Evans is the same person that signed all of these original documents that I'm laying before you, including Clay's and Jennie's marriage certificate, mortgage papers and others. This report was prepared by your favorite handwriting and signature verification expert, Hans Vanderhoest."

"Hmm," grunted Harry.

"Here's an affidavit," Jake said, handing it to the prosecutor, "from Dr. Blasé, your own dentist, Harry. It affirms that his examination of Clay's teeth last week match perfectly with the upper and lower x-rays for Clay Evans, which came from files prepared over twenty years ago by Dr. Joe Givens, Clay's dentist in Florence. That's also absolute proof that this Clay Evans, seated across from you, is who he says he is.

"Lastly, Harry, take a look at this photo of Clay in his 1949 high school yearbook, and this one of Jennie in her 1953 yearbook. Now look at them sitting across the table from you, and compare. They're virtually identical, except for clothing."

"Okay, Jake, you've got a winning case if there was ever a jury trial, no doubt. So go ahead and prepare your motions to dismiss and expunge. There's just one gigantic problem with all your evidence, though. How can they truly be the people that lived back then in the 40's and 50's, and still look as young today as they did back then?"

Harry looked squarely into the eyes of Clay, and said, "Tell me Clay, if you are 81 years old as you say and the documents prove, why the heck do you look like a teenager?"

Clay truthfully responded, "Mr. Stansfield, I went to bed feeling ill one night about a month ago, and woke up the next morning looking like I do now. That's it. And the same thing happened to my wife, Jennie, only three days later. I'm not going to complain about these body changes, would you?"

"No, I wouldn't. To be honest, I'm jealous. I wish it'd happen to me and my wife.

"Okay, Jake, I'll tell the judge hearing the motions, probably Rodriguez, that I'm not opposed and in fact concur with them.

"Clay and Jennie, I have only one piece of advice for you two; when you leave here, go on over to First Street and tell the Department of Motor Vehicles that you need replacements for your 'lost' ID's, bearing current photos. If they have a problem with that request, have them phone me."

The Evanses did take that advice from Harry, went to the DMV, and patiently stood in the usual long lines waiting their turn. Without looking at them, the gum-chewing clerk nonchalantly copied the data from their applications for replacement licenses into the computer, including their actual birth dates, as submitted. "Next," she shouted, as the Evanses were shuttled off to another line, awaiting their turn to have photos taken. An hour later, they walked out with temporary licenses in hand.

The following morning, Judge Rodriguez granted Jake's motions, and Clay became a free man again, with no arrest record. He and Jennie both hugged Jake, bid him farewell, picked up their new permanent licenses at the DMV, and headed for the Sanger's home in Montgomery. A backyard celebration lunch followed, highlighted by Glen's charcoal-grilled hot dogs, Sonny's potato salad, and accompanied by, at last, Clay's favorite beer.

As dusk approached, Clay said, "Glen and Sonny, you've played a key role in freeing us to enjoy our new lives. We can't thank you enough. You're the best friends we or anyone could have, and we look forward to continuing that relationship over the coming years."

Jennie added, "Thanks especially for rescuing me from that CPS dormitory, and taking such good care of me while Clay was working on his freedom."

Sonny said, "You two are wonderful friends to us too. We're so happy we met you, and know we'll be seeing more of you."

Clay added, "Jennie and I need to spend a couple of weeks alone together, so we're going from here to a cabin we own on Sardis Lake in Mississippi. When we're feeling rested and normal again, we'd like to come back and seek your help in applying for membership in that Renewables Society you promoted."

"Hot dawg!" said Glen. "We'll sure be available to do that, and to tell you a lot more about how it all works."

≈ ≈ ≈

After darkness fell that same evening, a shadowy figure squeezed through the brush and bushes outlining the property of "The Fountain of Youth" attraction in Old Town, St. Augustine. The figure quickly walked to the rear of the building housing the Fountain pool, placed a footstool beneath the window of the Ladies Room, stepped up to the top and pushed up on the upper edge of the lower pane. It was unlocked, and easily opened. The figure climbed through, and using a small flashlight, found and got into the pool, climbed out, closed the window and left the building and grounds behind. Following a long drive home dripping wet, the individual went to bed. The next morning, on awakening, that person went into to the bathroom, turned on the light, looked into the mirror, and moaned with dismay, "Damn! It didn't work." Jake Harding was crushed. "Oh well," he said, "it was worth a try."

CHAPTER 17

SARDIS Lake proved to be the perfect tonic to reinvigorate the shaken lives of Clay and Jennie Evans. Sardis Lake wasn't just a vacation. Three weeks on their treed vacation plot at the water's edge, living in a rustic cabin built by Clay's dad, or motoring out on the lake itself in their classic varnished wooden Chris Craft, or swimming at a nearby sandy beach, were all just what a savvy doctor would have ordered. Even though they'd been married more than 54 years, Clay and Jennie began to feel and act like young teenage newlyweds again.

"Last one in is a chicken," shouted Clay one night, as he literally ran off the edge of their lot into the lake's dark water, which then glistened across its surface with a thousand sparkles as his naked body splashed down in the moonlight."

"Oh, I don't know if I want to do this, Clay; are there any fish prowling at night that can bite me?" Jennie replied, as she gingerly put one foot into the water. "How deep is it, I don't remember?"

"If you don't come in, I'll have to swim away by myself," laughed Clay.

"Okay, I'll come in, but please don't swim away." With that, she splashed forward, landing on her belly, and swam quickly toward Clay, trying hard not to touch bottom.

He splashed a handful of water toward her face as she approached. "Oh please, honey, don't," she cooed, literally thrusting herself into his waiting arms. "And no swimming away, I want you to just stay with me right here, and hold me up, and hug me and kiss me."

Clay laughed with delight, pleased to oblige as he cuddled the slippery smooth body of his youthful playmate.

After the month and a half of separation that had been thrust upon them just two days after their astonishing body changes took place, they now truly looked, felt and acted like teenagers again. Moreover, they were completely free. Free from state-imposed confinements, free from responsibilities, free from the need to work, free from the health problems and restrictions of old age, and free to be totally and completely in love.

But all good things eventually come to an end, including vacations.

Bowing to that logic, Clay finally suggested, "Baby, we really need to pack up and take off soon. We've got to kiss Sardis Lake good-bye, and head back to Montgomery. Remember, we promised the Sangers we'd be back in a couple of weeks, and we've been here more than three."

"Yeah, we better get going, honey," she responded. "We really do need Glen and Sonny's guidance to help us plan for whatever lies ahead. We know that it certainly could involve joining that Renewables Society thing."

The following afternoon, the Evanses drove back to Montgomery, and pulled into the Sanger's driveway. Glen and Sonny came out the front door to greet them as they exited the car.

"Welcome back to the working world," yelled Glen. "Did you two have a good time over there at that lake?"

"It was super. We didn't want to leave," Clay responded. "But we decided there that you two might really help point us towards an exciting and meaningful future. Are you guys still up for that?"

"Glen was chomping at the bit for you two to come back," said Sonny. "He's so anxious to get you involved with the Society that's he's been online for hours. He's gone through all the latest procedures for bringing in new members."

"You mean the Renewables Society has their own website?" asked Jennie, as they all walked into the living room and sat down.

"Yes," Sonny said, "a very secret one that only members can access. All of the Society's activities are viewable online. There's no actual Society office or authoritative leadership. All members cooperate to keep the website current and meaningful.

"Well, if we decided that we wanted to join, how would we go about it?"

Glen took over, "First of all, candidates for membership must be sponsored by at least two current members. In your case, that'd be Sonny and me. Each of you would also complete a multipage application. That will help the Society to extensively probe your lives before you became Renewables. Good thing your arrest was erased from the records, Clay. Trouble with the law can block admission in some cases, according to the procedures I've been reading.

"Then, assuming your background checks were acceptable, you two must prove that you're worthy to become members. A three-person Membership Committee will decide that. Worthiness is measured by the completion of an initiation requirement. That's the heavy-duty part."

"We really did hear what you said the last time we were here, Glen, about us doing something for humanity But we've been hoping to start doing all the things we missed doing for lack of money while we were young, lack of time during our middle age, or because of health issues in recent decades. Things like foreign travel, sports and rugged outdoor adventures."

"The Renewables Society wouldn't slow you down in achieving those objectives, Clay. In fact, it'd probably speed you up, as you'll come to understand. In addition, membership has some wonderful benefits. All members get free healthcare, life insurance for the benefit of any living heirs, professional financial and investment advice, legal advice, an estate plan, and free lodging in many countries around the world as you travel."

"Whoa, where's all the money coming from to pay for those fancy benefits?" asked Clay.

Glen responded, "Remember, Clay and Jennie, you're renewable, not immortal. Someday, maybe multiple lifetimes from now, you will die. All members are required to update their estate plan to name the Society as a beneficiary for fifty per cent of their estate. That only takes effect however, if, when you are both deceased, you have no living children, grandchildren or great grandchildren heirs. Members are free to specify where the other fifty per cent goes, such as distant descendants, colleges, charities, etcetera."

"That makes a lot of sense. One more question, Glen. During one of our visits here, you mentioned the Society's

'Grand Project.' But you avoided telling us anything about it. Can you tell us now?"

"Nope. Only members can know. You have to be a full-fledged member first. Frankly, it is now, and must stay, a bona fide secret to the rest of the world. Someday, I'm certain you two could become deeply involved in it. You'd find it to be a huge challenge, and a great privilege."

Clay shrugged his shoulders and looked questioningly at Jennie, who nodded 'Yes,' and asked, "Tell us what our initiation requirement would be, Glen."

"Okay, you must select one from a list of three proposed missions that I've picked out from the Society's master list. Then you must plan and execute it successfully. All three are overseas, but are straightforward, and don't require having to learn a new language. All can be completed in less than the two-year-max timeframe."

"I have to admit, this initiation requirement is starting to intrigue me," said Clay.

"Me too," added Jennie. "Tell us about the three you picked."

"Okay. One is fulfilling the need for a couple to teach English in a Tibetan village at the base of Mount Everest. Another is to invest your sweat labor in a Habitat for Humanity project in Bangladesh. The third is to drill a well for drinking water in a Kenyan community in Africa."

"Oh, they all sound so exciting, so adventurous!" exclaimed Jennie.

"I guess then, Glen, that we probably do want to go ahead and join. Tell us a bit more about the initiations you picked," said Clay.

Glen then briefly fleshed out the scope of each of the three that he had selected, and proposed that the Evanses stay for supper. During the meal, he suggested, they could discuss the options and everyone voice their opinions. Then Clay and Jennie could make a firmer decision. After the meal, they could delve deeper into the minutiae of that decision as presented online by the Renewables Society website. While Sonny started preparing the meal, Clay and Jennie retreated by themselves to the Sangers' back yard, where they sat on a bench beneath a huge flowering apple tree.

Clay spoke first, urging caution, "Jennie, we seem to be rushing a bit headlong into this Society-thing. Then again, maybe we should commit at least to the background check. If we're approved, then we can decide whether or not we want to continue and go for the mission."

Jennie whimpered, "I keep thinking what he said about those poor girls and women in Kenya having to walk all those miles every single day to collect river water. Just so their family members can stay alive. It makes me want to cry, just thinking about their babies and little kids getting sick or dying because the river water they get isn't pure. I think we absolutely should join the Society, and try to do something to help."

Clay cautioned, "I'm not sure we should take such a mission on. We know nothing about drilling a water well."

"Jenny put on a sad face, and whined, "Oh, Clay."

Clay, taking note of Jenny's dismay, quickly softened his stance. "Perhaps we should go look online for details of that project after the meal. In the meantime, let's not count our chickens before they hatch, okay?"

Jennie, seemingly ignoring what Clay had just proposed, said, "I really believe we should go ahead, join the Society and do the Kenyan mission, Clay. Especially since we've never been to Africa, and it'd be a great adventure for us."

Clay again cautioned, "As I said, babe, before we make any rash decisions, let's get more of the facts from the website. You know, when you get right down to it, we don't have to do any of these initiations. We don't have to join the Society. We can just live our lives any other way we choose."

"B-o-r-i-n-g," she groaned.

After the dinner meal, Clay and Jennie headed for the Sanger's computer, had Glen log on, and spent an hour and a half reviewing details for the three options, concentrating mainly on the Kenyan mission.

Finally, Clay sighed and concurred with Jennie. "Okay, agreed! We should join. I'm willing to settle on the Kenyan option too. It'll take only months, not years."

"We should go tell Glen and Sonny about our decision," she said as she grabbed Clay's hand and pulled him towards the living room."

"Fantastic!" said Glen, on hearing their decision. "Before you two start doing anything, we've got to get you tentatively approved. I've downloaded the application forms. I suggest you complete them now, before leaving.

"Say, where are you two staying tonight?"

Before Clay could respond that they intended to return to their home in Florence, Sonny said, "Why don't you just stay here. Jennie's room's now vacant."

They did, gratefully, thus avoiding a 300-mile drive in the dark.

CHAPTER 18

AFTER breakfast the following morning, Clay and Jennie said their goodbyes to the Sangers, with hugs and cheek kisses, and headed out for the six-hour drive to Florence. That afternoon they opened up the house.

"Oh Clay, it smells musty in here," said Jennie as she walked in.

"Well, except for the day I came to Florence to get the files and safe deposit papers that Jake needed, the house has been locked up tight. It's been that way ever since we left on our Anniversary trip to St. Augustine," said Clay.

"Uhh, I forgot one other time," he added. "The local police came in one day to get our toothbrushes, combs and other stuff that might've had our DNA on them.

"Keep any house closed up a couple of months in this part of Alabama, Jen, and it's not going to smell nice inside."

"I'm going to fix that right now," she said, as she started opening windows and doors leading outside. "I'm glad that it's breezy and not raining."

"You do that," said Clay, "I'm going to my desk now to see if my computer still works. I hope those forensics IT guys at the Dothan PD didn't screw it up. Jake said they'd disassembled it, looking for some kind of incriminating evidence stored on the hard drive."

To his delight, the computer still worked fine. Clay went to Google Search and typed in "Samburu Project," remembering Glen's suggestion that it had be a good starting point to do research about drilling wells for water in Kenya.

From the website display, Clay read: *The Samburu Project´s primary initiative is aimed at providing easy access to clean, safe drinking water to communities throughout the Samburu District of Kenya. This is a community where women and children walk up to 12 miles every day in search of water. Often, this water is contaminated. With clean water, it will become possible to impact other aspects of community life including education, healthcare, income generation and women´s empowerment. With water, development happens.*

"Glen's right about this website," mumbled Clay. So he plunged headlong into researching the whole concept of how charitable organizations go about bringing fresh water into the lives of remote Kenyan peoples. The Samburu website provided an extensive starting insight into the methodology of such an undertaking.

In subsequent days, Clay expanded his research elsewhere on the web, and also made contact with Americans who'd actually visited some of the Samburu well sites under construction or previously completed years earlier. It became clear from their reports that he and Jennie should do the same; that is, they should actually visit some of the Samburu Project sites as a critical first step to their own mission.

Clay called Jennie into the office, and showed her some of the photos and information on the Samburu pages. "Jen, if we're really serious about drilling a well in a remote Kenyan village, we need to witness first-hand how the big boys make it happen. We need to go see the action at one or more Samburu Project sites."

"You mean in Kenya?" she asked.

"Right."

"Okay, hon, I'm on board, but have a lot of questions running around in my thoughts. When do you think we should go? What do we need to do in preparation? How do we get there? How much is providing a well going to cost? Can we afford to pay for it ourselves, or do we need to start a fund for contributions? And, how safe is it for us to do this?"

"The answer to your last question, Jen, is a qualified 'safe.' The Americans I interviewed said it was perfectly safe in the villages, but that in Nairobi, we'd have to be careful about our movements, especially at night. We'll flesh out answers to your other questions during the coming weeks.

"More important right now than an African trip, I believe, is that we need to start figuring out how to handle the possible near-future arrival of one or both of our kids and their families."

"Oh Clay, that's right! Joshua and his family could show up on our doorstep any day, but almost certainly for our usual Thanksgiving celebration. That's only two weeks away. It's unlikely that Deborah and Ken will come this year; they were still in Paris the last time we spoke."

"I doubt that either family would just show up unannounced," he observed, "but then again, it's happened before."

"I think we should phone Joshua today, and find out if they're coming," she said.

"Good plan," said Clay, "but I think I'll call Glen and Sonny first. They said they knew how other Renewable couples coped with the trauma from their kids' first visitations. Maybe we'd profit from that info."

"You do that. I'll go start putting some kind of a lunch together. The fridge is empty, you know. We've got to go get some groceries soon."

After phoning Sonny Sanger and chatting with her for almost an hour, Clay phoned his son.

"Hello, Joshua?"

"Yep, it's me. Who's this?"

"It's Pop; how are you and the family these days?"

"Your voice sounds different, Pop. Younger, sort of. You got a cold or something?"

"Nope, I'm fine. Mom and I were wondering if you guys were planning to come by and have Thanksgiving dinner with us this year."

"Funny you should call. We just decided to do that at breakfast this morning."

"Wonderful! Are the kids coming too?" Clay asked.

"Briana's 20 now, and is planning to have Thanksgiving dinner at her boyfriend's house; he wants his parents to meet her. But Cody will be there if I have anything to say about it. He'd rather be skateboarding with some of his teenage buddies, or chasing girls at the mall, but I know how to twist his arm. You know, Pop, I can't remember being that interested in girls when I was 15."

"You weren't, Joshua. You were only interested in Citizen Band radio. You had one in your room, and only came out to eat once or twice a day, or on weekday's to go to school. But, times have changed, Son. In other ways too, as you'll see when you get here."

"What's that mean?"

"You'll see. By the way, have you spoken lately to your sister?"

"Nope, been too busy. I guess Debbie's been busy in Paris too, since she didn't call us as usual this month."

"I assume you'll be staying overnight, considering the distance you have to drive."

"Yeah Pop, we thought we'd get there Wednesday evening and leave Friday morning, if that's okay with you and Mom."

"I'm sure Mom will be thrilled to have you and the family here for both nights. She's calling me now for lunch. Gotta go, son. Bye."

"Bye, Pop. See you soon."

For the next week and a half, Clay and Jennie looked forward to Joshua's arrival with some trepidation. They knew all would be well by Friday morning following Thanksgiving day, but wondered how well they'd be able to control the initial shock and disbelief of their son and his family when they walked in the door Wednesday night. They took Sonny's advice to heart, and had gathered and laid out on the coffee table all the family photo albums and miscellaneous pictures of Jennie and Clay when they were young, as well as their wedding pictures.

They also displayed their new driver's licenses, as well as copies of the original ones they'd replaced. With help from Jake, Clay was also able to obtain and display copies of the newspaper articles and pictures, police report, DNA comparisons, and court documents from Dothan, as well as

CPS intake records on Jennie. During his phone conversation with Jake, he'd also invited Jake to come to the celebration, knowing his bachelor status. Jake tentatively agreed.

The Evanses were as ready as they could be for the impending trauma.

CHAPTER 19

JOSHUA Evans and his wife, Eve, exited the parked SUV, and walked to the front porch just before dark. Cody Evans remained in the car, watching the final half hour of the DVD movie *The Bourne Legacy,* playing on the back-seat monitor.

Joshua pushed the doorbell button. Coming from inside, they could hear the muffled sound of chimes playing the first stanza of 'Three Blind Mice.' The door opened, and there stood Jake, with a drink in his hand.

"Hi Joshua; hi Eve. Come on in and have a seat in the living room. Clay and Jennie are in their bedroom, and will be right out."

"Jake, it's so nice to see you again. It's been a couple of years, I think," said Joshua.

"It has been awhile, indeed. Your dad prepared a pitcher of whiskey sours, knowing how much you prefer them. I've already got mine; why don't you pour one for Eve and yourself. You may need them."

"Huh, why is that? Is something wrong?" responded Joshua as he made the pour.

Clay and Jennie walked into the room, hand in hand. Jake said, "Joshua, say hello to your Mom and Pop."

Joshua jumped up, his jaw dropped, and he blurted out, "What is this, Jake, some kind of prank. Who are these kids?"

Jake replied, "The name of that young good-looking man there is Clay Evans, and his lady's name is Jennie Evans. This is not a joke, Joshua; they really are your mother and father."

"Preposterous!" shouted Joshua, "My Dad is 81 and Mom is 77!"

"Joshua, take a swig of that there drink in your hand, calm down, and have a seat," said Jake.

By now, Eve had gulped all of hers down, and was pouring herself a refill.

Clay walked over to Joshua, grabbing his hand and saying, "Son, remember when I phoned you two weeks ago about this visit, you mentioned that my voice sounded young? Well it's because I am young again, at least in my body. My mind, emotions, knowledge, wisdom, soul and all that stuff are just the same as they were a few months ago, when my body was that of an 81 year old."

"I don't know how to respond to this situation. I'm speechless. I need another drink, a big one," said Joshua as he plopped down on the couch.

"Give me your glass, honey, and I'll pour you one," said Jennie, in her sweet teenage voice, as she took the glass out of his hand.

"Okay, all of you. I simply cannot believe all this without some kind of proof," Joshua said after a few more swallows of his second drink.

Eve, who'd been quiet up to this point, added with an ever-so-slight slur in her voice, "Old people just don't get young again. It can't happen. You must all be actors playing some kind of cruel game with my husband and me."

Jennie responded, "Oh Eve, we're so sorry that you're confused by our appearance. We love you both very much, and aren't trying to make you feel uneasy."

Jake by now had stepped way back near the hallway to the front door. It shortly opened, and in walked Cody.

"You're Mr. Harding, aren't you," he said to Jake. "I remember going to your Attorney office in Dothan once with my dad."

Without waiting for a response, he looked around the room; saw his mother and father seated on the couch, and two teenagers standing nearby, all with drinks in their hand, and all participating in a heated conversation. Not wanting to interrupt, he continued standing next to Jake, and whispered, "Where's grandma and grandpa?" And after a slight pause, "Wow, that's a cute little chick standing there, just about my age. Could you introduce me to her?"

Jake almost broke into laughter, but suppressed it, and seeing the opportunity to inject a little merriment into the all-too-serious conversation in the room, gently pushed Cody along as he walked toward Jennie, saying, "Jennie, this young man thinks you're cute, and wants to be introduced to you."

Cody said, "Hi Jennie, want to go watch a new DVD movie with me in my folks' SUV?"

Clay couldn't suppress his laughter, and let it flow all the way out from his belly up through his mouth into the otherwise silent room.

Jake quickly interrupted, "Cody, Jennie is your grandma."

"She is not my grandma; my grandma's an old lady!"

Jennie rushed over and kissed Cody on the cheek and said, "Oh Cody, we all love you."

He was one confused 15-year-old boy, so he turned on his heels and stormed out of the room towards the front door.

"Cody, where are you going," shouted his mother, Eve.

"I'm going outside; all of you people are acting nuts!"

Up until that point, Clay had said little, but he knew he must take charge of the deteriorating situation. "Joshua, I've located some photos and other things that I'd like to show you and Eve."

He sat down between them, displaying materials that Jennie, in turn, was placing and removing from the coffee table in front of them. "Look here, son, at this picture of me in my college fraternity's yearbook. I was 19 then, about the same age that my body now appears to be. Compare that with me now." Clay stood up and struck the same pose as the photo.

"Here's one of me a few years earlier, when I graduated from high school. And here's one more to compare, when I was an army officer at age 21. Do you see the unmistakable resemblance?"

Joshua said, "Yes, but . . . ." Shaking his head, his voice trailed off as he stared back and forth between the photos and Clay's features, adding, "How is this possible?"

Clay continued his display of proof, "Not too long ago, I was arrested and jailed. That's another story that I'll fill you in on later, or tomorrow. You can also read about it from these newspaper clippings. Here are official Dothan police documents that show that DNA swabbed from my mouth upon booking is identical to the DNA removed from my toothbrush and comb that were removed from this house a day later by Florence police. These documents were critical to my release from custody. You should also look at these official results of court experts that tested me on a lie detector machine, and made handwriting comparisons.

"Placed over there on the coffee table are dozens of other photos, including Mom's when she was a teenager, when we were dating, and our wedding pictures."

Joshua's eyes were transfixed on the paperwork. After minutes of delay, he looked up at Clay, and said, "Okay, D-D-Dad, but you've got an awful lot of explaining to do to help Eve and I digest this situation . . . like how did you two become young again." Joshua nearly choked getting the word 'Dad' out of his mouth.

Jennie said, "Tomorrow's another day, and we can explain more then. But soon we've to get some rest. Cody can sleep on the floor in the study, and Joshua and . . ."

Before Jennie could finish, and anyone head for their sleeping quarters, the front doorbell rang. Once again, Jake was closest, and opened the door. There stood Cody's sister, Briana, and some guy, presumably her boyfriend. "Come on in, Briana, your family's in the living room; they'll be pleasantly surprised to see you."

"Hey, hi, welcome Briana," shouted the group. "You look terrific," exclaimed Joshua.

"Hello everybody, sorry to surprise you guys so close to bedtime. Glad you're still up," said Briana.

"Have a seat you two; can I pour you each a drink," said Eve.

"Right on!" said the new guy, with emphasis. "Got any moonshine?"

Briana spoke up, "This is my new boyfriend, Billy Bob."

Billy Bob was close to six feet tall, built like a football lineman with broad shoulders and huge hands. He wasn't particularly handsome, but noticeably a standout, thanks to his two missing front teeth, ear rings, and nose ring. He was wearing a plaid flannel shirt and bib jeans. A pair of muddy work boots protruded out from his threadbare trouser cuffs.

Briana introduced the others in the room to him. "This is my dad, Joshua, my mom Eve, brother Cody, friend Jake and, uh, I don't know these other two teenagers."

Joshua, somewhat grimacing, answered Billy Bob's query, "No moonshine, Billy Bob, just whiskey sours."

Billy Bob responded, "That's all right, Dad (click); my pappy says if it's got a kick to it, drink (click) it down (click) anyway. Do (click) you have a bigger glass?"

"What the heck is that clicking sound I'm hearing?" asked Joshua.

Billy Bob said, "Oh, just ignore that. That's me, yup. Every time I use a word that starts with a "D" (click), the pair of studs in my pierced tongue click together. Ya'll get used to it after awhile. Briana's having trouble getting used to it, but she puts up with it because she likes the studs when we kiss."

Joshua and Eve both touched a hand to their forehead, looked down, softly groaned, shrugged their shoulders and glanced toward each other with dour expressions on their faces.

Clay smirked, but Jennie looked distraught.

Jake chimed in at this point. "Briana, you need to know something about these other two teenagers . . . ."

"Where's the toilet; I need to take a whiz," Billy Bob interrupted.

Jake answered, shaking his head, "It's down that hall, last door on the right." Billy Bob moved quickly in that direction.

Jake, taking comfort in Billy Bob's departure, as he realized he'd almost disclosed something that should remain a family secret, continued what he was about to say to Briana. "Briana, those teenagers are Clay and Jennie. They're your grandparents. I won't take time to explain, because your mother and father can do a much better job to help you comprehend that. Talk with them, but please don't keep them up all night doing it; they need to help Clay and Jennie make a big Thanksgiving dinner tomorrow. And, Briana, please don't repeat that to Billy Bob; it's a family secret. Also, Joshua and Eve, top secret, right; it's up to you to please help Cody understand that he cannot talk about it anywhere outside of the family."

Cody, quiet until then, objected, "I still don't believe it."

Jennie tried to conclude the conversation, "Okay, everybody, let's start over on the sleeping arrangements. Cody and Billy Bob sleep on the floor air mattresses in the study, Jake takes the small bedroom, Joshua and Eve get the larger guest bedroom, and Briana sleeps on the floor air mattress in her parent's room."

Billy Bob said, "Hey, can't Bri and I be together in the same room."

"Too bad, Billy Bob. The logistics of space allocation simply preclude that possibility," countered Jennie.

"Shucks, 'logistics' sure messes up my plans for tonight. We weren't going to have a logistics problem when we going to stay with my folks."

"Hey, Billy Bob, how come you're here and not there at your folk's house?" asked Joshua.

"Because my mama and pappy had an automobile accident this afternoon."

"Oh my gosh," said Eve. "Are they alright? Are they in the hospital?"

"Nah, they're in jail. Mama, who was driving (click), got arrested for DUI (click), and Pappy had so much moonshine in his gut that he tried to beat up the cops. He got arrested for that."

Clay took over, "Good night everybody, lights out in three minutes."

In the dark, Briana and her parents talked about Clay and Jennie well into the wee hours before finally falling asleep.

CHAPTER 20

IT was Thanksgiving morning. The men were still sacked out or showering, but Jennie and Eve were busy in the kitchen, preparing the turkey and all the fixings for the afternoon feast. Briana was off someplace applying her makeup. Cody had been up since dawn, and was outside somewhere. Nothing was cooking yet, but the turkey had been cleaned and stuffed with dressing, and most of the vegetables cleaned and cut up. They decided the bird had to go into the oven at 9:30 am in order to be on the table ready for carving at 2:00.

Just about then, the front doorbell rang. Eve said, "That must be Cody back from wherever he's been." She headed for the hallway, and opened the door.

"Oh my god, hello Deborah! What a surprise. And I can see Ken unloading the luggage from the station wagon's back door. Oh, here come all three girls, piling out of the back seat. Your parents are going to be so thrilled to see you. And, I might add, for you to see them."

Deborah responded as she entered, carrying a bag of groceries. "We just got back from Paris earlier this week. Ken's been transferred to the home office in Montgomery. At the last minute, we decided to come here for Thanksgiving as a surprise, rather than just phone; it's such a perfect opportunity to see the family after such a long time. We were really hoping you and the family would be here too, and are delighted that you are!"

Jennie intentionally stayed in the kitchen when she heard that the rest of the Evans clan had unexpectedly arrived. She wanted very much to hug Deborah and her granddaughters, but decided to wait until Clay came downstairs.

That wasn't meant to be. Deborah walked directly into the kitchen to put the groceries down, hoping to see her aged mom there, but saw only a teenage girl. "Hi, I'm Deborah, Jennie's daughter. Who are you, young lady?"

Uh oh, this is where it hits the fan, Jenny thought. "Hi Debbie, I'm . . . uh . . . Jennie."

"Oh, you have the same name as my mom, isn't that nice."

"No, you don't understand, I am Jennie Evans, and I am your mother."

"Hey, little girl, don't try to feed me that kind of baloney; what kind of stupid game are you playing? I've got a daughter as old as you."

"I'm not playing a game, honey. I'm your 77-year-old mother, but I've got a wonderful new young body, no kidding."

Deborah yelled out loud, "Ken, Joshua, Eve . . . someone come into the kitchen and help me!"

Jake, who had heard the yelling, rushed down the stairs into the kitchen, and arrived at the same time that the others did. "Hi Debbie, remember me, trustworthy old Jake, one of your family's best friends?"

"Jake, thank goodness you're here to put the fear of the law into this twerpy teenager," gasped Debbie.

"Debbie, you know I'm not a kidder, and that I tell the truth. This beautiful young lady is really your mother, Jennie Evans."

Ken stepped quickly behind Debbie to support here, as she was starting to wobble.

Just then, Clay walked into the kitchen. "Hi Debbie, I'm your dad."

Debbie felt light-headed, and then everything in her vision turned silvery, then black. She slumped in Ken's arms. Just for a minute or less. Joshua put a kitchen chair beneath her, and Ken sat her down. When she opened her eyes, she was surrounded by everyone, including her daughters who had just entered the kitchen, and were saying, "Mom, are you alright. Mom. Mommy."

Debbie soon spoke, "Oh I'm so embarrassed, I'm sorry. I must have fainted. That never happened to me before."

Clay spoke, "I'm sure all of you are confused and trying to understand all this. But let me assure you, your mother and I are real, and healthy, and we love you all. I promise to explain how Jennie and I became young again when the children and Billy Bob are elsewhere. But please, not now, or we'll all miss our dinner, as no one is cooking. Ladies, please continue what you were doing, and the rest of us will get out of the kitchen."

Billy Bob, who had stayed in the living room, welcomed the returning men, saying "Co-o-o-l, now that you guys are back, we all can start drinking (click) again, right Dad (click)?"

Ken said to his three daughters, "Girls, for now, come on into the living room and say hello, but don't talk about what happened in the kitchen. Then you can all head right upstairs to the attic game room to play, or go outside."

Deborah felt normal after a few minutes, and announced, "We suspected that you might not have enough turkey and fixings to feed five more hungry people, so we stopped at the store in town and bought a ham, veggies, a couple of pecan pies and some ice cream. Now, ladies, what can I do to help?"

Jennie said, "How about cooking the ham in the bottom half of the double oven. There's a perfect pan in the stove's drawer. Briana can help you, as well."

Clay prepared another pitcher of whiskey sours, and also opened and brought a bottle of white wine and glasses, plus a few cans of beer into the living room. As the men started conversing over drinks, the three daughters chatted about whether they wanted to go outside or up to the game room.

The doorbell rang again. Ken said, "One of you girls, get that, please."

Dawn walked into the hallway and opened the door. There was Cody. He stood there outside, staring at Dawn, and said, "Hi, I'm Cody, your cousin. We met before at my grandpa's lake house. Remember? Say, how'd you like to watch a neat new DVD movie with me in my folks' SUV?"

"Come on in, Cody. In case you forgot, I'm Dawn. I'm 15 now. My sisters and I are going up to the game room. Wanna come? And later, I'd love to watch that movie with you."

The girls and Cody headed upstairs. He had a huge smile on his face.

After the turkey was in the top oven, Jennie said, "I'm going to go set the table. I think I need to do a head count."

She entered the dining room and counted. There was son Joshua and his wife Eve, granddaughter Briana and her boyfriend Billy Bob, and grandson Cody; daughter Deborah and her husband Ken, granddaughters Cindy, Dawn and Kristen; Jake, Clay and herself. Thirteen in all. Even with the extra leaves in place, the table would be too small. So she decided to set up a card table nearby, where the grandkids could eat.

It was a memorable Thanksgiving dinner indeed. At its conclusion, Billy Bob left the table and went into the library to watch the football game with Cody. A few of the adults, still seated around the table, jested that the clicking phenomenon thankfully left with him.

Over dessert, Clay and Jennie, with Jake's help, laid out the facts leading to the change in their bodily appearance, as well as the presumed biochemical and genetic causes. Clay noted, in passing, that it was possible that inherited DNA might beneficially impact the future lives of both children and grandchildren. The planned near-future visit to Kenya was also briefly discussed.

No one seated there, except for Jake, ever truly believed in the deepest sense of their being that 81-year-old Clay and 77-year-old Jennie had bodily become young teenagers again. That reality simply clashed with their intelligence. But they all, nevertheless, verbally acknowledged it, as there was no alternate explanation to the proof presented to them.

Even if Billy Bob had heard the discussion and seen the evidence, he wouldn't have really given a hoot, one way or the other. To him, other folks made their lives too complex; he'd learned well from his pappy to just go with the flow, roll with the punches, and not try to figure out anything that required real thought. All that really mattered in life was food in your belly, moonshine that didn't taste foul, and pretty women to woo.

The grandchildren simply accepted subsequent secret explanations as fact, but totally ignored them in their hearts, because they knew without a doubt that their real grandparents, Clay and Jennie, were old, feeble and grey. It was simply pointless to dispute what their parents told them, as they knew the place of children in society . . . behave nice, be quiet, do what they're told, and don't argue.

After the meal, Jake said his goodbyes and left for the long drive to Dothan. Clay followed him to the car, and thanked him profusely for coming to help minimize the traumatic transitions from disbelief to acceptance.

The rest of the participants continued the celebration all afternoon, with leftover snacks and desert at dusk. No one got drunk, but Eve again had a noticeable slur in her speech while they were playing charades. The kids stayed upstairs for hours until they came down to watch television. Cody asked Clay on two occasions if he could possibly find some mistletoe in the closet, or out in the yard where it sometimes grew in the trees.

Finally, it was getting close to bedtime, and Jennie re-allotted the sleeping areas. The girls would sleep on air mattresses in the game room, Cody and Billy Bob in the studio, Joshua and Eve in the large guest bedroom, Briana on an air mattress in her parents room, Deborah and Ken in the small guest bedroom, and Clay and Jennie in the master bedroom. Everyone slept well except Cody; Billy Bob, lying on the air mattress next to his, snored loudly, with a click at the end of each respiratory vibration.

CHAPTER 21

BY 10:30 am Friday morning, the visiting members of the Evans Clan had departed, leaving Clay and Jennie thankfully alone and at peace. While cleaning up and picking up the remains of the celebration, Clay commented, "I don't want to go through that same experience all over again at Christmas. Our kids finally seemed to believe us, but the grandkids are adamant that we're fakes. Moreover, I'd rather not experience the presence of Billy Bob in our home again. I can't imagine what Briana sees in that character."

Knowingly, Jennie said, "I can."

Clay let that matter drop, wisely choosing not to probe the insights of the female mind. Instead he suggested, "Let's bug out of here before Christmas; let's go to Africa. Let's take on that initiation mission so we can become members of the Renewables Society."

Jennie responded, "I'm on board with that, hon; but first, we'd better touch bases with Glen and Sonny to see if the Committee approved those applications we filled out."

"Yeah, I'll do it right after we finish making this place look acceptable again."

≈ ≈ ≈

"Hello, Glen? Hi, it's Clay. Have you heard anything yet from the Society about our applications?"

"No Clay. I suppose I should've checked by now. I'll do it pronto, and get back to you soon."

"Okay, Glen. As soon as you give us the go-ahead, we'll start serious planning on our first trip to Kenya."

A few hours later, Glen called back. "There's a problem holding things up. The Dothan police records show that you were arrested on suspicion of robbery. Apparently, when the court expunged your arrest record, they only did so for the child molestation charge. Someone dropped the ball, and it's jeopardizing your admission to the Society."

"Doggonit! Look, I think I may be able to have Jake fix that. Would the Committee be willing to reconsider?"

"I think so, but only if the error is corrected fast. They won't meet again for weeks."

"Okay, assuming I can get it fixed in a day or two, how's the Committee going to pick up on that correction?"

"I can ask them to re-check the police records if the error can be corrected promptly, say in one or two days. Do you think that would give Jake enough time to put the fix in?"

"I don't know. I'll call Jake right now and ask. Bye."

≈ ≈ ≈

"Hello Jake. Once more, I need your help."

"Don't tell me you're in jail again."

"No, nothing like that. My false arrest for robbery was never expunged! It's creating a real problem for us with the Society."

"Those dumb court clerk jerks. Relax, Clay, I'll do my best to get it fixed."

"I knew you would, Jake, but it's got to be done immediately. Glen's going to try to get them to review the police files again; I don't know how long that Committee would be willing to wait. How many days should he suggest?"

"Let me see if I can get it done in two days. I'll let you know after I talk to my court and PD contacts."

Clay didn't hear from Jake the rest of that day. He and Jenny didn't sleep well that night. Nor did Glen.

Jake called back the following morning. "Sorry for the delay, Clay, but one guy I needed to cooperate was out of town. He returned this morning, talked to the judge, court clerk and the PD captain. Everyone apologized and agreed to have the record corrected before day's end."

After thanking Jake, Clay called Glen and asked whether he could arrange to have the Committee recheck the records the following day. They did. The matter was resolved.

Jake closed with, "Stay out of trouble Clay. Please, no more problems. Bye."

≈ ≈ ≈

Three days later, Glen phoned. "Your applications are approved, Clay. What can we do to help you two move forward?"

"Well, as we mentioned, we've decided on the Kenyan water-well mission. Could you find out from the Society where the village is that expressed their dire need for a water well, and who's the primary contact in that village?"

"Will do, Clay. It might take a little time. I'll get back to you ASAP."

Another day passed before Glen called with the information.

"Clay, there's a tribal community of about 800 people that live in the Turkana region of northern Kenya. They're the ones that pleaded for help from the Samburu Project, but were too remote. They're actually hundreds of kilometers away from the region where the Samburu wells are being drilled. But the Samburu people made sure the word got around about the Turkana need for help up north. One of our Society's members heard of it during his travels, and added it to the website missions list more than two years ago."

"Jennie and I are ready to tackle one, Glen, and now we know that's the one. We'll start our plans and preparations at once. How do we get there, and who's the contact?"

"All I can tell you is that the community is about 15 km northeast of the junction of a primary road, A1, and a secondary road, B4. You'll have to find the exact location with the help of locals. The contact, once you've found the place, is a Turkana tribal chief named Waitimu Iweala."

"Thanks, Glen; great information. We can take it from there. We plan to go see some of the Samburu Project wells first; maybe they'll be able to help us locate that village."

"One other thing you need to know, Clay. Apparently, some kind of government drilling permit from Nairobi is necessary. It costs 12,500 Kenyan shillings, which works out to about $145. But there may be bribes that have to be paid too. You'll have to learn about that on your own. Also, be sure to document your whole mission adventure. Keep notes and take pictures.

"Oh, and finally, Sonny and I put a package in the mail for you two. Our Society traditionally provides member candidates departing on their initiation mission journey with identifying good luck charms. Sort of like carrying a rabbit's foot. Keep them with you to identify yourself should you happen to meet another Society member. They each consist of a tiny sealed plastic vial containing a few drops of PDL water, a ribbon bearing the initials RS, and a key chain. There's one for each of you in the package. We'd have liked to have handed them to you personally, but won't see you again before you leave. Good luck, God speed, have a great trip."

≈ ≈ ≈

Jennie asked, "How many changes of clothing do we need to pack? How many dress outfits should I bring? Oh, and do we need to get immunizing shots at the doctor's office?"

Clay responded, "Hey babe, we're going only on a short fact-finding trip this time. A few days there, and we'll return home to plan and do the real long-term preparation. That's when we'll get the shots. This time, you may want one dressy outfit for a stopover in London going and coming. That's it. We need to travel light. But don't forget to pack your new digital camera."

Clay subsequently determined that no advance visa was necessary to enter Kenya. It was simply obtained at the airport on arrival. The Evanses booked a British Airways flight to London and from there to Nairobi, with an open return date. On arrival, they checked in at the Hilton Nairobi for a one-night stay.

"Clay, I'm hungry, and I saw a very nice dining room from the lobby. I know it's a little early for dinner, but couldn't we go now?"

"Okay, Jen, but first I have to phone my contact from the Samburu Project, as he's only in the office 'til 5:00 pm. Then after we eat, we can make our final in-country travel plans. We'll probably be returning to London within the week if all goes well."

≈ ≈ ≈

"Hello, may I speak with Mr. Burnside please."

The Samburu office receptionist's response, "Who may I say is calling?"

"This is Clay Evans. I spoke with him before we left the United States."

"I'll see if he's in."

"Hello Mr. Evans, Ralph Burnside here. Hope you had a good trip."

"Yes, thanks. You suggested we contact you on arrival for help getting to a few of the Samburu Project well sites."

"Indeed. I recommend that you first travel to Isiolo. I suggest that you do not drive a rental car. Instead hire a bilingual guide and his vehicle. Or for much lower expense, you can ride one of the regular *matatu* public mini-buses. They're slower but inexpensive.

"Once in Isiolo, you can rest, and perhaps take in a lunch."

"Mr. Burnside, we'll probably go with the guide idea. What's the next leg?"

"That's going to be noticeably less comfortable, but shorter. The matatu ride northward from Isiolo is even more crowded, and quite hot. Perhaps the guide you hire in Nairobi would be willing to take you on that next leg of your journey, as well, heading for Archers Post. That puts you right into the heart of the Samburu region. It's a total trip of 316 km from Nairobi to Archers Post, and will take you about five hours travel time."

"Okay, thanks. How do we get to the well sites from Archers Post?"

"I've arranged for one of our staff there, a nice chap named Luke, to host you and take you to two typical Samburu Projects in different villages. He can also answer any of your questions about how these wells are sited, drilled, financed and maintained."

"Thanks, Mr. Burnside. We appreciate your help."

"My pleasure, Mr. Evans. I'm glad to be party to your and your wife's own drilling venture. Good luck. Call me if you ever need more help."

CHAPTER 22

CLAY was unsuccessful in his try to hire a Nairobi driver and vehicle for the trip to Isiolo. Apparently, none wanted to tackle that long round trip during Nairobi's 'Kenya Music Festival', a weeklong event that attracts throngs from all over Africa. Too many local fares and tips to for a driver to earn, compared to a multiday trip. So the Evanses boarded an 8-passenger matatu that was headed for Isiolo.

When they arrived about four hours later, they were more than happy to get out and stretch their legs. Isiolo seemed like a frontier town from the Old West, but with an eclectic mix of peoples and cultures, outdoor markets and a Barclay Bank.

"Jen, let's grab a quick bite; there's a little food place that we passed just down the block. I could use a local beer."

"Maybe I could get a margarita," she responded.

"Yeah, probably made from fermented potatoes and goat's milk," he quipped.

"Okay, so I wasn't thinking; a beer will do, if they'll serve me."

After a snack of *bhajia* (potato slices dipped in spicy batter and then fried), chased with Tusker Premium Lager, they boarded another matatu getting ready to depart for Archers Post, only 20 miles distant. This one had 14 seats, but somehow 17 passengers crowded on, along with the Evanses and driver. Fortunately, that cramped trip took only 40 minutes, and the Evanses gleefully stepped free of the bus. Clay reminded Jennie to take lots of pictures, and even some videos if possible.

"Hello there," shouted a nearby man dressed in khaki shorts and flowered shirt. "Are you Clay and Jennie Evans?" It was Luke.

"I hope you're not too tired from your journey from Nairobi. We still have another 50 kilometers to reach Wamba, our headquarters for the Samburu Project," he said, as they all climbed into his ideal backcountry vehicle, an old well-used Land Rover.

Clay responded, "In this relative comfort, we're up for another couple hundred miles."

Luke proudly added, "The road's dirt, and a bit bouncy here and there, but this car will make good time. Be there in less than an hour."

After he briefly stepped into the Wamba office on arrival to verify he had the Evanses in tow, Luke returned to the Rover and said, "I've picked out two different well sites for you to visit this afternoon."

Luke headed down a different dirt road. After about 20 minutes, he turned off the road into the bush, and drove cross-country another half hour, stopping only after they entered an inhabited community, with stick-and-mud homes scattered over many acres.

"There're about 1500 people that live here. It's called Lendadpoi, and it was the first Samburu Project well site. That's the well over there to our right, with the women standing nearby."

"Luke, can we speak with those women?"

"Sure, I'll stand with you and interpret."

Clay and Jennie approached the women, smiled and nodded. Jennie spoke, "Good afternoon, ladies. Would you mind telling my husband and me what difference this well has made in your lives?"

"We used to spend so much time each day walking miles to meet our water needs. Now we just push that handle up and down. We get all the water we need. And it's clean. Our children don't get sick so often. They attend school more regularly. We women have more quality time in our lives. And because of the water, our community can now make and sell bricks."

After thanking and parting from the women, Luke said, "So far, the Project has built 30 such wells in different villages throughout the Samburu region. Currently we have applications from 50 other communities waiting for funds to be built."

"So how does the development process take place?" asked Clay.

Luke explained, "Each community's women's group signs a contract agreeing to specific conditions and responsibilities. These include clearing the area of brush for well construction, and collecting and delivering materials, such as sand and concrete.

"The women must also attend hygiene and sanitation workshops. After the well is built, they participate in maintaining it. They also must pool money from the community's members to fund a portion of the ongoing maintenance."

Then Luke said, "Jump into the car, and we'll go visit another well site," and off they went through the bush, another dozen miles.

Luke pulled into a clearing amidst hundreds of acres bearing scattered stick-and-mud houses, some with roofs made of pieces of scavenged tin, and others that were thatched. Each family unit had considerable acreage, a main house, other smaller shacks or buildings nearby, and an abundance of animals: goats, sheep, cows, even a camel.

As they exited the car, Luke said, "We completed this one, the Lauragi well, in 2011, and already it's making a big impact on the people's lifestyle."

A young man of the village, Michael, who was the son of an elder, joined them at the well as Clay pumped the handle a few times, watching the water spurt out onto a concrete pad. Michael explained, "The community's people spend more time closer to the village now, and the proportion of girls attending school has increased."

A few chattering women in colorful flowing dresses approached the well, carrying containers. So Luke, Clay and Jennie stepped a few yards away, watching them. Clay asked, "Luke, tell us about the process once the village people submit an application."

"Assuming the Project accepts the application, we bring in a hydrogeologist to select the best location for the well, one where drilling will most likely yield a sufficient quantity and quality of water. Sometimes it's right within the community; sometimes further away. Strategically, a well is best if it's located near to a dry riverbed if one is not too far."

"Who drills the well?" Clay asked.

"The drilling rig and crew are hired from a nearby town," answered Luke.

"What's the typical cost for completing a well, start to finish?"

Luke offered, "Rule of thumb is $15,000. The average depth at that cost in this region is 230 ft.

"We'd better head back to Wamba, as dusk is approaching," said Luke. "You really don't want to be out in the bush after dark. Have you made arrangements for sleeping quarters there?" he asked as they pulled out of the community, heading back into the bush towards Wamba.

Jennie responded, "I made reservations at the Matthew Heights Guest House for tonight. We're planning to visit our Turkana village starting tomorrow."

As they neared Wamba, Clay inquired, "Hey Luke, maybe before we part company today, can you can give us some guidance on how we can get to our target location tomorrow. All we know is that the nearest place is Marich Pass, and the community is northeast of the road junction of A1 and B4."

"That's easy," Luke said. "Hire one of the bilingual guides from Wamba, one that has a good vehicle. He'll get you there, and can be your interpreter while there. They're not really all that expensive, but you'll also have to pay for his gas and food for the round trip, and any extra days you're there."

"How do I locate one of these guys?"

"I'll set one up for you this evening, okay?"

"We'd be most appreciative. Would you care to join us for dinner at the town restaurant?"

"No thanks. My family expects me home tonight. But I'll leave a message about the guide for you at the Guest House office before I go to bed. I suggest you plan to start early, because the trip to the vicinity of Marich Pass is probably going to take you the better part of a day."

As they departed, Clay and Jennie thanked Luke profusely. He said, "Drop a note to Mr. Burnside about your day with Luke. That'll mean a lot to me. Good evening."

That night, while lying in bed in the dark, Jennie said, "I'm so glad we decided to do this, Clay. It's really opened my eyes to the needs of others; people we can help in our new life."

CHAPTER 23

HEEDING Luke's suggestion of the previous evening, Clay and Jennie arose at dawn, found some food nearby, and stopped at the Guest House office shortly after 7:00 am. The message left there by Luke read: "Your driver-guide's name is Eli. You'll find him and his vehicle next to the Samburu Project office any time after dawn, awaiting your arrival. My satellite phone is 327-378 if you need me. Good luck, Luke."

Clay read the message aloud. Jennie responded, "We better get over there right away. Eli must have already been waiting over an hour."

≈ ≈ ≈

"Are you Eli?" Clay asked the only man near the office, leaning against an old Defender vehicle. Even though Luke had briefed him about their youthful appearance, Eli marveled that his fares for the next two days were mere teenagers.

"Yes, I am. You must be the Evans couple."

"Hello," said Jennie, reaching unsuccessfully for his hand. "I'm Jennie."

"And I'm Clay."

"Pleased to meet you Mr. Clay," said Eli, while half-bowing. "And Miss Jennie, too," nodding toward her. "Luke told me you want to go almost all the way to Marich Pass. That's a very long trip. We must first head part way back towards Nairobi for 100 km, and then go north more than

500 km. It will take us about 11 hours if the roads are in good condition. We should bring food and plenty of water from Wamba, as there are not many places to find it on the way."

Clay said, "Fine. Take us to the place where we can buy it. Do you need any gas for your vehicle?"

"It is full now, Mr. Clay. You can buy more later, and fill it after we return."

"Do we need to pay you anything in advance for your services?"

"No, you can settle with me when we arrive back in Wamba, a day or more from now."

It was a long day's ride, but in relative comfort, as the A1 road was in excellent condition, and Eli's car was well appointed for travel. Along the way, Clay and Jennie explained their objective to Eli: to install a water well for a Turkana village that had been trying to find someone to do it for more than two years. Eli was most impressed that an ordinary private young couple from another country so far away would travel to a remote Kenyan community to spend their time and their money to help strangers live better. He knew the same thing was going on for years in the Samburu region, but that was being done by a huge organization, with donations from all over the world.

Eli said, "My religion preaches that we should love and care for one another, so what you are doing is correct."

Clay asked, "What religion is that, Eli?"

Eli responded, "I am a Christian. Long ago, missionaries converted my ancestors to Christianity, and my parents urged that I and my brothers and sisters put our faith in Jesus, and we did."

Jennie noted, "Clay and I are Christians also." And then for the next several hours, the discussion turned to local foods, traditions, music and the growing predominance of hi-tech gadgets like cell phones in Kenyan population centers.

Suddenly, Eli hit the brakes hard and swerved to the right, avoiding a zebra that sprang onto the road from the left rangeland. The Defender went into a skid to the right, dropped about a foot off the raised highway escarpment and plowed into light brush, stopping only after hitting a small but jagged outcrop of ancient rock.

"Is everyone alright," Eli shouted anxiously, still seated at the wheel. After stepping out of the car, Clay stood up, checked his body movements and clothes, and said, "I'm Okay, I think. I don't hurt anywhere. Jenny, how about you?" he said, looking through the rear open window.

"I'm okay too," she said, "but my nose is bleeding a little. I think I banged it on the window frame I was looking out of at the time. I don't hurt anywhere else." She took out a handkerchief from her zipper bag, held it to her nose and applied pressure, hoping to stop the bleeding and avoid blood drops onto her clothes.

Eli got out of the car, uninjured, and checked the front of the vehicle where it struck the rock. "This old Defender is built like a tank. Just a small dent in the bumper, I think. As he continued inspecting the car, he uttered, "Uh oh. A flat tire on the right. Must have got cut on that sharp outcrop. No problem, I have a spare and a jack."

Jenny got out and looked at the tire as Clay was coming around the front of the car to see. For the next twenty-five minutes, Eli and Clay wrestled the front wheel off, and replaced it with the spare. Eli backed the car out of the brush, with Clay standing behind yelling directions. After the car had backed about 30 yards through some high grass, Eli drove it forward and gradually to the left until it was up over the escarpment and back onto the highway.

"I apologize for that accident, Mr. Clay, and especially for your nose injury Miss Jenney," said Eli.

"Oh, it doesn't even hurt, and the bleeding's stopped. I'll be fine."

"Actually," said Clay, "you did a great job avoiding what could have been a disastrous crash with that zebra, Eli. Good job."

After six and a half more travel hours, Eli stopped the vehicle. "That road off to the right up ahead is B1. So this is the junction you targeted. I see some herdsmen up there on that road. Do you wish to speak with them to help find your village?"

"Yes indeed, please do so," said Clay.

Eli pulled the car to the side of the road near the walkers. He got out and started speaking with them. Clay got out too and joined the group.

Eli looked at Clay and said, "They want to know the name of the community that you are seeking."

Clay said, "I don't know the name, but they're a Turkana people, and the chief is a man named Waitimu Iweala."

Eli translated Clay's statement. The herdsmen were nodding understanding, and chatting among themselves and with Eli, and pointing up the road.

Eli said, "Yes, the community you speak of, Lotuxo, is about 15 km from here in a northeasterly direction. They say we should continue on A1 for about 10 km, and we will then see a dirt goat trail into the bush that leads to that village."

"Please thank them for the help, Eli." He did so, and they continued on their way.

"If the goat trail is in fair shape, I can drive right to the community. If not, we will have to park and walk."

"Let's go, I can't wait to see the village and meet the people," said Jennie, excitedly.

"Me too," said Clay. "Don't forget to keep notes and take lots of pictures, hon, but be careful not to offend anyone."

The goat trail was quite bumpy, and had some large rocklike mounds that almost caused the Defender to bottom out, but they made it all the way, about 5 km, to the edge of the populated area. Eli turned the engine off and stepped out, along with Clay and Jennie. They walked into a relatively cleared area, and stopped before reaching any of the stick-and-mud dwellings, waiting for the native men to notice them, approach them, and hopefully invite them into the community.

A few male villagers did see them, and started chatting with each other about 50 yards away; they were soon joined by a dozen or more others. All were speculating with one another why two white teenagers were standing at the entrance to their community. Finally, two left the group, and approached Eli, Clay and Jennie, carrying their herding staffs alongside.

Eli spoke in their native language. One of the two men turned about face and quickly walked back towards one of the houses. Soon, another man exited that house, and the two of them joined the strangers standing at the edge of the community. The third man spoke briefly with Eli, then approached Clay and Jennie, and extended both arms in welcome fashion.

Eli said, "This man is the community chief, Waitimu Iweala. He welcomes you. Grab his outstretched hands with yours, and nod. He does not speak English, so just say 'Hello Waitimu' and smile."

Clay did exactly that, and the chief spoke some unintelligible words, and patted Eli on the back. Jennie stayed back, as she noticed none of the native women moved while the men's conversations were underway.

"Eli, what did you tell him about me, and about Jennie?"

"I told him that you and your wife came from America to this community to build them a water well in response to the application he filled out over two years ago. I explained that, despite your youthful appearance, you were going to work with the men here, and that your wife would be working with the women's group to make this happen. I also told him that you were going to pay for the construction out of your own wealth."

"Eli, thank you. Please also tell him that we're first going to make an initial survey of the community, then return to our home, make preparations and contact authorities to make all this happen. Then we'll come back to start the well construction in about a month. We'll only stay overnight and tomorrow for now. When we come back, we'll probably stay in the community for several months, and will need a place to sleep, cook and eat. We're hoping that one or more of the younger men or women here or nearby speak English, enabling us to communicate and complete the well's installation."

Eli turned to Waitimu, and translated what Clay had just said. Waitimu nodded his understanding, and smiled. He spoke at length to Eli.

Eli said, "You are a most welcomed guest, Mr. Clay, as is your wife, Miss Jennie. Aware that daylight is now fading fast, he will see to it that the three of us have a place to sleep tonight, as well as enjoy meals by the local ladies here during our stay. When you return for the working stay, you will have your own house, which they will build while you are away. He also said that there are a few young people here that can understand and speak English, and he will introduce you to one or more tonight. For now, he would like you to come to his house and meet his family." Waitimu turned and started walking towards his home, with the Evanses and Eli following.

From the outside, the Iweala family's house appeared to be a shade larger than most of the visible dwellings in the community. But to enter the stick-and-mud dwelling, they had to stoop down, as the opening was not very high. The interior, then lighted by kerosene lamp, was sparse. Homemade wooden furniture, mainly low tables, stools and storage boxes, was placed according to use, while rolled up mats and bedding lined one side of a separate room.

Waitimu proudly introduced his family, with the translation help of Eli: Adani, his wife, Bakkir, his 17-year-old son, Keriuki, his 13-year-old son, and Farhani, his 15-year-old daughter.

Clay and Jennie didn't really know at first how to respond as each was introduced: handshake, bow, nod, smile, or what? So they simply copied Eli's actions, which varied depending on whether a male or female was being introduced. Nevertheless, it was an awkward few moments of doing the wrong thing, and then correcting while mouthing the Turkana words of greeting as best they could. All the while, Waitimu grinned, thinking, *What wonderful but strange white people. How is it possible that they can be so young, so rich, so self-sacrificing, and yet so stupid culturally? I must be understanding, and try very hard to help them adapt.*

During the subsequent meal of *sukuma wiki* (leftovers), *ugali* (maize staple) and small portions of goat meat, supplemented by neighbor women, Eli translated conversation. His skill was a real blessing, making sure everybody understood what everyone else was saying. Eventually, they had to move outside the small dwelling, as neighbor visitors and some of the community English-speakers joined the gathering. The evening Iweala meal thus gradually turned into a neighborhood party. The unplanned affair, when supplemented with various local beverages, created merriment into the late night.

When all revelers departed to retire, Clay and Jennie were provided mats to sleep on, and placed them on the hard earthen floor of the Iweala kitchen area. In the darkness, Clay whispered, "Jen, how are you enjoying our African adventure now?"

"It sure is different," she said, "but I love it."

"Me too. Our Kenyan mission to Lotuxo is finally underway, and is off to a good start."

CHAPTER 24

THE next morning just before dawn, Adani Iweala entered the kitchen area to start the morning meal, trying very hard not to awaken their guests sleeping on the floor. Farhani had already left to get water from the distant river.

Clay and Jennie soon arose, and stepped outside to kiss and watch the sun rise through the bush growth surrounding the community. Neighbors could already be seen starting their day, women hanging wash, men moving herds toward pasture and water, and boys carrying wood.

Clay said, "I'd like to walk around the entire community with Waitimu. I want to get a feel for its size, amount of bush, location of community-owned property, small hills or depressions, and dry riverbeds, if any. Not that I could really tell one if I was standing in the middle of it. But when I speak to a hydrogeologist to line him up for well-site selection when we come back, he may ask a few questions, and I don't want to appear stupid."

"What do you mean, community-owned property, Clay?" asked Jenny.

"Property not individually owned by a family. Each family in the community actually owns a couple acres. It's theirs. We can't put a well in someone's back yard, or where they keep their animals."

"How do you know about all this?" she asked.

"It was in some of the stuff I read on the Samburu Project's website."

"I guess you aren't stupid after all," she quipped, giggling.

He grabbed her and feigned giving her a spanking, an action that did not go unnoticed by one of the Turkana men nearby. He politely turned away, silently shaking his head and wondering, *What's with these white people?*

Just then, Clay noticed Eli walking out of one of the distant dwellings. Their eyes met, and they waved and walked toward each other, Jennie close behind.

"We lost sight of you after the meal and party, Eli. We're going to need your translation help as we walk the community grounds with Waitimu. By the way, where did you sleep?"

"Oh, one of the community widows graciously offered me a mat to sleep on in her house."

Clay, casting a quick peek at Jennie's demeanor, asked, "Did she cook breakfast for you too, or are you going to have the morning meal with us and the Iweala family?"

"I'm still hungry," Eli responded and added, "How long will our walk take? Remember, we need about 12 hours to drive back to Wamba, if we're going today."

"I'm guessing we should be able to leave between 8:30 and 9:00," said Clay, "maybe before. Wouldn't it be a shorter trip for Jennie and me, though, if we went directly to Nairobi? We'd pay you there, and add a fee for your time and fuel to return to Wamba from Nairobi."

"Good thinking, Mr. Clay. Yes, let's do that. It will only take 10 hours, I think."

Just then, Waitimu stepped out of his dwelling, and approached his nearby guests. "Good morning," said Clay.

Waitimu responded with a grouping of Turkana words, which Eli translated as, "It looks like it will be a nice day."

"Eli," Clay said, "Please tell him that we'd like him to lead us in walking around the entire community's boundaries, and specifically to point out all sections of community-owned land as we go."

Waitimu nodded agreement and took off walking at a moderate pace, with the others following. The boundaries encompassed at least four hundred acres, by Clay's estimate, and were basically oval in outline. He made a rough sketch on a pocket pad, denoting approximately the location of patches of land that weren't owned by any villagers. Clearly, he could see, most of these patches were covered by heavy brush, rocky outcrops and debris.

During the continuing conversation between Waitimu and Clay, with Eli as translator, Clay made the point that able community men would be responsible for clearing the land for the well site. If their assistance was needed, they'd also be asked to help transport needed supplies, like sand, concrete and well casings, along the goat trail if the delivery truck couldn't make it all the way from the A1 road.

Jennie asked Waitimu, "Does your community have a women's group that meets to develop solutions to community problems?"

Waitimu responded with a laugh, "Ha, they do, and they practically run this place! I, as Chief along with the elders, are supposed to be the leaders here, but the women somehow manage to get their way and control what really goes on. The women's group certainly makes most of the social and financial decisions. The men are too busy with their work and herding."

Clay joined that conversation, "Waitimu, when we return, Jennie would like the opportunity to meet with that ladies group, and solicit their support for the process of building and maintaining your new well here."

"That will not be a problem," said Waitimu. "I'm sure the ladies will welcome Miss Jennie during the time she is here. Perhaps she might also be willing to help some of the teenage children learn a few words of the English language."

"Oh, yes," said Jennie, "I'd love to do that."

As they finished their circumnavigation of the community, Clay checked his watch, and noted that it was 8:27.

"Waitimu," Clay observed, "we must leave soon, as we plan to drive all the way to Nairobi today. We plan to return to our own country and home over the next three days of travel."

"Adani has prepared a simple morning meal for you. Will you have time to eat before you depart?" asked Waitimu.

Clay looked at Eli. He nodded 'yes' to Clay, and answered Waitimu, "Yes, we'd very much appreciate your kind offer of a meal."

Following the meal, the Evanses grasped Waitimu's and Adani's extended hands, nodding their heads slightly as they did, while Eli thanked them for their hospitality. They climbed into Eli's Defender, and headed down the goat trail toward the A1 road.

CHAPTER 25

ALMOST as soon as the Defender was out of sight, two of Lotuxo's senior elders walked the community's grounds, inviting other elders to join them for a group conversation. When most of their number had assembled near the village center, a few began to question, "Why are we gathered here? Where is Chief Waitimu?"

"Leaders of Lotuxo, I am concerned about the events of the past two days," responded one of the two senior elders. It seems that our Chief has not only welcomed white strangers into our midst without seeking our guidance and consent, but he has also apparently opened the door for them to come back and live here, supposedly to provide us with a water well. How is that possible? Those strangers are mere children! Who invited them to come here? And why aren't we, as leaders, involved in such decisions?"

One of the other elders responded, "I briefly chatted with Waitimu yesterday afternoon, and he told me that the white couple came all the way from the United States. They wanted to familiarize themselves with Lotuxo and its people as a preliminary step to building a well here in response to an application that he, as Chief, had sent to the Samburu Project people more than two years ago."

"Do you mean those strangers were part of that organization, the one putting all those wells in villages much further southeast in Kenya."

"I don't know. You'll have to ask Waitimu. Here he comes now."

Waitimu, having noticed the unusual gathering of the elders, was briskly approaching the gathering. "What's going on," he asked as he arrived in their midst.

"We're concerned about those white strangers showing up unannounced, spending two days here, and apparently coming back soon to supposedly build a water well here," replied the senior elder. We weren't brought in on this event, and wonder why, and we're amazed that two kids are being welcomed to undertake such a venture in Lotuxo."

Oops, thought Waitimu, *I've inadvertently stepped on a few toes.* He responded to the group, "Gentlemen, this was a preliminary visit, sort of a fact-finding effort on their part. We . . . Lotuxo . . . have made no commitment other than a willingness to cooperate if they indeed can prove that water truly exists many meters below our feet."

"But they're only kids, Waitimu, the same age as two of your children. How can they do anything?"

"They are indeed young in physical appearance, but they are unbelievably mature in wisdom, speech, intelligence, and I might add, wealth. They have come here as volunteers on a mission that Lotuxo initiated over two years ago, when we applied to the Samburu Project to build us a well. The Samburu people knew they couldn't do a well here because of our great distance from Wamba, so they forwarded our desire for help to an organization in the United States, to which the young couple belongs. They took it upon themselves to fulfill our need with their know-how, time and money. Why shouldn't we welcome this blessing?"

"We knew nothing about such an application for a well?"

"Gentlemen, your memories are getting shorter as you age. We brought this matter up at one of our meetings almost three years ago, and it was decided that we should indeed try to get a Samburu well."

Two or three of the elders, silent to that point, spoke up, "I remember that decision. We told you to go ahead and apply, Waitimu." "I remember it too." "As do I."

Waitimu continued, "In any event, as matters now stand, they plan to return in a month to start the installation. Do you want me to cancel that mission? I only need to get word to the Samburu people in Wamba."

"No, no," shouted many of the group with emphasis.

The senior elder that initiated the conversation relented, but added, "I agree that we should allow them to come back and proceed, but I personally am going to watch what's going on like a hawk."

"Wonderful," said Waitimu with a grin, "we need someone to defend our traditional lack of water."

The group disbanded with laughter as all the elders returned to their homes for dinner.

CHAPTER 26

AFTER three days of travel back from Kenya and London via car, airplane, bus and limo, the Evanses finally reached the comfort of their home in Florence, AL, just in time to go to bed shortly before midnight. Since no alarm was set, they slept late the following morning. Jennie awakened first, and as she lay there in the warm comfort of her own bed, her thoughts drifted back to the people of Lotuxo, sleeping on their dirt-floor mats in their humble mud-and-stick dwellings. They had so little: scant belongings, no flowing water, no electricity, no heat or air conditioning, no refrigeration, and only meager food quantity and variety.

"We're so fortunate," she mouthed softly, but the whisper was enough to cause Clay to stir. She continued her thought train, aloud to Clay. "You know, hon, I've been lying here thinking; the poorest people in our country, even in Mississippi, live like kings compared to the Kenyan people of that Turkana tribe."

Clay concurred, adding, "Yeah, according to some facts I read online, the average national per capita annual income for all of Kenya is less than $800 a year. Compare that with the U.S. median of about $50,000 for a family of four, or with our economy's poverty level of about $23,000. But for the rural indigenous pastoral peoples, like the Turkana, it's perhaps only a tenth or less of that $800 national average. However, for the people we met, currency income is a minor or negligible consideration, since their local economy depends on bartering to supplement individual needs beyond their own herds and grown foods."

"Clay, we're truly wealthy and so fortunate. I really don't want to employ a fund-raising methodology to acquire the $15,000 to 20,000 that it'll cost to put in that well. We can afford to pay for it all ourselves. I want to feel that it's you and I alone that are financially helping those wonderful Lotuxo people."

"I agree wholeheartedly, Jen. But, right now, it's time to cut off this pillow talk and get up. We have to start preparing for our next trip, the actual well-drilling work."

While Jennie prepared a brunch, Clay got onto the phone, almost too late to talk with the contacts in Kenya, considering their seven-hour advance time differential. But he did reach Ralph Burnside in Nairobi. "Hi Ralph. I need a bit of help from you, if you have the time. First, though, I want to compliment your man Luke. He was a wonderful, obliging guide and advisor for our first visit to Kenya."

"That's nice feedback, Clay. I appreciate it. What do you need?"

"I'd like to get answers for a series of questions. I'll send them to you via email also, but I'd like to hear your initial responses now, as best you can. Here's the list verbally:

1. What's your email address? Do you have Skype? What's Luke's email address?

2. Start to finish, what's an estimate of the number of weeks to complete a typical well?

3. Can you point me to a reliable hydrogeologist for siting the well in Lotuxo?

4. Ditto, Ralph, for one or more drilling contractors.

5. I understand that we must get a drilling permit from a government agency in Isiolo after we have the hydrogeologist's report. What's their physical address, email address, phone number, and name of the main contact?

6. Where do you recommend we buy our supplies: sand, cement, etc.?

7. We'll need a vehicle, perhaps a used pickup truck, for about three months.

Could we buy one in Isiolo, or would we have to get it in Nairobi?"

Clay and Ralph chatted for about 20 minutes, and all information relayed was detailed and complete.

"That's all for now, Ralph. I truly appreciate all your help enabling us to go forward on this project. Can I contact you again in the future if I run into a roadblock? Thanks. Bye."

During the meal, Clay and Jennie discussed what he'd learned during his call with Burnside. The main finding was their need to be there two or three months, and plan accordingly. They decided on a date to start the next trip. They also agreed that for the rest of that day, they'd share the tasks of setting up a visit with their doctor to get necessary shots and medical supplies, book airline reservations for the flights to London and Nairobi, make hotel reservations for those cities, and prepare lists of clothing and other needs to last them three months. Decisions on these lists led to some considerable disagreements.

"I think I'll need both of our 28-inch suitcases, Clay, and also the long green clothes bag. I've been thinking about what to bring for three months use, and believe I'll need that amount of space to pack all my clothes, outerwear, shoes, toiletries and cosmetics."

"Huh? Jen honey, we're not going to Las Vegas in the winter with clients again. We're going to a rural hot wilderness area of Kenya. You've been there, remember?"

"What do you mean by that?"

"Well, you won't have to avoid wearing the same dress twice; spangled jeans and boots will be too hot; we won't be going to cocktail parties or stage shows; there're no formal banquets to attend; your high stiletto shoes will be unwearable in the dirt; there's no weather in Kenya that justifies heavy outerwear; and none of the ladies in Lotuxo wear pants or makeup."

"Okay, Mr. Ralph Lauren, what do you recommend?"

"All the ladies I've observed there seem to be wearing long, loose-fitting, very colorful, lightweight, willowy dresses and sandals. There must be a reason. Pick or buy two or three light dresses, two week's supply of underwear, one outfit suitable for London and Nairobi hotels, one sweater, a windbreaker and a broad-brimmed hat. You can buy additional native dresses in Isiolo. For footwear, something comfortable for London, and one pair each of sandals, sneakers and walking shoes."

"Impossible! That's not enough for three months."

"You asked me. That's my recommendation, babe. You can wash clothes occasionally, you know, in the river if necessary."

"Well, what are you bringing, Clay?"

"I think I'll limit my packing to two pairs of lightweight pants, two pairs of shorts, three plain polo shirts, a long-sleeved white shirt and one of my Hawaiian shirts, plus two weeks supply of underwear and socks, a windbreaker, sweater and brimmed hat. Also, a pair of sandals, loafers and my walking shoes."

"Maybe I'll only need one big suitcase, plus one or two smaller ones for incidentals," she said.

"I don't think that's the way to go, Jen."

"Now what's wrong with my selection?"

"I recommend instead that we buy two 30-inch wheeled duffel bags. They'll hold everything we'll want to bring besides clothing, including some camping cookery, LED flashlights, air mattresses and ultra light sleeping bags. For carry-on stuff like computer, medical supplies, vitamins, soap, toiletries, etc., we can each wear a small backpack."

"Backpack! We're not going on a hike, Clay."

"I'm positive they'll be the most convenient way to lug our miscellaneous stuff around, easy to store in the plane's overhead, or under the seat, and easy to get into on the way; cameras and cell phones at the ready, each stored in an accessible zippered pocket. Think about it, hon, before you reject that approach. Think how much more practical they'll be in our stick-and-mud house."

"Okay, I'll think about it. But don't count your eggs before the chickens are hatched," she said with a forced grin on her face, eyes cast upwards.

"That's my girl," said a happy Clay Evans. "I'm going to go now to see if I can buy those duffel bags. While I'm gone, why don't you try to get us a near-future appointment with Doc Nichols for shots and supplies?"

"Hey," she said. "I thought I was gonna have time to think about it!" Too late, he was out the door.

Two days later, while getting shots to prevent what seemed like every imaginable disease, Clay asked their doctor, a former green beret medic, "Dr. Nichols, if you were going to a village in Kenya so isolated that it'd take ten to twelve hours of driving to reach the first real hospital in Nairobi, and were going to be there for two to three months, what medical supplies other than the usual first aid stuff would you want to bring?"

Dr. Nichols said, "Well, I'd surely want to have some oral antibiotics for respiratory illness, some pain pills for minor injuries, and malaria pills. I'd also want to bring a few ampoules of morphine for severe injuries, and an intravenous antibiotic like cephazolin for severe life-threatening infections."

"Doc, take a look at these air travel tickets; as you can see, we're really going to a place and duration like that, and we'd appreciate it if you'd fix us up with prescriptions for all of those medications you mentioned, and any others you think we should bring."

"I guess I could, but I'm a little concerned about giving habit-forming drugs to young folks like you two. What did you say your names were?"

"Clay and Jennie Evans," responded Clay, hoping that their occasional general practice doctor wouldn't start trying to link their relationships to the elderly couple having the same names he'd cared for over a five-year period in the past.

"Well, it's clear that you need them, so I'll write the prescriptions. And I'll give you a half dozen syringes too. I'm trusting you two because I knew your grandparents, and they were truly trustworthy. I haven't seen them for quite a while; I hope they're still around."

"Yup, they still are," said Clay, winking at Jennie.

CHAPTER 27

CLAY and Jennie stepped into their newly made stick-and-mud hut, which would be their home for the next few months. The visible interior, dimly lit by a kerosene lantern hanging from an unseen rafter, was basically an open dirt-floor room for living and cooking. A high divider at the far end concealed a small area for sleeping. The kitchen area was furnished with a few pots and pans, and two buckets for water and washing. Two wooden crates and crude chairs served as the meal table. The sleeping area had two rolled-up mats lying against the wall, a low table, and two shelves attached to the divider.

"Ah, home sweet home at last," said Clay. "I'm pooped from all the travel since we left London, and would really like to lie down and take a short nap."

"Me too," said Jennie. "Let's bring in our bags and backpacks, and get the air mattresses and sleeping bags out." They went outside to their 'new' pickup truck, a used model purchased in Nairobi that morning, grabbed their luggage and brought it in.

Clay unzipped and reached into his duffle bag and pulled out a large, folded-up piece of thin plastic sheet. "I brought this sheeting along in case our new house had a dirt floor like all the others in Lotuxo, and it does."

He unfolded it and placed it on the dirt; it more than covered the entire sleeping-area floor. Next, he unrolled the sleeping mats and positioned them on the covered floor, blew up the air mattresses and put them on the mats, and finally put the unrolled sleeping bags in place.

Lying down, with his backpack for a pillow, Clay said, "Wake me up after you've prepared a nice dinner, Jen."

"Sure, right after you build me a cooking fire in the outside pit," she responded as she too lay down. "How long do you want to nap; I'll set the travel alarm?"

No answer. Clay was already asleep.

≈ ≈ ≈

"Hello in there! Is anybody there?" A male native, in his early twenties stood at the entrance to the Evans's house, shouting in.

Jennie awoke, and shook Clay until he responded, "Yes, we're here. Just a minute and we'll be right there." Both got up, quite groggy, and walked to the entrance.

Clay extended his open hand, and the native grasped it, saying, "Greetings, I'm Abasi, but you can call me Abe. Waitimu has designated me as your interpreter while you're here."

"Wow, hello Abe, you speak clear everyday English."

"Thanks, Mr. Evans; I studied it while at the university in Nairobi."

"Please Abe, just call me Clay."

"Waitimu and Adani know you and Miss Jennie have been traveling all day, and wouldn't have time to prepare anything, so they'd like you to be their guest for the evening meal."

"Well that's so nice of them, Abe. Please tell them we'd very much like to do so. When do they want us to come to their home?"

"Now would be a good time, Mr. Ev . . . err . . . Clay."

"Please tell them we'll be there very soon. And, Abe, I hope you'll be there too, so we can converse with everyone."

"Yes, indeed. I'll be like glue to you every day."

"You mean 'ever present,' right, Abe?"

"Yes, of course, that's what I should have said, 'ever present.' Thanks for correcting me. I hope to learn much better English from this assignment. I'll see you momentarily."

"Soon."

"Yes, of course, 'soon.'"

≈ ≈ ≈

The evening meal with the Iweala family was a delight, not so much for the food, but rather for the company with their new friends. After the meal, Clay and Waitimu, along with Abe, left the ladies behind and went for a walk through the community. All of the elders and many other men made a point to briefly meet and welcome Clay as he and the Chief walked nearby.

Speaking to the Chief through Abe, Clay said, "Waitimu, I've been in contact with the people that are in charge of the Samburu Project, and they've kindly provided me with a lot of information on how to effectively develop a well for the Lotuxo community. Jennie and I'll manage and finance its construction, as we mentioned the first time we visited you. But we will need much help and support from your people."

"Our people are at your disposal, Clay, and anxious to help you bring this wonderful blessing to our families. I will be your principal intermediary for the men, and Adani will be for whatever Miss Jennie wants to accomplish through the women."

"Waitimu, the Samburu people told me that once the well site is determined and properly prepared, it only takes about one week until the well is drilled, the pump installed, and the water flowing on demand. We're many weeks away from that kind of completion. Jennie and I believe it'll take us two or more months to finish the project, as we're starting from scratch."

"We have been without a local water source since our tribe's history in this part of Kenya began. A few months longer will be like single raindrop in a mighty storm," responded Waitimu.

"My first task, Waitimu, will be to hire a hydrogeologist from either Nairobi or, possibly, from Isiolo. He'll help us decide where to place the well within or near your community. A hydrogeologist is a person that's studied how to locate underground water of sufficient quantity and quality, and at a shallow enough depth that a drill can access it. There aren't many such experts in the world, and fewer in Kenya, so we may have to wait a long time until one is free to come and work for us here.

"Once he determines the right spot, we must clear the land of trees, boulders and brush all around it. That'll be a job for your people. Then I must hire a drilling contractor, a company that provides the truck-mounted machinery that typically drills for water at depths of as much as 100 meters or more. The average depth for the Samburu wells has been 75 meters so far. Sometimes, water is found at much shallower depths, like 25 meters.

"As with the hydrogeologist, after we hire this drilling service, we may have to wait many days or weeks until they can come to work for us here in Lotuxo. There's a possibility that the truck cannot drive into Lotuxo on the goat trail without your men widening it substantially. We won't know about this for certain until after I determine which company will come.

"As you must have noticed, Waitimu, we now own a pickup truck available to help with deliveries of materials needed for the construction, since many of the delivery vehicles from Kitale or Isiolo and beyond are also too big for the goat trail from the A1 highway. So, again, your men will be needed to load and unload all these goods to and from my truck, as they arrive."

"Clay," said Waitimu, "as I said before, my people will do whatever you say is necessary. We will be thrilled to participate in this great undertaking."

"Well, it's getting dark, and our families are probably wondering why we're taking such a long walk. We'd better get back. It's so nice to have discussed this with you again, Waitimu."

"Good evening, Clay. I hope you sleep well tonight."

CHAPTER 28

"CLAY, tomorrow is our once-a-week meat night. Do you want flame-broiled goat or diki-diki stew for the evening meal?" asked Jennie, as she washed dinner's plates in a bucket.

"What the heck is diki-diki?"

"It's a miniature antelope," she said. "Bakkir, Waitimu's oldest son, caught one in a snare this morning, and Adani has offered a hind quarter to us."

"I'm game," chuckled Clay, pleased with his pun.

Three weeks had passed since the Evanses arrived in Lotuxo. They were not yet fully acclimated to living the native lifestyle, but they were becoming more adept at life without the modern conveniences of the Western world.

As Clay put it, during pillow talk that night, "Living here is sort of like camping out when I was a Boy Scout. Live in a tent, sleep in a bag, cook over a fire, carry your water, wear dirty clothes, bathe in a river, dig a pit toilet, and so on. Except our shelter is a mud-and-stick hut instead of a tent."

"Well, that's why it's easier for you to do this. You had a lot of practice as a kid. I didn't," said Jennie.

"Honey, you're doing just fine. We can do this, really. Especially with all the help we get from our neighbors. They sure are showing their appreciation for what we're doing here."

"Yeah, I'm really trying. But you could support my efforts the next time you go to Kitale by buying some canned or boxed food for emergencies, and other things I need for the kitchen. Oh, and some bread in a package; I haven't been very successful at baking it myself yet. We can't continue to live on donated bread from the other families."

"Jen, you're in luck. I was actually planning to go there tomorrow morning to meet with the Nairobi hydrogeologist so he can follow me back here. Did you forget? He said he wouldn't come otherwise, since he'd never even heard of Lotuxo, and couldn't find anyone who knew how to get here."

"Okay, Kitale tomorrow, that's fantastic. I'll put together a shopping list for you before you go. What time are you leaving?"

"About 7:30 am. Kitale's 59 miles from here, and I want to get there by 9:00. Hey, don't make that list too long. I can only afford an hour, max, to find your stuff; we're paying that guy by the hour, and the clock starts when he gets to Kitale, not back here. By the way, I've promised to take Waitimu with me. Do you think Adani might need something that we could buy for her?"

"I'll ask her and do the list the first thing in the morning. Hon, it's getting late. Don't you think we should get some sleep now?"

"Yeah, in a little bit, maybe."

≈ ≈ ≈

By the time Clay arrived back in Lotuxo with the hydrogeologist, Jennie was almost back from the river, carrying her daily water supply. For their first week there, other families shared their water with the Evanses, but she decided it was only fair that she get her own. Initially, she walked with Farhani, the Iweala girl, but didn't like leaving in the semi-darkness of dawn. She soon learned that she could always find some older women walking during midmorning to join for company. Of all the women in the community, Jennie was the most impatient while waiting for the new water well to be drilled.

Percy Raleigh, the white hydrogeologist from Cape Town, South Africa, slowly trailed behind Clay, Waitimu and Abe, as they all walked the perimeter of the community. He'd periodically stop, gaze toward the central area, or look in the opposite direction beyond the perimeter, eyes almost always cast down towards the ground. If he saw a heavy patch or line of greenery, he'd walk over to it, kick the dirt, or turn over and inspect some boulder. At the least inhabited portion of the community grounds, due to a large rock outcropping, Percy pulled a hammer out of his pocket and tapped away on the rock face until he broke off a piece of stone, and inspected it with a jewelers eyepiece.

After a complete loop around Lotuxo, he went to his own pickup truck and grabbed a small suitcase containing a computer and a cell-phone-size instrument, walked about twenty paces, and set it down. He called to Clay, "I need the help of one of the stronger men living here." Abe translated.

Waitimu, standing nearby, walked over to a group of houses and yelled towards the closest; a very large native walked out, and Waitimu brought him over to Percy at the truck. They shook hands, and Abe said the man's name was Kanja. Percy asked Kanja to gather two metal probes, a sledgehammer and a foot-wide thick steel disc from the truck's bed, and set them down next to the suitcase.

Communicating with Kanja through Abe, Percy said, "Please use the sledge to bang the two four-foot rods halfway into the earth, about two meters apart, anywhere near the suitcase." When this was accomplished, Percy connected one of two wires from the instrument to each probe. He then placed the metal disc between the probes, picked up the sledge hammer and said, "Please ask Kanja to watch what I do, and then mimic my actions." Percy took a mighty swing with the sledge, landing squarely on the metal disc. Then Kanja did the same.

"Tell Kanja to swing with all his might five times now." He did so, while Percy studied the instrument in his hand. He then sat on the ground, turned on the computer, and input readings from the instrument. "I'm using the Electro Seismic method to map the formations and aquifer beneath the surface in hopes of finding the best place to drill the well," he said.

"Abe, please ask Kanja if he can do this with me for the next hour or two," said Percy. The big man nodded yes, and the three of them walked off, and repeated the procedure a dozen times at various places around the community.

Finally, Percy told Abe that Waitimu needed to alert the community that there'd be a small explosion, so as not to surprise and alarm them. After studying the modeling of the subsurface structure on his computer, Percy chose the place for the final test, placed the probes, and half-buried the black-powder explosive device, and ignited it. Kaboom! He recorded the data, added it to the computer, and thanked Kanja for his help.

Percy studied many screens on his computer, turned it off and returned all of his gear back on the truck. Clay had observed all these final activities close up, and asked the big question, "Do we have water?"

"Yes, there's water here indeed," said Percy. "There's one shallow aquifer about 75 feet down, and another deep one at about 185 feet. That one alone will provide more than enough water for Lotuxo's 800 people and their animals, and at a high flow rate. There's even another aquifer at 290 feet, but there's no point drilling that deep. I recommend that the well be drilled to a depth of 200 feet, and be located near that rock outcropping. I've placed a wooden stake at the exact spot I chose.

"I'll prepare my recommendations and official Kenyan documentation tomorrow, and deliver them to the Water Resource Management Authority, the permitting agency in Isiolo. I'll also send copies to you along with the bill for my service. If you don't have one already, you'll need to get a postal box in Kitale.

"Clay, you'll have to go to that Isiolo agency, see Director Mutua, and apply for the drilling permit. The fee is 12,500 Kenyan shillings, which is equivalent to about $145 in your currency. I suggest you wait a week before applying to make sure they have my paperwork in hand. Don't be surprised by delays of several weeks to acquire your permit after applying. I've been told, however, that sometimes a little money on the side makes the process proceed faster. Good luck."

Clay thanked Percy, invited him to stay for the night in Lotuxo, but he declined, citing something about a sick wife. His truck soon disappeared down the goat trail as he drove off for an all-night journey back to Nairobi.

CHAPTER 29

A FEW days later, Jennie was getting ready to make her daily water run when she noticed that Abe was standing near the Iweala home. "Abe," she called as she walked up to him, "I need to speak with Adani; will you translate for us?"

"Yes Miss Jennie, I will."

Jennie walked to the house's entrance and said loudly, "Hello, Adani, do you have a few minutes to talk with me?" Abe translated the query.

Adani walked out, and both women smiled and nodded toward each other, touching hands.

"Yes, Jennie, I will always have time for you."

"Adani, during our first visit here, Clay mentioned to Waitimu that when we returned and were getting ready to construct the well, you might be willing to set up a meeting for me to address the women's group here about their role. Did he mention that to you, and is it possible?"

"Waitimu did tell me that, and I will be very happy to arrange such a meeting."

"Wonderful. When do you think we should do this?"

"It will take two days for the word to get around, so I suggest we meet in three days. But, Miss Jennie, since there are over 200 married women here, it might be too big a crowd. Perhaps if you spoke only to the wives of the elders and the other active women leaders here, your words would be more effective. Those ladies could then be responsible to organize and tell all their friends and other women in each of their neighborhoods."

"Adani, I certainly concur with your advice. Let's meet in three days. I suggest we meet at the large rock outcropping where the well will be constructed, perhaps at 2:00 pm."

When the meeting day arrived, Jennie was a bit nervous about her mission. "I hope I can pull this off, hon," she said to Clay during their morning meal.

"Well, with all the practice you've had speaking to those convention crowds before you retired, it should be a piece of cake for you," he said.

"Yes, but this is different. I have to speak through Abe and pace myself accordingly. And I don't know how they'll react when I ask for a commitment on paper for all the things we're expecting the women's group to do. I don't want to insult, scare, or anger those ladies."

"Jennie, you'll do just fine. After all, you're going to be helping them change their lives so much for the better. They'll love you. Trust me.

"By the way, you're not the only one who's going to be busy today. Waitimu and I are leaving shortly for Isiolo, and probably won't be back until dark. Today's the day we apply for a drilling permit at the Water Resource Management Authority. I hope they don't give us a runaround, as it's a 12-hour, 580-mile round trip. I wouldn't want to have to go there too many times. For the permit fee, I'm bringing that cashier's check for 12,500 Kenyan shillings, plus a pocket full of $10's and $20's in case I need them."

"Oh Clay, you're not going to try to bribe them, are you," Jennie cautioned.

"No, hon, I'm not going to try to do so. But we're in a foreign land, and cultures and customs may be different. I just want to be ready to do what's best for the people of Lotuxo."

"Well, keep in mind that the jails here are probably not as nice as the ones in Dothan."

"Good point! I'll keep that in mind. Love you; see you tonight. Bye."

≈ ≈ ≈

During the long drive to Isiolo, Clay and Waitimu were so engrossed in their attempts to communicate that time seemed to pass by quickly. Between expressive facial contortions, arms waved and hand gestures, both were trying to signal words or meaning. Scarce words occasionally blurted out clarifications aloud, breaking the silence, but adding little to the listener's comprehension. Despite all this distraction, Clay managed to stay on the road and avoid colliding with pedestrians or occasional passing vehicles. They arrived in Isiolo just before 2:00 pm.

Clay and Waitimu found the target building, and walked into the Water Resource Management Authority office shortly thereafter. Since there appeared to be no receptionist, they waited until a well-attired male seated at a desk looked up from his paperwork.

"Hello, do you speak English?" Clay asked.

"Yes, how may I help you?"

"Are you Director Mutua?"

"No, I'm Jimiu, his assistant."

"We're here to apply for a drilling permit."

"Oh, you must be Clay Evans. Percy Raleigh said you'd be coming around soon. You will need to speak with our

Director here. I will introduce you and Mr. . . . (looking at Waitimu).”

“I'm sorry, this is Waitimu Iweala. He's Chief of the Lotuxo people.”

“Thank you. Please, both of you come this way.” He led them to a glass-enclosed corner of the one-room office. He knocked on the door, which bore the sign “Jomo Mutua, Director.”

A voice from within said, “Yes-s-s-s?”

“Director Mutua, there are two men from Lotuxo to see you.”

“Please, send them in.” Clay and Waitimu walked in and stood before a very stout, balding black man seated at a large desk.

“Director Mutua, I'm Clay Evans, and this is Lotuxo Chief, Waitimu Iweala.”

“Greetings. Please be seated. I know, Mr. Evans, that you're here today to apply for a well-drilling permit. Percy Raleigh, whom we see frequently, told us that Lotuxo has a great abundance of water beneath the ground surface there. He also told me that you, Mr. Evans, as young as you may appear, have already invested much time and money towards accomplishing your objective to provide the Lotuxo people with running water.”

“Yes sir, that's my fervent desire.”

“Very noble of you, and of your wife, I understand. If only there were dozens of other couples like you; so many villages and communities in this part of Kenya need water. In fact, there's a group of philanthropy-minded Kenyans that have started a fund to help finance such projects. In the event you'd like to contribute to that cause, there's a bucket on that table over there for donations."

"Indeed, I would, as it's such a great cause. I only have about $200 with me, but I'm sure that could help. Would it be alright if I put my donation into the bucket?" Clay said, as he arose and walked over to the table.

"I'm sure it will be most appreciated, Mr. Evans." Clay dropped the wad of bills in, and returned to his seat.

"Where were we? Oh yes, we were about to approve your permit. All the papers that Percy brought here are in order. I trust that Chief Iweala is in accord with your plans on this project, is that correct?" Clay nodded.

Mutua addressed Waitimu in Swahili. Since the Turkana tongue was a modified Swahili, Waitimu understood his query, and responded with an affirmative statement.

"Did you happen to bring the fee with you," Jomo asked.

"Yes sir, I have the cashier's check for 12,500 ksh here," placing it on the desk.

The Director opened a drawer and pulled out a piece of paper. He laid it on his desk, and took out a rubber stamp and pad, and stamped the word "Approved" on the permit, signed and dated it, and handed it to Clay.

"It's nice to do business with you Mr. Evans. Thank you for coming."

"Oh, just one favor, Director Mutua; would you please summarize for Waitimu what has just transpired. I was unable to bring a translator with me, and I'd really like him to know that we have permission to proceed with the drilling process."

Jomo Mutua obliged, and briefed Waitimu on the entire session. Waitimu grinned from ear to ear.

CHAPTER 30

ABOUT the same time that Clay and Waitimu were getting their drilling permit in Isiolo, a meeting is underway in a small bed-and-breakfast near Hotel Nasa-Hablod, not many miles from the Mogadishu Airport. A man in Arab garb calls the group to order, and introduces the speaker, Mukhtar Abu Zubeyr, also known as Ahmed Godane. The six men in attendance are shocked, as Godane is the top leader of the Al Shabaab terrorist organization, a man that almost never appears in public places.

"Greetings, my brothers. Your presence here today bespeaks of your firm and noble desire to serve as martyrs of Somalia, and loyal servants of the Prophet. I have come personally to instruct you, owing to the importance of the mission on which you are about to embark. All of you come highly recommended by your clan leaders, and I desire to connect your names with your faces. Please stand when I address you: Ghedi; thank you, be seated; Khalid, thank you; Omar, thank you; Abidi, thank you; Nadif, thank you; and Ali, thank you. Please make yourselves comfortable in those easy chairs, as it will be the last time you will be able to do so for many months, or more likely, never again. Also, feel free to help yourselves to the refreshments on that table.

"My fellow jihadists, as you know, Kenya's involvement in the African Union has led to the death of many of our brothers. Those defeats must be avenged. Your role in a much larger-scale plan will be to infiltrate Kenya through our porous border with that nation, and journey with personal supplies many hundreds of kilometers to a terminal geographic area, specified by latitude and longitude coordinates. In that remote wilderness, you will establish a semi-permanent campsite amidst the heavy surrounding brush. That campsite will serve as a staging area for you and others for a future attack from the north on the Kenyan peoples in Nairobi. Other groups will be simultaneously attacking from the west and east.

"The site I have personally selected for your group is far-removed from major cities, towns and known native villages, but has access to river water, as well as a small resupply town, Kitale, about 95 km away. There you may replenish food and other needs when necessary.

Pointing by pencil laser to a large map on a projected screen, Godane continued, "You will be driven from Mogadishu by truck to your departure point, due west of here, about 1500 meters from the Kenyan border. Split up. Do not travel in a group. You will then continue in a westerly direction, passing near but not through the Kenyan towns of Wajir and Isiolo, thru the Samburu region and onward towards West Pokot, not far from the junction of Highways A1 and B4. Travel cross-country on foot, or on roads and highways by vehicle, as Allah provides. Always keep a low profile.

"You may not carry any weapons. They will be furnished to you at the campsite the day before the attack. You will carry dried food for your journey, a change of clothes, sleeping and cooking gear, tent, Swiss Army knife, water containers and roadmap, all in a backpack. You will travel in pairs, not in a group. Each of you will have a compass, and the leader of each team will have a GPS to locate the exact coordinates chosen for your camp. One of the teams will also carry a satellite telephone to notify us here at headquarters once the campsite is set up,

"Your mode of travel will most likely be primarily by foot, but you are permitted to use stolen bicycles, scooters and cars. Anything stolen must be abandoned within 12 hours. Minimize contact with Kenyan people, and hitchhike only if necessary. Do not, under any circumstance, hurt anyone. If questioned by authorities, you are to say that you are on a cross-country trek to improve your endurance for an upcoming race event.

"Do not alert family or friends about your pending departure. Dispose of all personal identification before leaving. You will each be given all necessary forged documentation. Ali, Khalid and Ghedi are the leaders for their respective two-man teams. You will meet here and depart at 4:00 am in two days. Allah Be Praised"

"With that said, Godane abruptly turned and walked out the door. The Somali that introduced him said they were free to relax for the rest of that day and enjoy any of the refreshments.

CHAPTER 31

BEFORE leaving the WRMA building, Clay stopped by Jimiu's desk and asked, "Does the drilling contractor that works on the Samburu Project have an office here in Isiolo?"

"Their home office is in Nairobi, but they do have a branch office and local equipment here as well. It's behind the corner building a block down the street, opposite side."

Following those directions, Clay and Waitimu walked to that structure; the sign on the door read, "Kenyan Construction and Drilling, Isiolo Division." On entry, they learned from a receptionist that the general manager-operator was out on a local job.

"However," she said, "our office manager, Mr. Keinos, can probably help you. Would you like to speak with him?"

"Yes, please," responded Clay, anxious to get something started on the Lotuxo well.

Keinos appeared, saying, "How can I help you, Mr. . . .?"

"I'm Clay Evans. We've just received our permit to drill a well in Lotuxo, and are looking for a contractor to do the job. Percy Raleigh tells us that there's plenty of water under our community, and recommends we drill to 200 feet. Do you want the job?"

"Where's Lotuxo?"

"It's about 100 km north of Kitale, very close to the intersection of A1 and B4 highways."

"That's quite a ways from here. There would have to be a two-extra-day premium above the normal drilling cost to cover the travel time for our equipment and operator."

"We understand, and expected that."

"Okay, yes, Mr. Evans, we would like to do the job, starting in three weeks. We charge $80 per meter for drilling, and then there are the added costs for the casing, pump, concrete pad and incidentals. Experience tells me that your installed cost will run between $15,000 and $20,000. Do you wish to commit now, sign our contract, and write a deposit check?"

Clay answered, "I was hoping to get started sooner than three weeks, but yes, let's sign the contract now."

Contract in hand, they departed. As soon as they reached the street, Clay and Waitimu shook hands and grinned at each other. Clay did a little jig, much to Waitimu's amusement, and then taught the Chief how to do a high five. At Waitimu's insistence, they did it four more times. As they walked down the street, laughing at each other, Clay imagined Waitimu teaching that odd display of joy to all the elders of Lotuxo.

Since Isiolo was so distant from Lotuxo, Clay next took full advantage of their presence there to stock up on a few needed supplies and rare grocery items not available in Kitale, nor anywhere near their community. While in one shop, he noticed that Waitimu's eyes were like big saucers as they peered over displays of goods he had never seen, or even imagined. Clay gifted several items that Waitimu clearly wanted, including a Swiss Army knife. He also wisely purchased colorful native dresses for Jennie and Adani. After filling the pickup truck's gas tank and a pair of spare

20-liter plastic fuel containers, they left town for the long drive home, arriving there late that night.

≈ ≈ ≈

Three days later, Jennie led her meeting with the women leaders of Lotuxo. Abe was there to translate.

"Good afternoon ladies. Before talking about the new water well, I want to thank you all for the warm reception you've given Clay and I, and especially for all the help getting us settled in our house, and for sharing your food and water with us until we were able to subsist on our own. I'm so happy that my neighbors are also my friends.

"I've asked you to be here for this meeting because the successful transition of the water well, once completed, into your community's service will depend on proper well management. Samburu experience shows this is done best by a governing Water Board. During the next few days, your group should select five women who'd be willing to serve on this Board.

"Each member of that Board, representing all the people of Lotuxo, will sign a contract binding the community to specific conditions and responsibilities, one set for the men and another for the women."

Adani asked, "Miss Jennie, what kind of responsibilities will the women have?"

"The most important one, Adani, would be to create a community fund to be used for ongoing well maintenance. A fund to which all families make an initial small money contribution to insure that necessary repairs and replacements will keep the well operating properly over time, long after Clay and I are no longer here.

199

"Clay and I will start the fund by making an initial donation of 14,000 ksh, and we'll donate at least 14,000 ksh every year after the first. The goal for the community contribution is 21,000 ksh per year. Based on experience learned from the Samburu wells, maintenance costs per well will average 35,000 ksh annually.

"Ladies, a second Water Board responsibility is to assure that they and other women leaders will participate in workshops that I or an expert will teach on hygiene, sanitation and well maintenance. The Water Board must also choose two men to attend the workshop on well maintenance; they will be responsible for any manual labor necessary to deal with well maintenance problems as they arise in the future."

After the women's meeting was over, Clay met with Chief Waitimu and the Elders, and briefed them on the decisions made by the Women's Group. A few resentful statements were aired about the women being given leadership roles in managing the well, but Clay explained that the Lotuxo plan was simply following the very successful Samburu Project model.

It was decided that the work responsibilities of the men should start as soon as volunteers could be marshaled, since most work would have to be done part time, after herding and other responsibilities. Everyone committed to completing the work in time, prior to arrival of the drilling contractor.

CHAPTER 32

"**G**O tell him that I'm stuck here, and if he wants that well drilled, he'd better get a bunch of guys here to get my truck off this damn mound." Abe, who was awaiting the drilling contractor truck's arrival on the goat trail, took off on a dead run towards the Chief's house. Clay and Waitimu were just outside discussing the plans for that day, with interpretation by one of Lotuxo's other English speakers.

Abe ran up to them, panting and shouting, "The drill truck is stuck on the goat trail! Its bottom is resting on a big rock or a dirt mound. We need a lot of men with tools or sticks to remove it. The driver is very unhappy."

That promised big day had finally arrived, and was starting off poorly. Weeks of preparation, brush removal, ground smoothing and leveling, fund raising, and expectation weren't going to be thwarted or even long delayed by a mere bump in the road. The fervent effort of twenty or more men poking, pushing and scraping at the baked, hard-packed mound beneath the undercarriage of the truck soon leveled it. Within an hour, the truck moved slowly through the community towards its destination.

"Over here," Clay yelled towards the approaching truck, while pointing at a particular spot on the ground. As the driver-operator stopped the vehicle, motor still idling, and dismounted to walk over to him, Clay said, "This wooden stake was placed by Percy Raleigh. It's where the hole should be drilled."

The men shook hands as one said, "I'm Clay Evans, the well's financial backer." The other said, "I'm Stan Borden, owner of Kenyan Construction and Drilling. I also operate this drilling rig. Nice to meet you." Clay then introduced Waitimu as the community Chief.

"Hmm, the stake is awfully close to that big rock outcropping," said Stan. "I'll have to jockey the truck around a bit to be able to back the drill directly over it. Chief, please ask all these people, especially the children, to step way back so I don't run over anyone."

After the crowd cleared, Stan positioned the truck, and operated onboard machinery that lowered equipment into a position where the drill rod and bit, once attached, would be directly above the stake. When all mechanical connections were completed and checked, Stan turned on the motor that rotated the drill bit, and lowered it to touch the ground where the stake had been.

As the bit started turning into the earth, churning up the first clumps of fresh hidden dirt, a loud cheer went up from the crowd of onlookers, some jumping up and down while others clapped in place. Lotuxo's water well was no longer a long-anticipated dream; it was actually being drilled.

Later that afternoon, Clay, Waitimu and Abe were chatting in the shade thrown by a large bush, not too far from the drill site. Stan called out to them, "Hey, come on over, we just hit some water."

The trio quickly walked to the drill, and watched mud rather than earth being expelled from the hole. Stan said,

"Just as Percy Raleigh predicted, we broke through to the first aquifer at a little over 70 feet. As soon as the drill drops through to the bottom of that small pocket of water, we'll continue drilling towards the big aquifer below." Soon, the sounds emitted by the rotating equipment changed from a high pitch to a lower groaning sound. "Uh oh," said Stan, "We seem to have hit something hard, most likely a shale layer. That'll slow down our rate of progress until we get through it. In light of the late hour of the day, this is probably a good point to stop work. I'll give the equipment a rest, and resume drilling in the morning.

"Where can I wash up," Stan asked, looking at his grimy arms and hands, not to mention his now dirt-and-mud-splattered clothes.

As Abe translated, Waitimu offered use of a bucket of wash water positioned outside his house. As they all walked in that direction, Clay asked, "What provision have you made for food and sleeping during the days you'll be working here, Stan?"

"I sleep on the truck bed, next to the machinery; I have a mat and pillow there. If it rains, or if mosquitoes get bothersome, I sleep in the cab on a shelf behind the seat. I've brought enough food and snacks for the first day, and assumed I could buy more nearby."

"Sorry, pal," said Clay. "No stores for 60 miles. But my wife, Jennie, and I'd welcome you to eat meals with us at our house over there," nodding his head accordingly. "If you'd prefer a roof over your head, you can sleep there too."

"I see no ring on your finger, Mr. Borden," said Abe. "If you are not married, you might prefer to have your meals with one of our community's widows? But if not, and you want real good Turkana native food instead of what this young American offers you," chortled Waitimu, "come to my house. You'll be even more welcome."

"Thank you all; I accept, and will enjoy the wide variety offered me, I'm sure," said Stan.

≈ ≈ ≈

For the next two days, the whine and groaning from the drill truck could be heard throughout Lotuxo. Just before daylight faded on the last day, the sound stopped. The drill bit had breached the big aquifer at 189 feet.

The following day, a Wednesday, Lotuxo men poured a concrete pad into the forms Stan had constructed around the casing. By Saturday, the concrete had cured enough that the manual pump could be attached to the casing, and bolted into place. About mid-afternoon, the task was completed.

At 5:00 pm on the second Saturday of the third month since the Evanses had arrived in Lotuxo, the well was scheduled to be tested. Virtually every man, women and child of the 800-person community had gathered around the project, waiting to see if water could really be coaxed out of the earth by merely moving a steel handle up and down.

Waitimu addressed the crowd, joyfully shouting at the top of his lungs, "Friends and neighbors of Lotuxo. Our lives are about to change forever. This well will end the need for long daily walks to the river for our wives and daughters, carrying life-sustaining water back here to our homes. Our children will no longer get sick, or even die from polluted water we sometimes had to rely on. Our animals will benefit, and someday we may even be able to grow some of our food nearby. The water that will issue from this well, coming up from a depth of 65 meters beneath our feet, will be clean and pure. It will be cool to the tongue, and taste delicious.

"I have been told by authorities from Nairobi that because we now have a well, and because women will now have free time to use teaching and supporting the education of our children, the government of Kenya will soon build a school here. We will become a more integrated community, with more activities and organizations to hold us together as one united people. Truly, this is a great day in our history, and we owe it all to the young Americans, Clay and Jennie Evans, whom you've all learned to love. Their generosity and boldness to enter into our very different world from theirs for the past three months will always be remembered and honored. When our school is built, we will name it 'Clay and Jennie's Schoolhouse.'

"Now, based on a decision by the Women's Group and Elders, Adani Iweala will have the honor of pumping the first water from our new well. Before she starts, let me remind all of you that a community-wide celebration will begin immediately after the water flows. The women's Water Board has donated food and drinks for everyone. And the elders have brought in native musicians and drummers from Kitale to keep the celebration going until well after dark. Everybody, ENJOY this wonderful day!"

Adani stepped up onto the concrete pad, walked two steps to the pump, which previously had been primed with filtered river water, grasped the handle and started lifting it up and down. Almost immediately water poured forth from the spout. A deafening shout went up from the crowd. For the remainder of that day, and into the early evening, the people of Lotuxo did the same, pumping the handle, one after another, filling their buckets for later use. Children pumped into cupped hands, and splashed it at each other, something never seen before except at the river. That day, March 10, 2013, was to be memorable for the Evanses for another reason as well.

The celebration went on and on into the wee hours, with hundreds dancing to the music and drums in a circular flow around a huge bonfire. Some of the locally brewed adult beverages kept merriment alive. The last few couples finally left for their homes only an hour before the sun came up. That night, three black and one white children were conceived.

CHAPTER 33

AFTER a late morning meal, Jennie said, "It seems our tour of duty here is drawing to a successful close. I guess we'll be packing up pretty soon to head for Nairobi."

Clay retorted, "Not so fast, honey. Remember, you still have to teach that hygiene and sanitation class to the ladies, and we still have to get the Samburu Project to lend us someone for a day to teach well maintenance. On top of that, we really ought to hang around for at least a week or two to make sure the well keeps working, and no problems develop. I propose we plan to leave ten days from now, and schedule our return flight from Nairobi to London accordingly."

"As usual, your logic prevails, Clay. I agree."

For the rest of that day, Clay and Jennie hung around the well site, chatting with friends they'd made, and meeting neighbors they'd not yet met. It was a real joy to see the locals lining up for their turn to fill their buckets. Two men had hollowed out a long, arm-thick dead log they'd recovered near the river, and half buried it next to the concrete pad positioned to catch runoff water; this semi-pipe sloped down with the terrain, leading spilled water towards a bucket buried in the dirt about 20 feet away, a convenient safe place for animals to find a drink.

Clay was awakened early the next morning by Waitimu, shouting via Abe into the front door, "The pump is gone! The pump is gone! Clay, please get up and help us!"

Clay jumped up, almost falling sleepily forward from lack of balance, rubbed his blurred eyes, pulled on a pair of pants and headed towards the well. Sure enough, all that could be seen was the top of the terminal casing and the ends of some bolts sticking up out of the concrete pad. Some women stood nearby wailing and weeping.

"Someone stole it during the night," Clay shouted. "Now who the heck would do that?"

"I can assure you that it was not a member of our community, Clay," said Waitimu.

"Who else could do it; there's no nearby villages that I'm aware of?" said Clay, now starting to regain his composure.

"True," said Waitimu, "but there're always transient natives camping out in the bush. One or more of them must have heard the celebration last night, crept close by and seen the pump. He or they must have assumed it had some resale value, perhaps in Kitale."

Clay thought for a minute and said, "It'd take them a week to get it there, assuming they'd be walking through the bush country. And that thing is heavy, hard to carry."

"Not so," said Waitimu. "Many people signal passing traffic, asking for a ride. Sometimes a neighbor with a vehicle will oblige; it's the neighborly thing to do."

"Yeah, we call that hitchhiking. That being likely, it could be arriving in Kitale as we speak. After breakfast, I'm gonna go there and find out. Wanna come?"

"Yes," said Waitimu and Abe together.

Around noon, Clay drove up to the Kitale general store, the most likely place in town to pawn a pump, and parked.

The three travelers walked in, and were met immediately by the proprietor.

He said, "I bet you're going to ask me if anyone brought in a water pump to sell. The answer is 'Yes,' they did, and left about two hours ago. Realizing it had to have been stolen, and that someone would soon be around asking for it, I bought it from them rather than raising a ruckus."

"Halleluiah!" said Clay with emphasis. "Will you sell it back to us?"

"I gave them 5000 ksh, about $58, and a box of beef jerky. They smiled their delight through broken teeth, and took off. For them, it was a big haul."

Clay followed up that comment quickly with, "To recover your expenses, and a bit for your wisdom and trouble, will this $100 bill be sufficient to reclaim our pump?"

After completing the deal with the pleased proprietor, shaking hands and buying a few supplies, Clay and his passengers placed the pump on the truck bed, and headed back to Lotuxo. By late afternoon, women and children were again joyously pumping water from their new well.

≈ ≈ ≈

Two nights later, Clay was awakened by faint unusual noise. His ears picked up the unmistakable sound of metal clinking on metal. It took a few seconds to break through his drowsiness, but a repeat clinking tone finally tore though his dulled mind, and he knew what it was: someone was in the process of stealing the pump again. He leapt out of bed, and started running while still pulling up his pants. As the Evans house was one of the closest to the well, it took him only seconds to reach the solitary figure hunched next to the pump.

Clay threw his body at the transgressor with a loud growling shout, knocking him right off the concrete pad. The two men grunted, punched and wrestled on the damp dirt in the dark, with Clay shouting curses at the top of his lungs. Momentarily his opponent was atop him, a mere second or two. And then, sudden blinding, searing pain accompanied by loud involuntary screams from his own lips shattered the community's peace and quiet. Near-superhuman strength from his convulsing body flung the transgressor rearwards onto his backside. Clay, enraged by pain, jumped up and moved to attack the dark figure, but sudden weakness from traumatic shock overcame him, and he fell to his knees. The other man staggered up and melted into the bush.

Within less than a minute, community men were at Clay's side, staring at the knife protruding from his right shoulder. One reached for it to pull it out, prompting Clay to shout, "No, no. Don't pull it out." Despite his pain, he knew that extracting it might cause him to bleed out. He needed to get to his house where there was light, where Jennie was able to see what damage was done or might be if careless actions were taken.

Even though she was no nurse, her career in the medical equipment field dealing daily with doctors had equipped her medical understanding beyond basic first-aid knowhow. His neighbors gently lifted him to his feet, supporting him but avoiding his right arm and shoulder, as he wobbled into his front door, and helped him sit down.

Jennie was now wide awake, and aghast at the sight of a knife protruding from her husband's torso, with blood running down his chest to meet a widening damp red stain on his pants. She wanted to draw back and cry, but knew she had to take action. She put her face close to the visible part of the blade, studying the angle of entry. She knew that it was possible that the steel had penetrated his right lung, and was very close to a large artery. Nevertheless she decided to very carefully pull it out, following in reverse the angle by which it had entered his shoulder. It came out easily, with no spurt of blood, a clear indication no artery had been damaged.

The blade was about four inches long, but only three-quarters-inch wide; she laid the knife aside. The wound was deep, perhaps close to three inches, and bleeding freely. She grabbed the Evanses first-aid kit off the divider wall shelf, took out some large gauze pads, and applied one directly over the wound, applying pressure to stop the blood flow. Over the next 15 minutes, the wound continued to ooze blood, but it gradually ceased as she reapplied more clean compresses. Eventually, she taped a clean compress in place.

Clay was calm, but woozy from shock, pain and blood loss, and emitted soft moans periodically. Jennie grabbed one of the syringes that Doc Nichols had given them, took out one of the kit's ampoules of morphine, and extracted enough to half-fill the syringe. She hesitated, trying to decide where to inject it, in his arm, shoulder or butt. The butt won. In just a minute or two, Clay's pain ceased, and he perked up.

"Good job, Doctor," he said to her. "You're hired, permanently. How much do I owe you?" He was not breathing heavily, and had no trouble speaking, so hopefully the lung had not been damaged.

"A kiss will do just fine," she said. He obliged.

"You've got good drugs," he said. "I feel great. How about another shot?"

"No way, hon. We may need to use more of this tomorrow, I mean today," she corrected herself, as she realized the sun had already come up. It was pretty clear to both Jennie and Clay that the wound was not fatal, and that he would soon recover.

CHAPTER 34

THREE weeks after they left Somalia, Ali and Nadif had arrived within yards of the designated campsite coordinates, according to their GPS. No other team members appeared to be there or within shouting distance. Clearly, no one had checked out the physical accessibility of the exact site, as it was right in the midst of an acre-size patch of nearly impenetrable dense brush.

"I'm not up to chopping my way into that jungle of twigs with a mere pocket knife right now," said Ali. "We've had a long day's trek, so let's just rest. I'm exhausted and going to take a nap."

"I wonder how long we'll have to wait for the others?" asked Nadif. "It could be hours or days or weeks. What are we supposed to do in the meantime?"

Ali didn't answer. He was asleep.

≈ ≈ ≈

Four days later, Omar walked into the campsite, pushing a motor scooter along at his side.

"Where's Ghedi," asked Ali.

"Everything was going well until the day before yesterday," said Omar. "We rented two scooters in some town, rode away, and didn't return. Ghedi kept looking behind him, fearful that the police might have been summoned, and were following us. I kept telling him we were safe, and to keep his eyes on the road, but he didn't. He was riding just ahead of me. He turned around to look again, just as the scooter's front wheel hit a pothole. Ghedi flew through the air and landed just in front of an oncoming truck. He died instantly, blood spurting all over the road and me too.

"I didn't stop; there was nothing I could do. I left the road immediately and sped off across a barren plain. No one followed me, so I kept the scooter until it ran out of gas an hour ago. Ghedi, as my team leader, had the GPS, so I had to find my way here by compass, the road map and some lucky guessing. Sorry I'm late."

"Was that a martyr's death?" asked Nadif. "Ghedi never had a chance to fight the enemy and die in conflict."

"Yes, I'm sure it was," said Ali. "He is probably already enjoying the same great reward that we will soon get."

"Omar," continued Ali, "you need to pitch in and help us turn this brush jungle into a functioning campsite. We've cleared out barely enough space for four tents and a cooking area so far. We really could use a machete. More than anything, we need more river water, and will soon run out of food too. We must soon visit a store in Kitale for groceries. How much money does each of you have left?"

"I have just a few hundred Kenyan shillings," said Omar. "Ghedi had the team's bankroll."

"Me too," said Nadif.

"I must confess," said Ali, "that I overspent our team's funds getting here, mainly on gasoline for vehicles that we all-too-soon had to abandon. I hope that when Khalid and Abidi get here, they'll have most of their starting money."

Nadif added, "Leader Godane cautioned us all to be thrifty with our funds, but also warned that we could be here for months. He said that realistically we would probably have to find ways to replenish our finances, as necessary. Perhaps one or more of us could find temporary work."

"Unlikely," said Ali. "In this remote impoverished region, only a few businessmen in towns have an income. The peoples around here are herdsmen, and barter for their special needs."

≈ ≈ ≈

Weeks passed. Khalid and Abidi never arrived. The three men already at the campsite assumed their fellow jihadists were either dead, or in jail somewhere. Khalid's bankroll was thus unavailable. So was the sole satellite telephone that he had been carrying. The mission so important to Leader Godane's plans had fallen apart. Ali, Nadif and Omar felt abandoned, and were very hungry.

≈ ≈ ≈

It didn't rain one rare evening, and the wind had stopped blowing through the brush and high grass. Even the flies and mosquitoes were not buzzing. An unusual silence reigned. The three Somali men sat quietly around the fire, drinking river water, and savoring the last one-third piece of jerky that Omar found at the bottom of his backpack.

Breaking the silence, Ali said, "We must find something that has value, and sell it in Kitale so that we can buy some food. We truly are starving. We could sell the scooter there, but without gasoline, we have no way to move it a long distance."

They all lapsed into deep thought. In that moment of total quiet, for the first time on any night since they had arrived, the sound of distant drums could be heard.

"That's it," exclaimed Ali. "Those are sounds of a celebration in the distance. We must find where it is. There will certainly be food there, any maybe something we can steal to sell."

For almost an hour, they picked their way through the darkness-shrouded plain toward the noise. With no moon to enhance vision, they stumbled over rocks, walked into thorns, and fell into rabbit holes. Finally they could see flickering firelight through the bushes, and hear the laughter and other joyous sounds, as well as the strings, horns and drums of a band. Creeping close, they could see hundreds of people dancing around a huge bonfire. Ali noted the coordinates of that native village on his GPS. They all then carefully retreated back to the campsite.

The very next night they returned at 3:00 am to look for something to steal. Lotuxo's brand new pump was only a few meters away. It wasn't easy getting the hold-down nuts loose with just the small pliers in their Swiss Army knives, but they eventually did so. Omar and Nadif wrestled the pump back to their campsite.

The next day, Ali and Nadif stood on the A1 highway with the pump, eventually flagging down a pickup truck willing to take them to Kitale. They brought the pump into the general store, and were thrilled to sell it for 5000 Kenyan schillings and a whole box of jerky. They used the money to purchase enough basic food supplies for at least two weeks.

≈ ≈ ≈

Omar was disappointed when they returned without a container of gasoline he asked them to bring back for the scooter. Ali explained, "We thought it more important to use all the money for food. You can get the gas next time we have something to sell."

Two nights later, Omar left the campsite at midnight. He told Ali and Nadif earlier that he was going to try to find something else to steal in the native village, so that he could buy some gas. He didn't come back that night.

Omar returned shortly before 8:00 am the next morning, as Ali and Nadif were preparing breakfast. His torn clothes were covered with mud, his arms with bruises, and his face swollen and bloody.

He explained that the pump had been replaced, so he was attempting to steal it again. However, some white guy came flying through the air, hitting him in his mid-section, knocking him off the pump pad. "He was determined to kill me, so I reached into my boot, took out my old hunting knife, and stabbed him in the chest. He collapsed in a heap, so I ran off into the bushes, where I later collapsed from exhaustion. I woke up only an hour ago. I think I killed him."

"You fool!" shouted Ali. "You were told not to bring any weapons! Now the police will be combing the entire area searching for the killer. We can't stay here. We must leave now. We cannot escape successfully as a group. Everyone must be responsible for his own life and actions. I'm personally going to try to get to Nairobi. Perhaps I will be able to link up with another Somali team someday, assuming Godane's attack plans eventually go forward." Farewell. Allah Be Praised."

CHAPTER 35

POSSIBLY because of the side effects of the morphine, his physical struggle with the assailant, and the sleep he'd lost, Clay's eyes seemed intent on closing, so he decided to give in to a nap while still free from pain. Jennie had to inject him once more that afternoon when he awakened, but that ended his reliance on the drug. The pain gradually and naturally decreased over the next few days, but the wound seemed to be getting redder and more swollen day by day. By the fourth day, it had started to ooze fluid; it was clearly infected, and he knew the infection would get much worse if not treated.

"Jennie," he said, "I think you'd better get some of that antibiotic and another syringe from our medical kit, and stick me."

"Clay, don't you remember?" she said. "We used all of the cephazolin antibiotic that Doc gave us. You've forgotten that about two months ago we used it to treat that 11-year-old village boy's infected facial wounds and jaw fracture. You should certainly recall that, since you had to argue with his parents three days to allow you to take him to the hospital in Nairobi."

"Yeah, I forgot; too many things on my mind since."

"Well, what are you going to do about your infection? You'd better start driving yourself to Nairobi soon."

"Jen, I've been hoping we could hold off on that until we're all packed and ready to head home in two more days.

We've got to get on that flight to London on time, and a separate side trip to Nairobi would make that impossible."

"I'm afraid, Clay. Two days would be too long; look at that shoulder wound festering! You've got to do something now."

"Okay, to be honest, I have been concerned, so much so that I woke up at 2:00 am two nights ago, already starting to worry about infection, but then got an idea about healing. In the morning, I blew it off as a wacky idea. But maybe it's something worth trying."

"Tell me about it, please," she said.

"Okay. This is probably stupid, but remember the good-luck ID charms that Glen and Sonny sent us when we were readying to leave on this initiation mission?"

"Yeah, we each got one. As I remember, they're just a tiny plastic vial supposedly containing PDL water, wrapped in a fancy ribbon displaying the "RS" logo, and a key chain. Mine's in the bottom pocket on my knapsack."

"Jen, my 2:00 am idea was that the tiny bit of PDL water in the vial might have some healing power. After all, immersing in it made us young again. What if it were injected into my wound? Would it cause all the damaged surrounding cells to revert to healthy young ones; would it cause the wound to heal?"

"At this point, what have we got to lose, Clay? Let's try it right now."

"I agree. Get my charm, and bring a syringe; there should be one or two left."

For the next half hour, Clay and Jennie wrestled with the vial, trying to find a way to access the water inside without destroying the thing. The vial's plastic wall was too thick for the syringe needle to penetrate, so they were faced with the prospect of having to cut off the end of the vial with a knife. Clay didn't like that idea because of possible contamination and fluid loss. Eventually, Jennie remembered that she had a large safety pin in her sewing kit.

Clay was able to force the tip of that pin barely through the plastic wall. Once accomplished, Jennie threaded the syringe needle into the fluid, and was able to withdraw all of it. "It looks to me like enough to fill a quarter-teaspoon measuring utensil in my home kitchen," she said.

"Oh, good!" quipped Clay. "Now that we know that precise bit of recipe information, go ahead and stick it into my shoulder; put just a little in, say, three different places around the wound, and squirt the rest right into the center of it."

She did as he asked. Nothing happened. "Can you beat that," said Clay, "no sizzle, no smoke, no heavenly chorus. Maybe something promising will happen by morning; or perhaps you'll wake up to a boy baby in bed next to you. I can hardly wait."

"How can you make fun of this situation, Clay? This is serious! If it doesn't help even a little by morning, I'm going to insist you have to go to the hospital in Nairobi. We can always get other airline tickets home, but I can't get another you," she said, her eyes starting to tear.

"All right, I agree," he promised.

They spent the remainder of that day with the Iweala family at their house, enjoying the six-pack of warm beer and beef jerky that Clay bought on his pump-rescue trip to the general store in Kitale. Clay and Waitimu, with the translation aid of Abe, sat in the kitchen discussing what measures might be taken to prevent future theft of the pump. Jennie and Adani listened with interest nearby.

"One approach would be to modify the bolting system that holds the pump to the concrete pad," suggested Clay. "Perhaps the current hexagonal fastening nuts could be replaced with some that couldn't be removed without a special wrench designed for those particular nuts."

Waitimu nodded understanding, and offered an alternate solution, "Or, perhaps there's a way to use chain or cable to anchor the pump to the pad. In any event," he added, "I'm going to post a nightly guard there until we decide how to safeguard it and make those modifications."

Even though he'd napped that morning, Clay's eyes started growing heavy again, so the Evanses bid their friends goodnight and went to bed shortly after dark.

The next morning, Clay woke up and immediately noticed that the pain he'd been fighting all of the previous day was gone. Still in his sleeping bag, he reached over with his left hand and gently pressed on the right-shoulder bandage. No pain. He pressed harder. Still no pain, not even tenderness. So he arose and walked to the entry door, and stepped outside. The brightness of the new day caused him to squint for a minute or two, but he could see clearly enough to grip the edge of the adhesive tape holding the bandage firmly against the skin.

He peeled it away, wincing not from the pain of the shoulder wound, but from some of his fine chest hair being yanked out by the tape. Then he lifted the gauze off, and looked beneath. He gasped.

There was no wound! There wasn't even any scar tissue; not even a pink line! His right shoulder looked normal, exactly like it did before the knife was plunged in by his assailant. He stepped back inside, and sat down briefly on a nearby box, said a silent prayer of thanks, and stared again and again at the site of the injury, still in near disbelief.

Clay walked over to where Jennie slept, kneeled down and caressed her hair, speaking her name softly to awaken her. When she stirred and looked up at him, he said, "Honey, the PDL water injection worked like a miracle; the wound is gone, like it never happened."

She sat up, looked at his shoulder in the semi-darkness of that part of the house, and exclaimed, "Oh my God." She stood up and pulled him to the open door and outside, studying his shoulder. "Clay, this is miraculous. We've got hold of something wonderful. We have to find out how to use this knowledge to help others."

From that moment on, Clay and Jennie knew that their Kenyan mission trip had opened the door to their next second-lifetime endeavor. Although they'd soon be home in Florence, Alabama, it was already obvious that they were not going to be spending a lot of time lying on their backyard hammocks.

CHAPTER 36

IT was time to leave Lotuxo. The previous day, Clay and Jennie had packed about half of their clothes, some toiletries, necessary personal stuff and a few gifts and mementos into one of their rolling duffle bags. One memento, the knife that Jennie had pulled out of Clay's torso, had been carefully shielded by a leather-like sheath that Waitimu made from tree bark.

As soon as they rolled up their sleeping bags at sunrise that morning, they donated them, as well as everything else they owned, clothing, unused supplies, medical kit, the second duffle bag, etc., to the Iwealas to use or distribute as they saw fit to others in the community. At breakfast with those friends, they also announced that they'd decided to donate their truck to the Lotuxo Water Board, with the proviso that one of Lotuxo's English-speaking experienced drivers must come with them to Nairobi, and then drive the truck back.

Their departure at about 9:00 am was unforgettable. There were many warm words of thanks, handclasps, handshakes, and hugs from all of the elders and their wives, as well as Waitimu, Adani and their children. As several community singing groups joined voices in a farewell song amidst the crowd, tears flowed down dozens of faces, including Jennie's. Finally, they climbed into the truck and waved goodbye, and hundreds of hands started clapping, a chorus they could continue to hear through the truck's open windows as it headed down the goat trail to the highway.

Clay and Jennie stayed overnight in a Nairobi hotel, and caught their scheduled morning flight to London. After two days there, unwinding and sightseeing, they boarded their flight to the U.S., landing in Atlanta. They phoned the Sangers from the terminal after renting a car, and drove only as far as Montgomery, planning to spend their first night in the States with Glen and Sonny, before continuing on to Florence the following day.

≈ ≈ ≈

"Hello Afrikaners!" said Glen, as he met them at the door. "Come on in. Sonny's in the kitchen doing a stir-fry that she couldn't leave. Can I help you get your luggage from the trunk?"

"This is all we have," said Clay, pointing to the single mostly empty duffle bag he was holding.

Jennie gave Glen a hug and a kiss on the cheek, and rushed by him into the kitchen, to a squeal of delight from Sonny, "Jennie, I'm so happy to see you! It's been more than three months," she said, as the two women hugged each other, and started chatting about the meal being prepared.

Back in the living room where Clay had plopped down, Glen continued, "One limp cloth bag. You mean that's all you two brought with you for nearly three months in Africa?"

"Heck no," countered Clay, "We gave away most of our stuff to the natives there. Wow, they're so poor, materially speaking, but people rich with love. Poverty doesn't seem to bother them a bit. The whole community of 800 or so people we lived with seemed happy most all the time.

226

Especially when the well we drilled provided for their water needs. What a wonderful experience for Jennie and I. We're so thrilled to have been part of it."

"Clay, you've got to tell us all about it," said Glen. "Did you take any pictures and videos?"

"Tons," said Clay. "We'd be happy to share some of them with you tonight, if you want. Jennie took them all, and transferred them to two thumb drives, one each for photos and videos."

"Fantastic. After dinner, I'll set up a link between our computer and large-screen TV. In the meantime, how about a cold beer?"

"Yeahhh!" Clay responded enthusiastically; "I haven't had a cold one in three months. We had a six pack of warm local beer just before we left Lotuxo, and each had another warm one in a London pub, but I really miss good ole' American brew. If you've got the makings, I'd like to put together a margarita for Jennie. She's been on the involuntary wagon ever since we left Florence."

"I'll make one for her," said Glen as he got up and headed for the kitchen.

"I'm coming too; got to say hello to that wonderful good-looking wife of yours."

All four friends renewed and reinvigorated their friendship over drinks and the meal being cooked on the stove, until dinner was served. Afterwards, they moved to the TV room for the 'Evans Kenya Showtime.' Glen operated the equipment, but Clay controlled it via remote. Both Clay and Jennie shared narration duties.

"Our home for most of the last three months has been Lotuxo, which is located in the northwestern part of Kenya.

(Pic) This is what the community looks like from the goat trail access path."

(Pic) "Here's a photo of our home. The natives built it from mud and sticks. It's pretty dark in parts of the interior, as there's no electricity in Lotuxo. No water either when we first arrived."

(Pic) "This is a picture of the Iweala family, our principle host. The guy there is Waitimu, the chief of the 800-person community. His wife, Adani, was Jennie's best friend. Their children's ages range from 13 to 19."

Jennie added, "The teenage girl shown there had sole responsibility for getting the family's morning water every day from a river over five miles away; all that changed when the well was drilled."

"(Pic) This is a picture of the Chief and his elders. Adani got to know all their wives pretty well, and she eventually ran a seminar to teach them hygiene."

"Here's a photo of Isiolo, (Pic) the nearest major town, 290 miles away. It looks more like something out of the Old West when you walk down its dusty streets."

"I took this picture of Clay (Pic) watching the drilling rig you see there start boring the well hole. It eventually hit a big water aquifer at 189 feet down."

"(Pic) This is the most memorable picture of all. It shows dozens of women in their colorful dresses standing around the new well as Adani pumps the first water up from the depths."

"Now, Glen, please run the first video, and you'll see and hear the cheers and clapping of so many joyful people, and then watch some of them filling their household buckets. (Video) Look at the kids playing with the water, something never before possible. Let's switch back to the photo thumb drive.

"Before I click the next photo, I want to show you something else. Jennie, would you please turn on the lights for a minute." Clay stood up, unbuttoned his shirt, and removed it. "Glen and Sonny, look here at my right shoulder," he said, putting his index finger on his skin.

They both approached him, stooped over and looked; Glen said, "So, what are we supposed to see. I don't see anything but your chest and shoulder."

"Okay, lights back out, Jen. Now folks, watch as I click on the next photo." (Pic) Audible gasps could be heard. "Good grief, Clay, it looks like that knife is plunged deep into your shoulder," said Glen.

"Clay, whatever happened to you?" whined Sonny.

"Jen, put the lights back on, please. Glen, please turn off the TV for now. It's pretty obvious from the last photo that I was severely wounded by being stabbed. The wound was three inches deep, three-quarters inch wide, and within four days was so badly infected that it was swollen, bright red and oozing pus. And it all occurred within the past two weeks!"

"My first reaction," said Glen, "if I didn't know better, would be to ask, 'Did you die?' How did you get stabbed, and how did you survive? And how come the shoulder today shows no traces of the injury?"

Clay responded, "Shortly after the pump was installed, it was stolen. I was able to recover it the following day, and reinstall it. At 2:30 am two nights later, I caught a stranger trying to steal it again, and fought with him. He stabbed me during the fight, and got away."

"Why didn't you just go to the doctor or hospital right away?" asked Sonny.

"Because the nearest surgeon or hospital was over 10 hours drive away in Nairobi. Lotuxo is in the middle of nowhere. It's probably one of the most remote places in Kenya. But Jennie and I were prepared, or so I thought at the time. We'd obtained syringes, painkillers and antibiotics from our doctor before we left, so that we'd be prepared in case of an accident or sickness. After I was stabbed, Nurse Jennie injected me with the morphine and it worked fine; I thought I was on the road to recovery until infection set in. So I asked her to stick me with the injectable antibiotic. But I forgot that we'd used up all that antibiotic treating an infected jaw fracture of a small native boy two months earlier."

"So how come you survived," asked Glen.

"Jennie injected a few drops of PDL water into and around my wound; we got it from one of the RS good-luck charms you gave us. It was a last-resort attempt, and if it hadn't worked, I would have driven to Nairobi, and we'd have missed our flights home as a result.

"Glen and Sonny, try to grasp the full meaning of what I'm going to tell you next. The very next morning, only a few hours after those injections, that wound had completely disappeared, and looked exactly like you see it now, here in this room today!" Reaching into their duffle bag, Clay produced the knife, removed the sheath and handed it to Glen, saying, "Here's the actual weapon."

"Wow!" said Glen. Then after a few moments of contemplation, "I'm now certain that you two should definitely be involved as participants in the Society's Grand

230

Project. Finding out how to use PDL water in ways to benefit humanity is what that project is all about."

CHAPTER 37

OVER breakfast the next morning, Glen reminded Clay and Jennie to plan on attending the upcoming Annual Meeting of the Renewables Society. He also proposed they plan to make a multimedia presentation there, based on their Kenya photos, videos and healing story. "In the meantime," he said, "I'm going to advise the Membership Committee about the successes of your initiation mission, and urge them to approve you as full-fledged Members, enabling you to attend that meeting. After your presentation at the Meeting, I'll propose that you be invited to participate in the Grand Project. I'm certain that it'll be a done deal."

Jennie asked, "When and where does that Meeting take place?"

"Just a little less than two months from now, in Cleveland on May 22."

"I don't think we have any conflicts, do you Jennie?" asked Clay.

"We can make it," she said.

≈ ≈ ≈

After almost three months in Kenya, the Evanses finally arrived back in Florence. As Clay parked the rental car in front of their home, Jennie looked out and said, "Oh, I just love our house. It's so beautiful sitting there surrounded by a green sea of manicured grass, shrubs and flowers. No dirt, no mud, no sticks, windows all around to let in daylight and a doorway that actually has a door in it. We're so fortunate that we were able to complete our mission and walk away from that Lotuxo house and lifestyle."

Clay nodded agreement and added, "We'd better give our gardener a nice tip for keeping the exterior grounds so perfect."

Later, a bottle of beer in hand, Clay sat in an easy chair across the room from Jennie and said, "You know, when I think about the things that've happened in our lives over the past seven and a half months, it simply blows me away. Back at the beginning of last August, we were a just a couple of old folks celebrating our 54th Anniversary. Remember that week? Boy, did our lives ever change.

"Now we're a pair of teenagers that have just pulled off a miracle in the lives of a whole community of people in Africa. Yet, we're both still trying to cope with the fact that our children look older than we do, and our grandkids look like us. Add to all that, a door's about to open that we can walk through to perhaps help discover medical cures that could benefit all humanity. It's mind-boggling, Jen."

"Mind-boggling indeed, Clay, but we surely must walk through that door, and do our utmost, no matter what it takes. We've been given a rare opportunity and challenge like no other. We've got to devote ourselves to the task.

"That means that we've got to learn how to understand exactly how and why PDL water does what it does to people with our unique type of genes. I know virtually nothing of genetics, and I suspect you know even less, Clay. And neither of us knows anything about water beyond the fact that it's a molecule made of hydrogen and oxygen atoms.

"Jen, it seems pretty obvious to me that we're both in need of more education in appropriate specialized studies. I think we're probably headed back to college, babe. I'll go online after dinner and see where we might find those special courses."

"What courses do you think we'll need, Clay?"

"Well, my best guess is that one or both of us should take an undergraduate biology course centering on genetics and cell structure. That might help us understand what's unique about our peculiar genetic makeup that makes us susceptible to wild cell change under the influence of PDL water. Then, one of us should probably take a course that teaches us how we can use modern technology hardware to study PDL water in hopes of finding what makes it unique."

"Sounds like a good start to me, hon," said Jennie.

Subsequently, searching nearby colleges via Google for basic courses in genetics and analytical chemistry, Clay found that the University of Alabama in Tuscaloosa had a Department of Biology offering undergraduate studies of genetics and cell microbiology. Their Department of Chemistry also offered analytical chemistry lectures on topics such as Spectroscopic Methods of Analysis, Chromatography, Analytical Techniques, Electron Microscopy, and others, any of which might help expose the unique attributes of PDL water.

After sharing this information with Jennie, she suggested, "Tuscaloosa's not even a three-hour drive away. Why don't you head down there tomorrow and see if we could sign up for classes during the Summer Semester. I'd like to stay home today and get the house clean, our clothes washed and belongings put away."

"I'll leave after breakfast and should be back well before dinnertime."

≈ ≈ ≈

Clay parked the car in the University of Alabama's Visitors Lot, and walked onto the campus grounds, intending to find the Admissions Office. As he meandered through throngs of students, all rushing towards their next class, passing by pretty young coeds, jocks with their letterman jackets, and professors with their briefcases, he was reminded of his own college days. Memories flashed through his mind: fraternity blasts, girlfriends and blind dates, football games, and nights burning the midnight oil studying for the next day's exams. It was one of the happiest times of his life, he recalled.

With help from a couple of students, he soon found and entered the administration building housing the Admissions Office.

"Uh, hello," he said to the young female approaching the counter; "I'm interested in finding out where and how to apply to take some Summer Semester classes, but not for credit."

"Are you a high school graduate?" asked the voluptuous blonde-haired girl, smiling prettily.

"Yes, and I also have an MBA degree."

"Oh, I'm studying for an MBA now. Perhaps you can give me some pointers," she said suggestively as she raised her eyebrows and leaned toward him. "What degree would you like to pursue here?"

"No, like I said, I don't want to pursue a degree; I'm interested in taking only two courses, one in the Department of Biology and one in the Department of Chemistry. I'm not looking to acquire credit hours."

"I'm not sure that's possible. You really don't want to be a student?" she cooed with an air of disappointment.

Clay, starting to feel a trace of attraction towards the girl, found himself standing taller and smiling as he said, nonchalantly, "I really want to study and gain knowledge in two particular fields of science that your professors teach here. I'm willing to pay the necessary fees, buy the required books, do the homework and attend all the classes."

"Will you be sleeping . . . I mean staying on campus," she asked.

Clay then caught hold of himself, deciding to throw some verbal cold water on the girl, answering, "No, I'll be sleeping at home with my wife."

"Oh . . . well, this is the Admissions Office, she said bruskly. We admit candidates for particular degrees. Do you want to enroll as a student for a degree, or not?"

"No. Can't I be admitted to simply monitor a class?"

"No."

"But I could be admitted as a freshman intent on earning a Bachelor's degree from the Department of Biology?"

"Yes, providing you meet all the requirements. Here's a brochure that lays out those requirements. An application is included inside. You won't be able to enroll for the Summer Semester until May 13th and no later than May 29th."

"May I have two of those brochures, please? I've a friend who'll be enrolling at the same time. Thanks for your help. Bye."

"Yeah, have a nice day," she sourly concluded.

CHAPTER 38

AT the dinner table that evening, Clay explained to Jennie that they needed to complete their applications for admission as 'Bama' freshmen, working towards specific undergraduate degrees, and submit them between May 13th and 29th with the required fees.

"You could enroll as a candidate for a bachelor's degree from the Department of Biology," he said, "targeting the course 'Genetics and Cell Biology.' I'd enroll in the Department of Chemistry, and attend the 'Lecture and Lab Series on Analytical Chemistry.' I'm not positive, but I think we could also take each other's courses as electives, as well."

"Clay, I bet there's going to be a minimum number of credit hours we'll have to meet to stay registered."

"Yeah, you're probably right, Jen. There're hopefully some no-brainer courses that the jocks take to avoid homework. We could fill in with those, as necessary, and only show up occasionally for those lectures, just enough to keep the instructors happy."

≈ ≈ ≈

On the morning of May 9th, Jennie awakened, happily realizing it was her 78th birthday. She pondered whether instead she should consider it her 16th or 17th? Did Clay remember, and might he be planning a surprise? As Jennie sat up, she was suddenly overcome with dizziness, and quickly lay back down. But then she felt nauseous. She sat up again, not nearly as dizzy, but knew she'd better start moving hurriedly toward the bathroom. She reached the porcelain bowl just in time, dropped to her knees and vomited.

Clay, hearing her retch, shouted, "Jen, what's wrong, baby." Jumping out of bed, he walked quickly into the bathroom and kneeling down, comforted her, holding her head and hugging her, saying, "You must be coming down with a bug or something. I'm sorry for you, honey."

She said, "I've felt woozy on and off for the past couple of weeks, but this is the first time it's been this bad."

Clay stood up, walked over to the medicine chest, found the thermometer and said, "Jen, let's see if you've got a fever. If you do, you'd better go see the doctor because it might be the start of something more serious than a cold or the flu. It might be something you picked up in the Kenyan jungle before we left; something exotic that has a long incubation period?"

"Forget the thermometer, Clay; I feel so terrible right now I want professional medical help ASAP. Let's go."

They both quickly dressed and drove to Dr. Nichol's office. Because they had no appointment, the receptionist rejected their plea to see the doctor. However, Dr. Nichols overheard Clay dispute the rejection, stepped into the reception area and invited Jennie and Clay to step right into the examination room. "I heard you two were back in town, and I've been hoping neither of you'd be coming to see me with some kind of jungle rot or fever. What seems to be the trouble, Jennie?"

"Doctor, I've been slightly nauseous on and off almost since we returned, but it's been getting worse daily, and today I vomited; I just feel awful."

"Clay, please wait out in the reception room while I examine Jennie."

"Oh, she won't mind if I stay here and watch," said Clay.

"I know, Clay, but I will."

Clay obliged, sat down and started watching a soap opera on the elevated TV. About fifteen minutes later, he returned to the exam room at the doctor's request.

"Clay," said Doc, "we know what's wrong with Jennie."

"Is she okay; can you fix her up?" he asked, shocked at seeing the tears running down her face.

"Clay, Jennie is pregnant. Congratulations, you're going to be a daddy!"

"Oh, Clay, I'm so happy, I can't stop these tears of joy," she said. "We're going to have another family!" The doctor was a little puzzled by that statement, but said nothing.

"I'm speechless," said Clay, slowly shaking his head side to side, as if to signal 'No.' "I can't believe this. How's it possible?"

Doc said, "If you don't know the answer to that question, Clay, your family is going to be very, very large."

"How could this have happened, Jen; we've been taking precautions?"

"Always . . . except for that one night, March 10th, when we both got pie-eyed drinking native hooch in Lotuxo. Remember? We were all crazy happy, dancing around the bonfire in celebration of the well producing its first water," she responded.

"Oh yeah. Forgot about that night."

"Me too," she said, "until now. What a lovely surprise. Doctor Nichols did a little calculation, and came up with a delivery date of December 22nd. Clay, please tell me you're happy. We can make small changes to our plans, and it'll be wonderful!" she said excitedly.

Clay, taking hold of his emotions, wisely changed his frown to a smile, and said, "Sure we can. It'll be wonderful all over again, babe."

≈ ≈ ≈

Four days later, Clay and Jennie showed up the University of Alabama Admissions Office, and produced their letters of acceptance to the receptionist. They were directed to the table labeled 'D-E-F,' and stood in line behind three teenagers, all waiting for the volunteers at that table to locate and produce the documents officially designating their class schedule for the Summer Semester.

They jointly compared the schedules each had received. "It looks like you've got the Biology Genetics course at 11:00 am on Mondays, Wednesdays and Fridays, Jen. My schedule shows that course as an elective for me, same time. That ought to work out well, as we can have an early breakfast, leave at 8:00 and be here in ample time for these classes."

"Thankfully, our course schedules dovetail." she said. "Yours says you have the Analytical Chemistry lectures on Monday and Friday at 1:00, and the related lab on Wednesday from 1:00 to 3:00, and mine shows the same class times for my elective."

"They've really done a superb job setting up these schedules," said Clay. No time wasted sitting around waiting for each other, or for hours lost between classes. Best of all, we only have to drive down here three times a week.

"Classes generally start on Monday, June 4th," he continued, "but our first class will be on Wednesday. I'm looking forward to being a college man again. Jose Collegio, yahoo!"

"Yeah, but don't you start looking at all those other coeds; I'll be watching you," she said.

"For 54 years, you always told me I could look, but not touch," he responded.

"Well, I've changed my mind," she said. "Keep your eyes on the professors, and your mind on the class studies."

"If you say so, Jennie, but you'd have been the ultimate beneficiary of any stray glances that might have normally aroused my male instincts."

"I've changed my mind again. Look, but don't touch," she concluded, smiling slyly at him.

≈ ≈ ≈

After completing the registration process, and before driving home to Florence, Clay phoned Glen Sanger. "Hi Glen, we've been kind 'a busy lately, and haven't had much chance to chat, so I thought I'd call and learn whether you've heard back from the Membership Committee since giving them the report on our Kenya mission?"

"I just spoke with them this morning, as a matter of fact. They approved you both, with no conditions attached," said Glen. "And they do want you to do that multimedia presentation, with special emphasis on your amazing recovery from the knife wound. I don't think there's any doubt that ultimately you'll also be invited to join the Grand Project team."

"That's super news, Glen. Thanks for following up on our behalf. We've just finished registering at the University of Alabama for a couple of courses we'll need if that invite does come. We're going to start classes on June 6th. Between now and the Society meeting on May 22nd, we'll go ahead and start putting together that multimedia show. We've got plenty of photos and a couple of good videos, but it'll take time to merge them all with a reasonably interesting and informative script."

CHAPTER 39

MONDAY morning, May 21st, Clay and Jennie boarded a flight from Memphis to Cleveland. On arrival, they took a cab to the Hilton Garden Inn, checked in and unpacked their computer, projector and thumb drives containing the visual and music portions of their presentation. That afternoon, they practiced reading their typed scripts. Each had a specially marked copy enabling them to smoothly alternate their speaking roles as appropriate. Then they practiced again, that time while projecting visuals on the wall, and playing African native background music through the computer.

"It looked and sounded good to me," said Clay. "I hope the meeting room has a good screen and sound system, plus two microphones for us to use. I wouldn't want to pass just one back and forth."

Jennie said, "I think you'd better check that out today with the hotel's Meeting Support office. We don't want to get stymied tomorrow."

That evening, the Evanses planned to head for bed early, but as soon as Glen and Sonny arrived and started introducing them to dozens of other members, the conversation and cocktails captured them. It quickly became clear that most of the 178 Renewables that showed up were inherently party animals. Bedtime finally arrived near 2:00 am.

Clay and Jennie were a big hit during that Renewables Society convention. The vote on their participation in the Grand Project was unanimous. They were in, pending a final Project oversight committee review.

≈ ≈ ≈

'Bama's Summer Semester for the Evanses ended on August 17th; they'd studied hard and learned the basics they presumed they'd need to start working with the Grand Project team. Since Tuscaloosa was more than halfway between their home in Florence and the Sanger's residence in Montgomery, Clay and Jennie headed directly from their final class to see Glen and Sonny.

"Hi y'all, we're here as promised," exclaimed Jennie as Sonny opened the door to greet them.

A voice in the distant background, clearly Glen's, yelled, "The Crimson Tide has just arrived. Be right there." As he joined the Evanses, Sonny left for the kitchen.

Seated on the couch, Jennie proudly stated, "Today was our last class day at the University, and we successfully completed the two courses we told you about, and with top grades in both classes. We feel we're much better prepared now to dig in and do our part on the Project, when approved."

"You've been approved," said Glen, as he joined them. "The final ruling, based primarily on your performance at the Society meeting and subsequent voting, came down last week. They want you both on the Project team starting as soon as it's convenient.

"Well," asked Clay, "that being the case, Glen, can you now reveal to us what this so-called Grand Project is all about, how expansive it is, what progress has been made, and so forth?"

"Yup, we sure can. In a nutshell, the Project's goal is to determine if it's possible to use the unique properties of PDL water to help the medical community cure diseases and heal injuries that afflict all humanity; to extend and improve the lives of all the peoples on this planet."

"Glen, that's what Jennie and I assumed it might be, thanks to all the hints you've dropped ever since you first briefed us on the importance of joining the Society. If that wasn't the goal of the Project, we'd soon be starting to investigate the same objectives on our own. That's why we spent the summer studying as hard as we have. We've certainly seen firsthand what amazing capabilities PDL water has, but can only guess what its properties might accomplish in the future.

"So, tell us more, Glen."

"The Society has leased two substantial laboratories, one in Park City, Utah and the other in Memphis, TN. At considerable expense, the Society has equipped both labs equally with a wide variety of analytical instrumentation to study PDL water, both qualitatively and quantitatively. In addition, the labs are equipped with all the biotech tools necessary to employ genetic engineering techniques, as may prove to be necessary, during the endeavor."

"Why two labs, and in such non-strategic locations," asked Jennie. "Why not in Semicon Valley, or somewhere in Massachusetts, both hubs of scientific research?"

"Two labs so we can take advantage of the talent on both sides of the country," said Glen. "Most members involved in the Project can only work part time on it, owing to their other responsibilities and frequent mission trips. Keep in mind that there're only a few active Society members that have the background experience, qualifications and skills to do the work, so we want to make it as convenient for them as possible.

"City locations were based on the location of known surface sources of PDL water within an hour's drive of each. Some of the investigations require easy access to substantial quantities on demand.

"I can't brief you on the progress that's been made to date, if any. You'll have to find that out firsthand when you visit one or both of those labs. I presume that you'll be doing your work in the Memphis facility, since it's the closest to your home."

"Dinner'll be served in about thirty minutes," said Sonny as she stuck her head into the living room. "If you've been planning on a cocktail before we eat, better have it now."

"I'd like a margarita," said Jennie to Glen as he stood up, looked askance and headed toward the kitchen.

"I'll help if you need it," shouted Clay. "If not, make mine a beer."

≈ ≈ ≈

When Glen bought back the drinks, Sonny joined them. Seated across from Jennie, she said, "Jennie, I can't help but notice that you seem to have put on quite a bit of weight since we last saw you."

Glen, who'd also noticed the bulge under Jennie's tunic, but had avoided comment, felt chagrined that his wife would insult a good friend by implying she was getting fat.

But Sonny was grinning, and Jennie grinned back, saying, "I figure it came about sometime in mid-March while we were in Kenya; I guess I'm about five months pregnant now."

"What?" exclaimed a surprised Glen, "You're pregnant? Oh, wow! Congratulations, Jennie. Uh, you too, Clay."

"We're thrilled that we're well on the way to having a second family," said Jennie. "It doesn't seem possible considering our real age, but it's obvious now our young bodies are fully and completely functional."

"Are you guys aware whether this has happened to other Renewables as well?" asked Clay.

"No, we've never been made aware of that possibility, but that doesn't mean you're unique. There's no reason it couldn't have happened with other couples, I guess, but we've never met any."

"It sure is going to be interesting when our fifty-something children learn that they've a new baby brother or sister," said Clay.

"Or that our grandkids learn they have a new uncle or aunt that's a baby," added Jennie, laughing. "Boy, I can just see Cody's face now, and imagine him saying again, 'I still don't believe it.'"

≈ ≈ ≈

The following morning, after a delightful and informative day and evening with the Sangers, Clay and Jennie drove home to Florence.

CHAPTER 40

"MEMPHIS is 165 miles from Florence, according to MapQuest," said Clay staring at his computer screen after an early breakfast. "Our drive there's supposed to take 3 hours and 21 minutes. My iPhone's GPS app should get us to the lab's front door a few minutes later."

"Clay, that's obviously too far for a daily drive. We'll have to plan on being there a few days at a time, and stay in a hotel or motel."

"No way of knowing now, Jen. We may get a better idea after we talk with some of the other volunteers there today. Ready to go? We'll probably get there just before they break for lunch."

≈ ≈ ≈

"Hello, we're Clay and Jennie Evans," announced Clay as he shook hands with a middle-age man that unlocked and cautiously opened the steel door to the Society's Memphis windowless lab.

"Yes, yes, please come in. I recognize you and your wife from the Kenya presentation you made at the meeting. Super performance, indeed. I'm Roger Morris," he said as they shook hands.

"Nice meeting you Roger. I guess all the others have already left for lunch," said Clay, his eyes scanning all the distant equipment in the huge hall-like facility, but seeing no people.

"No, not really. I'm the only one working here today. You'll seldom find more than one or two of us here at a time. Sometimes no one. I'm thankful that you two will add to that number. But, yes, it's time for lunch, I suppose. Shall we all go together?"

"Yeah, sure," said Clay, eager to corner Roger and get answers to all the questions built up in his mind ever since first hearing of the Grand Project.

As they stepped onto the sidewalk, Roger turned and locked the heavy steel door, saying, "Always be careful to lock up when leaving this lab. Secret stuff going on here, you know, not to mention over two million dollars worth of hi-tech equipment."

Over lunch at a nearby delicatessen, Clay and Jennie excitedly deluged Roger with questions even before food was served: "What progress has been made? Has the team found out why PDL water is unique? Have there been any medical discoveries? How long have you been working on the Grand Project? Why did you get involved?"

"Whoa you two! I need time to chew my sandwich between answers," said Roger. "We don't have to rush right back to the lab. Let's enjoy our meal first. We've got plenty of time to get acquainted, and get you up to speed on the goings on here."

Clay apologized, "Sorry, Roger, we're just so wrapped up in our eagerness to get going that we lost touch with civility. I haven't even tasted whatever it is that I ordered. I see that Jennie hasn't either. Bear with us, please; we'll settle down. Right, Jennie?"

She just nodded, having just then taken a huge bite of her sandwich. For the remainder of the meal, conversation centered on sports, politics and the economy. When the bill came, Roger picked it up, paid it and verbally noted there were no other customers waiting for tables.

"Okay, let's talk about the Project now," he said. "This table is as good as any place. In answer to your first question, some progress has been made. The Park City lab people have been studying their own DNA, and believe they understand the unique structure that differentiates it from the norm. That's merely a starting point, however. It could potentially take years more of study to someday open the door to using PDL water to heal the general population."

"Yeah," said Clay, "but isn't that new Park City understanding of our unique DNA quite an accomplishment, Roger? How long did that work take?"

"Just shy of three years, part time of course. The Grand Project was commissioned by the membership at the 2010 annual meeting, and it took about four months to locate, lease and equip the two labs."

"What about progress here?" asked Jennie.

"We're rather excited with some of the findings we've made on PDL water," replied Roger. "Using our infrared spectrometer, we've discovered that PDL water molecules have much higher levels of the hydrogen isotope, deuterium, than standard fresh water does.

"Uh, let me digress. As you know, water molecules consist of two atoms of hydrogen and one of oxygen. A normal atom of hydrogen has one electron and one proton. The most common isotope of hydrogen also has one neutron, and is called deuterium. That's why water with elevated levels of the hydrogen isotope deuterium is called 'heavy water.' Is this news to you?" Roger asked.

"No," responded Jennie, "we learned about isotopes, including deuterium during our summer classes at the University of Alabama a couple months ago. But thanks for the refresher."

"Excellent. Then I'll continue. PDL water has over eight times as much deuterium as normal water. It's well known that biological systems are very sensitive to even small changes in deuterium level. For example, in one study, it was found that low doses of heavy water substantially increased the lifespan of fruit flies."

"Wow, that was an interesting discovery, Roger," said Jennie. "I wonder what effect elevated doses of deuterium has on human DNA, particularly a Renewable's type of DNA."

"That's something folks like you can work on here," said Roger.

"So," said Clay, "we've got access to equipment here that can quantitatively measure hydrogen isotope levels? That's really hi-tech stuff. Could it also measure for oxygen isotopes? In that same class we took, I remember hearing about a heavier type of oxygen that could be found in water molecules."

Roger responded, "I'm confident that our Fourier transform infrared spectrometer would do the job just fine, but we haven't looked at that yet. Interesting avenue to pursue, though. Another area for you two to work on, huh?"

"Jennie and I have just basic know-how about using such fancy equipment, but a little hands-on training by you would be appreciated, Roger. Are you up for it?"

"You bet."

"So, what's your background, Roger, analytical chemist?"

"Nope, stockbroker on Wall Street. Made the big bucks, retired early, traveled the world, got bored with it all, started drinking, lost my family, and tried to commit suicide by throwing myself off a cliff in the Adirondacks. There happened to be a pond of water below, a mere spring, and that broke my fall and saved me. Must have been PDL water. I climbed out, badly hurt, and lost consciousness. When I awoke the next day, I was a teenager again, just like you two. That was about forty years ago, and here I am today. I own a restaurant chain in seven states, but find this work on the Project much more fulfilling."

"That's quite a story, Roger. What's your real age?"

"Ninety-eight, I think. Don't really try to keep track, as it's sort of meaningless, it seems, since I plan to renew myself as necessary to see this Project bear fruit. Could be months, years or decades, but eventually we will succeed. Hey, enough questions for now; let's head back, and I'll show you around the whole facility."

CHAPTER 41

OVER the following three months of part-time work in the lab, Clay proved that PDL water also contained four times as much oxygen-18 isotope than normal water did. And Jennie's research had discovered not only routine levels of common minerals in PDL water, but also unusually high trace levels of rare earth ions. It had become clear to everyone that worked on the Project in the Memphis lab that PDL water, at least chemically, was far different than ordinary water.

One evening in their Memphis motel room, which had become a home away from home for far too many nights, Clay said, "Jen, you've been working here awfully hard, and in only a month more, you'll be a new teenage mother. I really think you should stay home in Florence from now on. The pediatrician wanted you to stop traveling here a month ago, and I think you should pay attention to her know-how."

"Clay, I've given birth twice before, and it wasn't a big deal except for the last 48 hours."

"Yeah, but you weren't 78 years old then; I know . . . I know you've got a teenage body now, but what if some unforeseen problems develop, and we're 165 miles away from the doctor you've been seeing. This delivery could really be a first in history for all we know. After the baby's born, you're gonna be real busy taking care of him or her . . . for a month or two anyway. I really want you to go and stay home. Please, honey."

"I'd be lonely, and wouldn't know what to do with myself, especially with you here in Memphis for three or four days every week."

"I'll make a deal with you. We go home together tomorrow. You stay home, and I'll work here part time for just two more weeks, and then stay home fulltime with you until the end of January. We can buy baby clothes and furniture, and fix up the baby's room and all that stuff together, and then share the busy first month of feeding and caring for him, or her then. Okay?"

"Deal," she said.

≈ ≈ ≈

The pangs of labor started on the morning of December 20. Clay phoned the pediatrician and drove Jennie to the hospital, where after an emergency room examination, she was admitted. The baby boy was born without complication just after 10:00 pm that evening. Mother and child were both fine. Clay was present during the delivery, watching through tears of joy. At his request, the baby's umbilical cord and placenta blood were saved, labeled and cryopreserved for possible future use.

"His name is Wyatt Clay Evans," announced Clay proudly, as he thanked the pediatrician in the room where Jennie was recovering. He and Jennie had the privilege of repeating that name dozens of times over as family, close friends and neighbors visited them and their new son over the following few weeks. Wyatt acquired an impressive collection of mostly blue apparel during those visits.

≈ ≈ ≈

Near the end of January, Clay departed from Jennie and his new son to head back to the Memphis lab, and resume his research. Since it was to be his first trip away from her in six weeks, he agreed to limit his stay to three days.

When he arrived, Roger greeted him, "Congratulations Dad. Glad you're back. We really missed you and Jennie."

"What's the latest on the research?" Clay asked.

"Not much to report here, Clay, as hardly anyone's been around because of Christmas and New Year's holidays and travel. A few of us got together to build on Jennie's rare earth findings, and obtained quantitative data that will eventually help us to make PDL water from tap water here in the lab, and run comparison performance tests with actual PDL water from the nearby spring."

For the next four weeks, part time, Clay busied himself actually trying to manufacture artificial PDL water in the lab. Much of that time was devoted to searching the internet for sources of heavy water and heavy oxygen isotopes, and all four of the rare earth metal oxides that would be needed. The lab's sampling and weighing-volumetric measuring equipment proved too crude for the work, so he had to acquire new equipment to supplement it. Eventually, he made a gallon of artificial PDL water, and used half of it to prove that its physical and chemical identity were extremely close approximations of real PDL water. The other half he carefully sealed and stored in the lab's cool room, clearly labeled "Artificial PDL, Do Not Use."

Back home in Florence, Clay observed that Jennie looked tired, and seemed a bit frazzled in her attitude. She clearly needed a break in her routine. He said, "I'm ready for a break, Jen. How about taking a skiing vacation somewhere?"

"What a super idea, honey. Have a particular locale in mind?"

"Yeah, how about Park City, Utah? They say the snow at all the resorts there this year is fantastic."

"Oh, Clay, I should have known. You just want to go see what the Park City lab's up to."

"Well, we could possibly fit it in between two weeks of total relaxation, don't you think?"

"Two weeks? All right!"

"I bet even Wyatt would like to get away for a little change, babe. We could hire a nanny, and bring her along so that we'd have more freedom on the slopes and evening après ski parties. I'll go online right now and get reservations."

"Okay. I'll go online too, Clay, and find that nanny."

"Good idea. May I suggest a twenty-something Swedish blonde?"

"Not too likely, Stud. Probably a seventy-something, grey-haired female wrestler on crutches."

≈ ≈ ≈

The reports of splendid snow in the Park City Mountains were totally accurate. Clay and Jennie had chosen the slope-side Grand Lodge as the resort of their choice, and checked into a delightful three-bedroom condo suite with an incredible view of Flagstaff Mountain. From their living-room picture window, they could follow the ascent of the Northside Express chairlift from its base to its terminus at one of the uppermost levels.

Bett, the newly hired nanny for Wyatt, was thrilled to have her own private room at the end of the luxury condo's hallway. As a 57-year-old widow and mother of seven grown children, she had been struggling for two years to avoid homelessness. But as an unskilled homemaker, she was only expert in raising babies. The meager paychecks she could earn from multiple part-time, minimum-wage jobs simply couldn't keep up with the costs of housing and supporting herself in the Memphis suburbs. In her mind, living with one of her kids was unacceptable, so she had decided to advertise herself as a nanny, hoping for full-time employment. The very first day Bett's online ad appeared, Jennie believed she had found the nanny she was seeking. Over a subsequent luncheon attended by Bett, Jennie and Wyatt, the deal was sealed, and Bett joined the Evans family just in time for their flight to Park City.

CHAPTER 42

ONCE again, Clay found himself knocking on a steel entry door to a windowless concrete building, this time the site of the Society's Park City lab. As was the case with the Memphis lab, the door opened only a few inches, and a male voice with a cautious tone inquired, "Yes, what do you want; we don't welcome solicitors?"

"I'm Clay Evans, actively working on the Grand Project at the Memphis lab, and . . . . " Welcome Clay," the voice interrupted as the door was opened. We know who you are, and about the very interesting PDL water findings you've uncovered. Come on in, and I'll give you a little tour of the facility. I'm Rudy."

Clay, pleased at the compliment, walked in while shaking Rudy's hand and said, "I've also heard a little about your success here, isolating the unique sequence common to the DNA of all Renewables. Nice going. My wife and I took a basic course in Genetic Biology, but we couldn't begin to do the kind of work apparently underway here. What's your background, Rudy?"

"Before retiring, I was Professor of Genetic Engineering at MIT."

"Man, I bet all those biotech firms in Massachusetts were after you. How come you didn't chase the big money in the corporate world?"

"Clay, it's one thing to have the book knowledge, but I lacked the hands-on experience that comes from years of research work in an industrial lab. Besides, I really preferred teaching young men and women who'd take the basic know-how I taught, and build upon it during their careers."

"So here you are doing genetic research now, finally. I get it. For the pure fun of it, right?"

"You got it, indeed."

"So, Rudy, what are you working on?"

"I . . . we . . . there are three of us part-timers here, we're trying to use gene splicing techniques to take a key fragment embodying the Renewables sequence from some of our own DNA, and combine it with common DNA. Then we'll see if there's any difference in behavior in the presence of PDL water between the two varieties when transfected into damaged human tissue cells.

"Come on, walk with me Clay, and I'll show you and explain how we're doing this study." For the next hour, Rudy led Clay through the lab, from instruments to chemical worktables to ventilated hoods and back to more analytical equipment, talking all the time.

Finally, Clay confessed, "I'm afraid it's all way over my head. But I wish you success, and ask you guys to keep in touch with us at the Memphis lab. Maybe working together will prove synergistic."

Then, in deep thought, he added, "I must tell you, Rudy, that Jennie and I didn't come all the way to Park City to meet you and see this lab. We're taking a two-week skiing vacation too."

"I never would have guessed, Clay. Where are you staying?"

"At the Grand Lodge, and I'd better get back there soon, or Jennie will be on my case."

"I'll see you to the door. Perhaps I'll visit you in Memphis some day when my wife twists my arm to take her to Elvis's place. Goodbye."

"Thanks for the tour and update, Rudy. Bye."

≈ ≈ ≈

Having lived most of their married life in Alabama, the Evanses were not lifelong skiers. But both had spent dozens of days on the slopes during their single years, and took occasional skiing vacations for the first few decades after marriage. Now that they were physically teenagers once again, they didn't hesitate to head for the upper, more serious slopes.

Early on a beautiful crisp morning of the third day, riding up the Northern chairlift, they decided to go to the very top, and enjoy a milk run over the champagne powder newly fallen on the Black Diamond before too many skiers packed it down. As they descended along together, edging down on opposite sides of the slope, the ground seemed to start vibrating, and there was a growing rumbling sound. A few voices from somewhere cried out as they skied past, "AVALANCHE!"

Clay carved sharply left, away from the center of the run, heading into a forest of trees, and stopped so he could turn and look up the slope. It looked as if the whole mountainside was breaking off and coming straight down. He turned the other way so he could see and shout to Jennie. She had snowplowed to a stop in place, and had turned so she could look uphill.

"Jennie, schuss to your left off the run, NOW," he yelled at the top of his lungs. She started angling at max speed toward the trees on her side of the slope. But didn't make it before the snow mass reached her, knocking her off her feet. As she screamed "Clay," the avalanche grabbed her and covered her over.

As soon as the head-high snow flood passed him, after knocking down some saplings closer to the run, Clay climbed up and out of the knee-high pile of snow that made it through the trees to where he took shelter. He immediately skied to the opposite side of the slope where he last saw Jennie. She was nowhere to be seen. Precious minutes passed as he started expanding his visual search, yelling her name repeatedly. As desperation started to take over his emotions, he almost hopelessly extended his gaze way downhill; there he saw a small dark speck, in contrast to the white snow mass. As he schussed to it, he could see it was part of a ski.

He dropped to his knees and frantically began scooping snow away from the ski, then saw a leg, and a torso wearing Jennie's colors. He scooped snow from where he thought the head should be, and there was Jennie's snow-covered face. A few wipes more, and a nose and eyes appeared. The eyes opened, and the mouth smiled; Jennie was alive! Thankfully, though she'd tumbled downhill with the snow mass, when it stopped, it left her covered with only a mere foot or two of snow. When he scooped the remaining bulk of snow from her torso, she was able to gingerly stand up with his help, still wearing one ski. He kissed her face repeatedly.

But she was hurt. As he tried to hug her, her left forearm complained with pain, and she responded by holding it up with the opposite hand, wincing as she came to realize not all was well. "Oh Clay, honey, I'm okay, but my left arm really, really hurts, and the pain seems to be getting worse by the minute."

Just about then, a ski patrol team arrived via snowmobiles, armed with long poles. One of the rescuers, observing Jennie's condition, quickly unzipped her coat, and carefully removed it so he could look at her arm. "It's broken," he said. "Sir, I'll take her down the hill to the medics; you can meet up with her there. Hop on Jennie, and hold onto me with your good arm." And away they went. The other rescuers zoomed away uphill, looking for other skiers in need of help.

Clay stood there alone, half-dazed by the shocking chain of events: the avalanche, the frantic search and rescue, the arrival of the ski patrol and Jennie's quick departure. Eventually, he regained reality, picked up her coat and skis, and edged his way down the steep slope toward the buildings far below. Heavy snow began to fall.

When he finally found the room where Jennie was being examined, the medic said to him, "Are you this young lady's boyfriend?"

Clay responded, "I'm her husband. How is she?"

"She has a fractured ulna, and the skin is broken. You need to take her to a hospital at once for surgery. The risk of infection for an open fracture is very high, and very dangerous. We've put on a temporary splint and sling to prevent further tissue damage."

Together with the medic, Clay helped Jennie on with her coat, the right arm in the sleeve and the other sleeve hanging limply at the side. It was a tight fit, but they got it zipped up. Seated in their car later, as they started heading through the falling snow for the nearest Park City hospital, Clay said, "Well, I guess we're done skiing for this year. We still have a week and a half of vacation. Got any ideas what we should do? Of course, I'm assuming repair of your poor broken arm won't keep you down for long, knowing you."

Jennie responded, "My big worry is that I won't be able to carry Wyatt around. Thank goodness we've got Bett. Ouch! I hope they give me something for pain."

CHAPTER 43

THANKS to his cell phone's navigation app, Clay quickly located and drove to the Park City Medical Center. As they entered the parking area and stopped, Jennie was quietly crying, both from pain and fear of what awaited her inside. Clay exited and ran around the car to open the door for her.

"Babe, it's going to be alright. They'll give you an anesthetic, and you won't feel a thing while the docs fix you up. We'll be walking out of this place in a few hours, and go find a nice restaurant where you can start dinner with a double margarita."

Jennie managed a feeble smile.

It was late morning as they entered the Emergency Room. After the usual delays for paperwork, Jennie was whisked away by a nurse. A volunteer Candy Striper eventually came by and moved Clay to a more comfortable waiting room.

In surgery, the doctors opened Jennie's arm to expose the ends of the bone break, and manipulated them back together, cleaned up the original open wound, applied medication to prevent infection, and stitched her flesh and skin back together. They encased the lower part of her arm in a plastic splint, and covered the top half with multiple layers of gauze, strapped the splint in place, and wrapped the forearm from elbow to palm with Ace bandage.

Clay saw her again late afternoon, as a doctor and an attendant wheeled a happy-looking Jennie into the waiting room. "Mr. Evans, I'm Doctor Ames, the surgeon who operated on Jennie's arm. Her arm is fine for now. The break was clean and easy to reset. We've applied a temporary soft cast, as we have to watch and treat the wound to prevent possible infection. Any time a broken bone breaks the skin, dangerous infection is a major concern. Since you're from out of town, bring her back here in two days for an x-ray, and so one of our doctors can take a look beneath the gauze, and treat her if necessary. We'll probably put on a fiberglass cast at that time. In the meantime, see to it that she keeps that arm in the sling."

"What if she has pain, doctor?" Clay asked.

"We've given her a prescription for pain pills if she needs them."

"How long will it take for her to be healed up?"

"She'll be almost as good as new in about six weeks," said the doc. "After that, she should see a physiotherapist to help her recover from her arm's immobilization."

≈ ≈ ≈

Later that evening, as they were awaiting menus in a restaurant recommended by the concierge at the Grand Lodge, Jennie said, "Clay, I haven't forgot what you promised about a double margarita. I'll settle for two singles though, because I doubt there's any doubles in this fancy place. What a day this has been!"

"Yeah, imagine. We both survived an avalanche. We were lucky, even though you broke your arm. I heard that three other skiers were killed."

After dinner, seated next to Clay on the leather couch in their condo, Jennie complained, "Six weeks is a long time to put up with a cast."

"Be honest now, babe, have you been thinking about what I've been thinking about?"

"I'm not a mind reader, Clay, but I bet we're both wondering if we should try using PDL water to heal my arm overnight."

"Exactly. We're both thinking logically. Rudy at the lab gave me the coordinates of the nearest PDL water spring. It's about 15 miles south of town, almost to Heber City. He said it's deep in a wooded area, and is a surface spring less than two feet across, overflowing slowly into a nearby dry gulch. It's hard to find without the coordinates, because it's just a hole in the dirt, sometimes covered by leaves or debris."

"Oh Clay, I don't know if we should put any of that on my wound, since it's probably contaminated with all kinds of bacteria and bugs from such a location."

"Hmm, maybe so. Here's another potential solution. The lab has a big glass jug full of it. I saw it while I was there last week. Rudy mentioned they'd treated it with high dosages of ultraviolet light to sterilize it so that it'd have a long shelf life without developing algae or scum. We could use that."

"Let's do it tomorrow Clay."

"Okay, but I'd prefer to do it when no one else was around. I don't have a key, so we've got to arrive during work hours. Let's go in the late afternoon, just before everyone goes home."

"Speaking of time, Clay, it's almost midnight. Let's go to bed."

"Music to my ears," he said.

≈ ≈ ≈

The Evanses arrived at the Park City lab about 4:15 pm. Clay chatted with Rudy about some new ideas he had, while Jennie studied the lab's electron microscope, which was more modern than the one she'd practiced with at the University during her summer classes. After the last volunteer left for home, Clay took Jennie to the lab bench where the container of sterile PDL water was kept. He carefully unwrapped the Ace bandage from her arm, gently supporting it.

"Now, lay your arm carefully on the bench, Jen, with the gauze side up."

He unstrapped the rigid plastic splint, but left it in place between her arm and the bench. Then he gently peeled the gauze from the top of the stitched-up wound, laying it to the side, still loosely touching the bottom of the splint. Next, he removed the protective wrapping from one of the lab's sterile syringes, and sucked up some PDL water from a beaker that he'd filled from the jug.

"Jennie, this is going to sting a bit, so grit your teeth and try not to move your arm." He pressed the needle tip about a half-inch through her skin alongside the wound, and injected a small amount; she had closed her eyes and made a face, but didn't make a noise or move a muscle. He repeated this procedure several times parallel to the incision made by the surgeon, which was several inches long. Then he flipped the gauze back over the wound, re-strapped the splint, and re-wrapped the Ace bandage.

"You are one brave lady, Jen! Not a peep or a wiggle while I did that."

"Yeah, but I'll find a way to get even with you for that," she said with a sneaky smile.

"Maybe I can do penance by taking you to that Mexican restaurant you pointed out last night in town. I bet they make super margaritas, and I know you wouldn't mind having them two nights in a row."

"Hmm, I might forgive you then."

CHAPTER 44

CLAY got up before 6:00 am. His normal routine was to pick up the paper at the entrance door, make some coffee, and sit in front of the TV watching the news and reading it simultaneously. As soon as the TV was on, Jennie awakened, moved her left arm out from under the covers, and winced in pain.

"Clay, my arm still hurts. The PDL water didn't heal it. Oh my god, six more weeks of this!"

Clay entered the bedroom just as Jennie sat up in bed. He reached for her arm and unwrapped the Ace bandage, undid one strap and lifted up the gauze. The skin and wound was just as ugly and bruised as the day before.

"I'm sorry, babe; I thought for sure it'd work, just like it did for my stab wound in Kenya. Something's wrong."

Jennie started crying. He kissed her face several times, and then, gently, her arm. He replaced the soft cast components, and left the room to think. After pacing the floor and stepping outside for a few minutes, he returned and said, "I got it. I know what's wrong.

"The lab's sterile PDL water is dead. The UV light did it. It killed or deactivated something that was previously functional. Therefore, natural PDL water must be ALIVE! There must be something within its natural state that has life, or borders on the edge of life. Perhaps strange microorganisms that are too small to observe with normal analytical equipment. If I'm right, we should treat you with natural PDL water, right at the spring. Come on, honey, get up and let's head for Heber City."

Along the way, they stopped for breakfast sandwiches and coffee to go. Then, using his iPhone's navigation app for guidance, Clay left the highway and drove onto a backcountry road, following it slowly. They stopped the car alongside a forest, then backed up a couple hundred feet. "Jen, we're there. We have to get out and walk from here. It looks to be in that direction, about two football fields away. Let's go."

After tramping around in circles where the GPS coordinates indicated the well should be, Jennie spotted something glistening alongside a large storm-felled tree. As they approached, they could see what appeared to be a rain-puddle nearly covered with blown leaves. Standing next to it, they could see that water was running out and heading as a small trickle down a mild slope. Clay knelt down uphill from the spring, and cleared the leaves and some twigs off the surface. He could see that it appeared very deep. He reached for a nearby dead branch about four feet long, and thrust it down the center of the water hole. It didn't touch bottom.

"I have an idea, Jen, that I think you'll like. Let's dispense with the syringe injection, and instead just put your bare arm all the way in up to your shoulder."

"I like that idea, for sure," she said.

"We have to do this very carefully to avoid screwing up the resetting job the surgeon did. Let's practice with the cast on. I'll help you get it out of the sling. Let your arm hang straight down, with my help supporting its weight. Now, without bending or swinging that arm, keeping it hanging straight down, lower yourself to your knees. Use your right arm and hand to help keep your balance. Make believe there's a hole full of water right where you're standing."

"Like this?" she said, as she went through the motion.

"Great," said Clay. Now let's take the cast off, and do the same thing for real, kneeling right next to the hole so that your arm goes into the water."

Clay gently removed the cast, and Jennie went through the motion, getting down right next to the hole, and then bent at her waist to put the arm in all the way to her elbow. Clay used his shirt to carefully dry the arm off as she stood back up. Then he reapplied the cast, and put her arm into the sling.

"You did it, babe. Nice going. Let's go back to the condo, and I'll make sandwiches for lunch. I guess I get to do dishes too, but hopefully not for six weeks. We'll know tomorrow morning."

≈ ≈ ≈

The sun sneaked up above the eastern horizon. Darkness fled westward. Jennie woke up. "Clay," she yelled, assuming he was in the living room reading the paper while enjoying his usual morning coffee.

"Huh," he said, as he rolled over next to her, having just been yanked from sound sleep.

"Oh, you're here. Honey, my arm doesn't hurt. At all!"

They both sat up in bed, stuffing their pillows behind them for support. Still half asleep, Clay said, "Hand me your arm."

"I can't; it's on the other side of me. You're on my right. The left arm's the one in the cast."

"Okay, I'll get up and go over to the other side of the bed. Now, let's take a look at your arm."

Clay unwrapped the Ace bandage, undid the straps holding the bottom splint on, and took off the soft gauze top cover. Even though some daylight was starting to stream into the window, he turned on the lights for a clearer view.

The wound was gone. Not a trace. Not even a pink line where the surgeons had sliced undamaged skin to allow access for resetting the bone. No bruises that had blackened half of her forearm. Two-dozen stitches lay loose in the now-empty bottom splint. Jennie exhibited the left arm of a normal, healthy teenage girl.

"Wow," said Clay. "I expected complete healing, but actually seeing this takes my breath away."

"I'm so happy," she whined, as her face wrinkled and she started to cry from overt joy.

Clay said, "We have an appointment this morning with the surgeon. Let's keep it, so he can x-ray to check the status of the bone fracture. Jen, I think we should reapply the cast and sling, and monitor the doctor's reaction to what's happened. We may need his endorsement someday."

"Okay, I guess I can put up with it for a couple more hours. And since my arm is therefore incapacitated, hon, you'll have to make breakfast and clean up again. Gotcha."

Clay groaned as he got up and headed for the kitchen. "Scrambled or over easy?" he asked.

≈ ≈ ≈

The surgeon met them in the visitor's lobby, and walked with them to the outpatient labs. "Have a seat, Mr. Evans. Mrs. Evans, come on over here and rest your arm on the bed of this x-ray machine. First we'll gently take the cast off, so

I can have a peek at your wound. Then the technician will take a picture of your bone so we can see if it's healing properly."

The surgeon was stunned when he removed the soft cast. "I don't understand this," he said. I've never seen anything like it before. I know I opened and entered your arm right there and touched your bone, but there's no wound, no scar." He looked questioningly at Jennie, then Clay. They both shrugged and remained silent. He called the technician into the room, and ordered an x-ray. When developed, the film was thrust onto a wall viewing stage, lit from behind. The film showed a perfect ulna, with no trace of a fracture.

"I don't believe this," he said, "but I know it has to be true." He shook his head and again looked at Jennie and Clay.

After the technician left the room, Clay said, "Doctor Ames, I can explain, but I won't for awhile, possibly even for a few months. If you'll give me your word to keep what you've observed to yourself, I'll give you my word to let you be the first surgeon in the nation to learn about an amazing new medical cure that could change the entire landscape of medicine. What do you say?"

Looking puzzled, the surgeon paused and said, "Mr. Evans, I'm required to document each patient's visit; what can I possibly write about this one for Mrs. Evans?"

"That's easy, Doc; just say, 'X-ray showed good healing. Patient coming along nicely. Discharged to family doctor in Alabama.'"

After a few minutes of thought, the surgeon agreed to keep the secret, and they shook hands. "Someday soon,

Doc, I may need you to address a large group about what you've seen today," Clay added, as he and Jennie walked out of the lab toward the lobby. Jennie swung her arm wildly and did a jig on the way out to the car.

CHAPTER 45

BACK in their condo that evening, as they watched dozens of flaming torches gliding in the dark down various slopes of Flagstaff Mountain, Jennie commented, "It's beautiful to see, but sort of eerie because you can't see the skiers holding them, except when they get almost to the base."

"Yeah," said Clay, "sort of reminds me of the microorganisms that must be in PDL water; you can't see them, but you know they have to be there. I'm going to have to go back to the lab tomorrow and share our experience with Rudy and the guys. Wanna come?"

"No, honey; I want to stay here and spend time with Wyatt. I want to give Bett a day off to get out of this condo, and go do whatever she wants somewhere else."

"Okay by me. I'll leave right after breakfast. Hey, now that your arm is normal, I won't have to make meals any more, or clean up either. That sure makes my day."

≈ ≈ ≈

"Jennie, it's too bad you weren't with me when I met with Rudy and the other guys at the Park City lab. You should have seen their faces and heard their rapid-fire questions when I told them about the avalanche, digging you out, your broken arm and your incredible healing. They were astonished hearing about our new suspicion concerning PDL water . . . that when natural, it's alive and potent, and when sterilized it's useless.

"You'd also have been fascinated, just like I was, to watch the work that those guys are doing there. Remember what Rudy told us during our first visit there; that they're playing with samples of their own DNA, and snipping key fragments embodying the Renewables sequence from them, and then sticking those fragments on ordinary DNA from other donors? Well, I actually watched that effort in progress. It's so exotic and impressive. They're hoping to be able to verify that their original DNA and the modified DNA behave equally in the presence of PDL water."

"That'd sure be a giant step towards meeting the Grand Project's goal," commented Jennie.

"True," said Clay, "but our aspirations to create fully functional artificial PDL water are perhaps just as important. Can you imagine how much PDL water would be needed to meet future worldwide medical demands if the Project ever yields fruitful results? I seriously doubt there'd be enough of the natural stuff to go around."

≈ ≈ ≈

Two days later, Clay said, "I've been thinking, Jennie. There may be another route to the same intermediate goal that the Park City team has. As impressive as the work those guys are doing, it occurs to me that we might be able to bypass DNA altogether, and work directly at the cellular level. They told me that if they were successful at the DNA level, their next step would be to implant or 'infect' damaged tissue cells with Renewable-type DNA to achieve the desired healing of those cells. They called that process 'transfection.'"

"I've never heard that word before," she said, "but I get the idea it conveys."

"Okay, here's my concept. Remember what we learned in our Genetic Biology class? That there's a special type of cell called a stem cell. That they're unspecialized cells that are able to become specialized cells capable of replacing any cell that has been lost in the body."

Jennie added, "I was there during that lecture too. The professor said there were two types: adult and embryonic, right? I recall that a lot of people in that class got upset when the he said he thought embryonic stem cells were best for most therapeutic applications. Most of our classmates sure didn't cotton to the idea of killing human embryos to harvest their stem cells."

"Right, a real uproar," said Clay. "But then the professor explained that there was a great source for embryonic cells that didn't involve killing an embryo at all. He believed that the best source for them was from umbilical-cord blood just after a child's birth.

"My idea is to study whether we could make a solution of placenta-cord embryonic stem cells in PDL water, and simply surround the damaged tissue cells with this blend to see if healing takes place. These special stem cells could only come from a Renewable donor. Then the right DNA would already be present. Of course, a big problem might be rejection of those stem cells by a patient's immune system.

"Jen, you and I know only too well how the presence of PDL water somehow hyper-accelerates our damaged body tissue cells to heal themselves. Look at how my stab wound was healed in the presence of PDL water overnight, as was your broken arm . . . bone, flesh and skin. Not only that.

PDL water made us both six decades younger, possibly by accelerating repair of age-damaged cells all over our body."

"I do understand," said Jennie, "but where do we get those special embryonic stem cells?"

"For research, we could use Wyatt's stem cells, on the assumption they carry the Renewable DNA."

"In a pig's eye! You're not going to touch my baby!"

"Hold on, honey, when Wyatt was born, I was there, remember? Well, I told the doctors we wanted to save his cord and placenta blood via cryopreservation. Parents are starting to do this as a common practice. Saving this rich source of cells for possible future use later in the child's life, should they need them, makes sense. We'd use just a little of Wyatt's for our research."

"What about the patient; where do you find one to do the research with?" she asked.

"We obviously can't experiment on humans, babe, but perhaps we could use a creature with DNA close to that of humans. In other words, a sick or injured monkey."

"Where do we find one of those?"

"Beats me. I'm still in the thinking phase. Hey, this is just a theory so far, babe. Let's kick it around. If we conclude that it makes sense to try, we can get the Park City guys involved. We're amateurs, but they'd know the feasibility right off, as well as the ins and outs of how to go about setting up a trial. If they needed more than a little of Wyatt's cells, they could probably culture them from his right there in the lab."

≈ ≈ ≈

The following day, the Evanses worked together to flesh out the theory, at least as much as possible, limited only by their lack of medical or biological professional backgrounds and experience. Jennie typed the finished proposal on Clay's computer, and since they had no printer, simply stored it on a thumb drive. That afternoon, they again visited Rudy and others at the lab, verbally briefed them, and gave them the thumb drive, There was quite a bit of skepticism voiced. However, everyone agreed they'd kick it around as a group for at least a week. Pending their decision, the Evanses promised to fly a cryogenically preserved sample of Wyatt's blood to them from Memphis. Clay and Jennie then said their goodbyes, spent a few more days of remaining vacation time in greater Park City, and then returned with Wyatt and Bett to Florence.

CHAPTER 46

FROM the day of their return to Florence, and through March to early April, Clay and Jenny spent about half of each week in the Memphis facility. Bett usually took care of Wyatt at home, except occasionally when Jennie brought him along to play in a crib at the lab.

The artificial PDL water development made excellent progress. Experimenting with the lab's electron microscope and special dyes, Jennie developed a way to see the life forms in natural PDL water. Two kinds of tiny microorganisms were visible. One type appeared to be single-cell bacteria. The other type, which was about 100 times smaller than the bacteria, could barely be seen, seemingly floating immobile in the fluid.

Jennie said, "Based on what we learned in class last summer, Clay, I'd guess those small ones are most likely some type of virus."

Clay nodded agreement. He then added ten percent by volume of that natural PDL water to his stored artificial PDL water, and found that the microorganisms survived and replicated in the blend. They even eventually reached the same population density as in the starting natural PDL water. The Evanses believed they'd created equivalent artificial PDL water. Yet, it hadn't been tested on a human to prove equivalency.

Meanwhile, the Park City team cultured Wyatt's stem cells to produce as many as they needed for research. They found that they were able to make a stable medium of living Renewable stem cells suspended in a mixture containing some PDL water, glucose and other additives. Mid-April, they acquired an injured chimpanzee from the Memphis zoo, and tried to treat his injuries with the mixture. The effort failed because the chimp's immune system rejected Wyatt's cells. Human trials were an ultimate necessity.

During a subsequent Skype meeting between the Evanses and Rudy, it was decided that work at both labs had progressed sufficiently far, with reasonable successes, that a presentation should be offered to the upcoming May 20, 2014 Annual Meeting of the Renewables Society. Where their joint effort would go thereafter would depend on the reception and outcome of that presentation.

≈ ≈ ≈

Less than hour after landing at Louis Armstrong New Orleans International airport, the Evanses traveled by taxi to the Drury Inn and Suites, their home and meeting hotel for the next three days. As matters turned out, Clay, Jennie and Rudy were scheduled to be featured speakers during the general assembly of that Society's meeting. They expected to also be involved with at least one of the committee conferences due to follow on subsequent days.

After checking in and reaching their room, Clay plopped down in an overstuffed leather easy chair, and checked his iPhone for emails and messages. Jennie busied herself emptying their two small suitcases and clothes bag. "Clay, everything's put away. What do you want to do now?" Jennie shouted from inside the closet.

As soon as the words escaped her lips, she knew she'd asked the wrong open-end question. She stuck her head out to look at Clay, expecting to see his Cheshire cat grin, coupled with a nod of his head towards the bedroom. Just as he prepared to say something witty and suggestive, she shouted, "Wait, let me rephrase that. It's too early for dinner, honey; let's go for a walk along that fun part of Bourbon Street. We haven't done that since your 60th birthday."

≈ ≈ ≈

The following morning, after the typical opening banter of most convention assemblies, the chairman said, "This Society has for almost four years financially supported two state-of-the-art scientific laboratories dedicated to our hope that one day our Grand Project would yield a methodology for using PDL water to benefit humanity's health and well being. We have as keynote speakers here today three dedicated volunteers that've labored in these labs towards this goal. I'm pleased to introduce Dr. Rudy Silverberg from our Park City lab, and Clay and Jennie Evans from our Memphis lab. They intend to bring you exciting news about their progress. Please welcome them with me."

Amidst clapping and a few soft cheers, the three speakers walked onto the stage, and sat down. Jennie was the first to stand up and approach the microphone.

"Good morning. I have a little story to tell you about my recent visit to Utah from our home in Alabama. My husband and I were on an extended skiing vacation at Flagstaff Mountain, not far from the Park City lab, which we had also been visiting. One morning, as we were heading down a difficult steep slope, an avalanche erupted a half-mile above us. Clay was able to escape the snow mass crashing down on us, but I wasn't. It caught up to me, knocked me down and covered me over. I couldn't breathe. I was suffocating.

"One of my skis was partially exposed above the snow. That's how Clay was able to find me, and dig me out with his hands before I died. After he helped me to my feet, I realized that my left arm was broken. It hurt like crazy. I had a compound fracture of the forearm. That means the broken bone had pierced the skin. But I soon cherished my good fortune in surviving at all when I learned that three other skiers had been killed.

"I was told by a ski patrol medic that drove me down the mountain that I was in imminent danger of life-threatening infection because of the skin break. I couldn't have my arm simply reset, and go on my way. I had to go to the hospital and have emergency surgery, wherein the surgeon enlarged the wound to access the bone ends, manually reset them, cleaned the wound, applied medication, sewed me up and immobilized my arm in a soft cast and sling. I was then released in Clay's care, who'll continue this story about our Utah trip."

At this point, Jennie returned to her chair on the stage, and Clay took over at the microphone.

"The day after her surgery, I discovered some UV-sterilized PDL water that was stored in a jug at the Park City lab. Remembering how PDL water had healed my stab wound in Kenya, Jennie and I decided we should try to do the same for her broken arm. After carefully removing Jennie's temporary cast, I used a syringe to inject some of the lab PDL water into and around Jennie's wound. We hoped for healing overnight, as had been the case for my stab wound. The following day showed no healing improvement whatsoever, which left us both in dismay. Puzzled, we eventually came to suspect that the sterile PDL water was somehow different than natural PDL water.

"So, we decided that we needed to repeat the treatment using natural PDL water. We drove to a forest about 15 miles beyond the outskirts of Park City, using a GPS to locate a known exposed natural spring of PDL water. After removing the cast, Jennie dropped to her knees and lowered her left arm into it, up to her elbow. The following day, we visited the surgeon. He removed her cast and was astonished to see no trace of the wound he had created and repaired. He took an x-ray that showed the bone as completely normal, with no evidence of a prior fracture. Needless to say, the doctor was shocked. However, he promised to keep secret what he had seen in exchange for my promise to brief him fully about the cure some day in the future.

"In a way, that ski accident turned out to be a blessing in disguise," said Clay. "Not only did Jennie experience incredible overnight healing, instead of the typical six-week immobilization and subsequent physical therapy. We also learned one of the major secrets of PDL water as a result.

"We learned that natural PDL water is alive! Using the Memphis electron microscope, Jennie discovered that it hosts both a strain of bacteria and a virus strain.

"Previously, we had also discovered that PDL water contains high levels of heavy hydrogen as well as heavy oxygen isotopes, and also several rare earth metals. Using commercially available reagents, we added duplicate concentrations of these elements to filtered deionized water. We believed that we had made artificial PDL water. After Jennie's life-form discovery, however, I knew we had more work. We subsequently added one part in ten of natural PDL water to my artificial PDL water, thus inoculating it with the bacteria and viruses naturally occurring. The microorganisms survived and replicated, eventually reaching a stable state that duplicated natural PDL water. So, we do now believe that the Grand Project indeed has the capability to make artificial PDL water.

"Your next speaker, Dr. Silverberg, will update you on accomplishments by the staff of the Park City lab."

"Good morning. What Clay and Jennie didn't tell you was that they are the parents of a new 5-month old baby boy, named Wyatt. That's why they only volunteer at the Memphis lab half-time. The rest of the time they're changing diapers!

"Let's congratulate that young couple." Rudy paused until the clapping stopped.

"By the time that kid's ready to graduate from college, both of his parents' real age will be over 100. Won't he be surprised some day when he finally finds out!

"He will, you know. He'll eventually learn that embryonic stem cells from his own umbilical cord and placenta have been cultured and reproduced at the Park City lab, and are the basis for all the recent research done there aimed at achieving the Grand Project health goals. In fact, our hope is that someday the ancestors of his stem cells conceivably could end up being used for healing in medical facilities all over the world.

"You see, we're hoping that a special blend made from artificial PDL water, Wyatt's stem cells, glucose, and a few other additives can be used to surround sick or injured human tissue, and accomplish lightning-fast healing. We tried this on a chimpanzee, but his body's immune defenses rejected it. Trials need to be done on humans. But this takes know-how and professional experience beyond our ability. Furthermore, because government entities like the FDA need to be involved, we'll need a much-expanded staff with diverse expertise.

"Oh yeah, we've done some other pretty cool things at Park City. One is that we've been successful using genetic engineering techniques to snip key pieces of DNA from a Renewable donor's cells and attach them onto other DNA in cells from any donor. We can't be sure what will develop from this know-how, but it's clearly a substantial achievement. Perhaps someday, we can thus modify and use a patient's own DNA as an alternative to the stem cell approach. For now, however, both Park City and Memphis lab staffs believe the stem cell methodology tried on the chimp holds the most promise for humans.

"Clinical trials must follow. The Grand Project has reached a turn in the road."

CHAPTER 47

AMID appreciative clapping by the Society's 290-attendee audience, Clay and Jennie joined Rudy at the microphone. After taking a bow with the others, Clay leaned toward the microphone, signaled with a raised hand for quiet, and spoke. "Members of the Renewables Society . . . all of you here today . . . it's now your turn to act. Yes, our research to date has promised eventual success, but we all believe that the Park City and Memphis labs, as currently constituted with part-time volunteer staff, have gone about as far as they should go on this Grand Project. It's time for change, folks.

"It's our joint opinion, reached after many hours of discussion, and the approval of your President, that today you should select a seven-member committee that will formulate the future path for the Grand Project. We propose that the starting point for their discussions should be to consider disassociating the labs from the Society, except for oversight, and allow them to be operated under a front non-profit corporate entity.

"Initially, this front entity would own only the land, buildings and scientific equipment of both facilities, but eventually would probably have to acquire office and manufacturing space. We also propose that the new entity must staff both labs with full-time scientific, clinical and medical professionals, working under secrecy contract. Initially, their effort should be aimed at proving efficacy of the research we've completed, followed by human clinical trials. Eventually, if all goes well, the long-term goal would be manufacture and worldwide distribution of healing products based on PDL water solutions and cryopreserved Renewable stem cells.

"As we are speaking, paper ballots and pencils are being passed out to everyone here today. We ask you to take a few minutes now and think about which members, in your opinion, should be on that seven-person committee. There are three spaces on the ballot. Use your judgment and write up to three names in those spaces. The ballots will be collected in ten minutes, and tabulated. The seven highest name counts will determine the makeup of the committee, pending their willingness to take on that responsibility, at least for the remainder of this convention.

"Lastly, I'll conclude our joint presentation by announcing that Rudy, Jennie and I will make ourselves available to that chosen committee, and ultimately the hired professional lab staff, for up to six months. Thereafter, we all plan to pursue other Society-related activities."

≈ ≈ ≈

The morning after the General Assembly, the newly formed committee held its first meeting in a private hotel room. Clay, Jennie and Rudy, all invited to attend as non-voting advisors, were surprised, but generally pleased, by the array of professionals selected: a famed genetic biologist, another Wall-Street broker, a retired corporate CEO, a retired IRS executive, a physician, and two attorneys, one of whom was retired.

Clay jokingly whispered into Jennie's ear, "That's two too many lawyers."

Over the course of the day, the CEO and one attorney committed to explore and legally set up a front company. The attorney explained to the other committee members: "'Front organizations' can act for the parent group without their actions being attributed to the parent group. Front companies are usually used to shield the parent from legal liability. In our case, the goal is to shield the secrecy of our Society's existence."

The other attorney and the IRS man agreed to study staffing requirements for different startup scenarios, and to propose organizational concepts. The remaining three members took on the job of proposing how the company would approach continued research, clinical testing, financing of operations, and coordination with government entities, such as the FDA.

≈ ≈ ≈

That evening, relaxing over a drink in the hotel's lounge, Clay and Jennie discussed their future. "Whew," exhaled Clay audibly. "Am I glad this year's meeting's over, and that we've successfully cut ourselves loose. No further participation in the Grand Project, beyond those six months of advisory commitments."

"I'm especially pleased," said Jennie. "Now we can spend some serious time with Wyatt. You know, they say the early months and years in a child's life are really the most formative. It's our responsibility to launch him in the right direction."

"True, Jen, but can we accomplish that, and still plan another mission trip overseas somewhere? Like maybe that one-year English-teaching stint in Tibet that Glen and Sonny told us was still open?"

"I don't see why not. Tibetan kids seem to get along fine in Tibet."

"Do you think Bett would be willing to come along?"

Jennie laughed, and said, "In a heartbeat."

Thus began a lifetime series of the Evans family's mission trips and great adventures around the world.

≈ ≈ ≈

Forty-three years and twenty-two mission trips later, Clay and Jennie returned to their Florence, AL home again. Both showed a few more wrinkles in their heavily tanned skin, and hints of grey hair. But Clay and Jennie weren't ready to retire just yet. Doing good and helping others was in their blood. One late July evening, as they began to review a list of the Society's new proposed missions, Jennie abruptly changed the topic. "Clay, do you realize that in a few days we'll have been married 100 years?"

"Really? I've lost all track of time. I can hardly figure out how old I really am. Um, I was born in 1931, and . . ."

"I don't want to scare you Clay, but you're 127 years old. Not only that, but your youngest son, Wyatt, is going on 44, and his kids are all in their teens. You're almost ancient!"

"How did you figure that out so fast?"

"Easy, you were 27 when we got married, and that's now 100 years ago. Voila, 127.

"Oh, I get it, since you were 23 years old when we married, you're now . . ."

"Don't you dare say it, Clay!"

"Okay, okay. Let's see if you're right on our Anniversary number; we were married on August 2, 1958, and it's now

July 28th, 2058. I'll be darned, Jen, you're right as usual; we'll be married 100 years in a few days."

"Clay, I have an idea. Why don't we celebrate by going back to St. Augustine again, just like we did on our 54th Anniversary?"

"Come on! I can read your mind right now, Jen. You're thinking about going back to that Fountain of Youth attraction. Right?"

"Well, why not?"

"And somehow finding our way back into that pool?"

"Clay, let's do it! Let's get young again. Let's do it all over again."

"Young again! Fantastic plan, babe! Yeah, let's do it all over again! Yahoo!"

THE END
(or is it just a New Beginning?)

Thank you for reading.
Please review this book. Reviews help others find me and inspires me to keep writing!

If you would like to be put on our email list to receive updates on new releases, contests, and promotions, please go to AbsolutelyAmazingEbooks.com and sign up.

ABOUT THE AUTHOR

Chuck Van Soye retired from the business world to reside in Key West, FL, where he stays active as Treasurer of both the Key West Writer's Guild and the local Gideons International camp. His career has ranged from Army officer to Chemical Engineer for Sun Oil to writer and editor for McGraw-Hill's *Chemical Engineering* magazine, to Sales & Marketing Executive for Du Pont. Chuck relaxes with boating, fishing and authoring books, such as his *Spy Mates, Pondering Life's Imponderables,* and *Confessions and Misadventures of Charlie the Fisherman.*

AbsolutelyAmazingEbooks.com or
AA-eBooks.com